CRYSTAL MAGIC
CLEARWATER WITCHES #1

Madeline Freeman

DEDICATION

To Dad:
For never forgetting the name of my first novel,
and for making me believe I can do anything I set my mind to.

And for the One
who makes the moon reflect the sun.

ACKNOWLEDGMENTS

Thank you, Rachel Schurig and Mary Twomey for talking me through things, reading crappy drafts, listening to my dithering, and pretty much being the best people ever.

Thank you Leah at Invisible Ink Editing for cutting through the sludge to help this story shine.

Thank you to Steven Novak for the beautiful artwork.

Chapter One

He thinks I'm lying.

With his mouth, Mr. Delaney, the assistant principal, says he wants to help me and would like to hear my side of the story. But his mind is already made up. He surveys me across the top of his disastrously chaotic desk, his gaze making me uncomfortable, like I've done something wrong.

"I didn't do anything," I say. It is my constant refrain whenever I'm seated in this chair. I fix my eyes on a blue ballpoint pen, which rests precariously at the edge of the desktop in front of me.

Mr. Delaney wonders what his wife is making for dinner. But what he asks is, "If you didn't do anything, then why does Kayla Snow have a welt on her forehead the size of a golf ball?"

I dig my nails into the palms of my hands as Mr. Delaney's mind circles around to golf and whether that new golfing video game will improve his swing. I have to focus. If I can focus, I can block out the flashes. The pain of my nails pressing into my flesh anchors me to the moment, to my own mind and body. "When I was leaving Mrs. Capella's class, someone bumped into me from behind and my books flew out of my hands. One of them hit Kayla in the back of the leg."

Mr. Delaney's thick eyebrows hitch upward, as if trying to connect with his graying hair. "That's not what Kayla said happened. She said you threw a book at her leg."

The pen on the desk rattles gently and I cover it with my hand, biting my lower lip. It shivers against my skin for a few seconds longer. I take in a breath, tamping down my anger and frustration, and the pen stills. My emotions have already gotten me into enough trouble today; I can't afford to have something happen here, in front of Mr. Delaney. "She probably thinks I threw it. Like I said, her back was to me. Anyway, she turned to me and... she called me a freak and a few other choice things, and I apologized, even though I wasn't trying to hurt her. And when I tried to pick up my book, she kicked it out of reach."

"Hm." Mr. Delaney's eyes express a willingness to entertain my version of the story, but his thoughts betray him. He thinks I'm making this up. Kayla Snow is on student government and the cheerleading squad. She's never in trouble. I, on the other hand, have been in this office three times already this year—and it's only October. His thoughts flick to the district's alternative school and out of the corner of my eye I see the monitor of his computer begin to flicker. I bring my hand to my mouth and bite down on the side of my thumb. The screen goes back to normal. The sharp shock of pain anchors my mind, but I don't have to be able to read Mr. Delaney's thoughts to know my behavior worries him. Biting yourself isn't normal, but neither am I. And sometimes pain is the only thing that makes me focus, keeps the chaotic thoughts of others from assailing my mind.

"I've already called your mother," Mr. Delaney says, his eyes shifting from me to the door to his phone. He's worried I might break into a fit and he might need help—or a quick escape. "We've barely been in school a month and this is the fourth incident you've been involved in."

"I haven't done anything."

"Destruction of school property is one thing, Kristyl." He turns to his computer and pulls something up on the screen. "A broken desk, a broken window, and a broken data projector."

I shake my head. "I didn't break those things."

"Oh, they just all happened to break while you were near them?"

I bite the insides of my cheeks. I was given warnings for each of those instances because in each case, no one could prove I'd been responsible. The desk I sat in during English fell apart when I stood up after an hour of enduring murmured taunts by the girls around me. The window I sat beside during history cracked clean in half when the teacher assigned a group assignment and every group refused me entrance. And in science, the projector slipped off its cart and crashed to the floor during our notes about plate tectonics when the students in class decided that calling me "Crustal" instead of "Kristyl" was hilarious.

"I don't know how those things happened. Just like I don't know how Kayla got hurt today. She kicked my book and I crawled over to get it and she kicked me in the hip."

"She kicked you?" His tone is dubious.

I nod. "I didn't want to get into a fight so I grabbed my book and ran out of the room."

"Kayla says you pushed her, that you knocked her into the corner of a desk. *Then* you ran out of the room."

I close my eyes. Of course that's what Kayla said. And of course it's the version of events Mr. Delaney believes. My version doesn't make sense. Even I know that.

Mr. Delaney shifts in his chair, squaring his shoulders and sitting taller. "When your mother arrives, we'll discuss the terms of your suspension."

"Suspension?" My stomach clenches. "Is Kayla being suspended too?"

The corners of his mouth twitch as an internal monologue plays in his mind. Of course she won't be suspended, she's the victim here. But he wants to be diplomatic. He opens his mouth to respond, but before the words come out, his office door swings open, banging against the adjacent wall, and he jumps. His eyes slide from the door to me and he pushes back from his desk, putting more distance between us. "Why don't you sit out in the waiting area until your mom gets here?"

I don't argue. It would be pointless. I stand and exit his office, passing through the short hallway to the waiting area, where the secretary has her desk. She raises her heavily penciled eyebrows at me as I pass, wondering what was going on to make me throw such a hissy fit. I bite back the urge to tell her I didn't touch the door and sit in a chair facing the hallway so I can see my mom when she arrives. I take in deep, slow breaths. I can't afford anything else going wrong today. I close my eyes, concentrating on the rise and fall of my chest, on my heartbeat. Now that I'm not upset, my thoughts are my own once more.

The creak of the office's main door makes me open my eyes, but it's not my mom who enters. It's a man with a round face and a thick thatch of blond hair atop his head. He wears the dark blue uniform of a police officer. My heart picks up its tempo, thudding rapidly in my chest. It'll be okay, I try to convince myself—he's just a cop. It's not unheard of for a cop to stop by the school. He walks up to the secretary and the two exchange murmured words. Then the secretary nods in my direction.

My skin tingles and a lead weight settles in my stomach as the officer turns to me. Has Kayla accused me of assault or something? Am I being arrested? Adrenaline courses through my body and I envision myself leaping off the chair and running for my life—running away from this cop, away from this school, away from my life, away from everything. But I won't do that. Instead, I sit stock-still, waiting for the officer to get out his handcuffs.

I study his face as he approaches, trying to determine how bad the news is, just how much trouble I'm in. His expression is clouded and I wonder if I'm the first person he's ever had to arrest. Or maybe he was expecting me to look differently—like a hardened hooligan instead of a small, plain girl whose face is half obscured by curtains of blond hair.

He comes to a stop in front of me, rubbing his left wrist with his right hand, his eyes not quite fixing on my face. I bite my lower lip, the pain interfering with the heat building in my abdomen. "Kristyl Barnette?"

I swallow hard. "Yes."

His eyes shift and the cadence of my heart increases. "I'll need for you to come with me."

I nod. It takes a moment, but I'm able to press myself to standing. "Am I being charged with something?"

His eyes flash confusion. "No..."

I don't like the look he's giving me. I dig my fingernails into my palm, but the sensation does nothing to allay the onslaught of emotions. It's bad, his reason for being here. But I don't want to know how bad. I don't want to hear it.

The officer's eyes slide away from my face and a muscle in his jaw jumps. His mouth works, like he's trying to figure out how to spit out what he has to say next. "Your mother is Amy Barnette?"

I feel like I've been punched in the stomach. The words don't come out of his mouth, but somehow, I know. An icy wave of dread envelops me and I know why he's here. There's been an accident. A bad one. And my mom won't be making it to her meeting with the principal.

Above me, the fluorescent light burns out, sparks flying from the edges of the bulb, as I realize my mom won't be coming home either.

Chapter Two

The three-story Victorian house looms before me, an immense monolith with pale blue siding and gray accents.

My new home.

It's been just over a week since the officer came to tell me my mom was killed in a car accident on her way to the school. If she hadn't had to leave work to come talk to my principal, she might still be alive. The corners of my eyes prickle and I rub at them with my knuckles.

My aunt, Jodi Barnette, nudges her way past me on the walkway and walks up the half dozen stairs that lead to the wraparound porch. She twists the doorknob and bumps into the door a couple times with her shoulder before it opens. For some reason, it isn't locked, even though Jodi hasn't been home in more than a week.

After the police officer told me about Mom's accident, he took me to the station so they could contact my next of kin. Both sets of my grandparents are deceased, and my mother is an only child.

Was. Was an only child.

My father... Well, the truth is, I'm not sure what to say about him. He may be dead too, for all I know. He walked out on my mom and me just after my twelfth birthday and we haven't seen nor heard from him for nearly five years. But my dad has a sister. Jodi.

Before last week, I hadn't seen my aunt Jodi since before my father left. When the officer located her information and called her, I can't say I was particularly hopeful that she would be sympathetic to my predicament. In fact, I fully expected to find myself in foster care. But Jodi surprised me by dropping everything, putting her life on hold, and driving over two hours from her home in Clearwater to Fraser. She totally shocked me by taking custody of me.

But by far the biggest surprise is this house. Jodi is in her early thirties and single, and I can't rectify those facts with the behemoth before me.

"You coming, Kristyl?" Jodi is watching me, and a flush rises in my cheeks. Here I am, standing and staring open-mouthed at her house while she hauls my meager belongings inside for me. I pick up the bags I dropped and hurry up the stairs.

"You can leave your things here for now. How about I give you a tour?" Jodi bounces slightly, swaying forward and backward. Her face is open and her lips curl upward in a slight smile.

I nod. "That'd be nice."

She leads me through the first floor and points out the living room—which is not to be confused with the sitting room, which is at the back of the house—and the kitchen. There's a dining room and a bathroom downstairs also. The walls are all painted in muted tones—mauve and gray-blue—and the furniture is heavy and wooden. It's probably at least as old as Jodi.

Her bedroom is on the second story, along with an office and a second bedroom. I expect her to tell me that's where I'll be staying, but she takes me to the third story. I figure this room will be full of a collection of dusty boxes, but it's not. Instead, the third floor opens up into a large suite. The space is surprisingly bright, with windows on all four walls. It feels spacious and airy despite the sloping ceiling. There is a queen-sized bed on the wall opposite the stairs and a desk to the left. Jodi walks around the stairwell to point out a small sitting area with a couch, along with the closet and a small bathroom complete with a shower stall.

"This is where you'll stay."

I look around the room, incredulous. "Seriously?"

"Unless you want the guest room on the second floor. That's fine too. I just figured you're sixteen and you'd probably like a bit of privacy."

Jodi's eyes are open wide, expectant. For a moment, I can see our family resemblance: she has my golden brown eyes, and our mouths are the same shape. But her hair is brown, wavy, and just brushes her shoulders, whereas mine is blond, pin-straight, and hangs down to my elbows. She bites her lower lip and a smile tugs the corner of my mouth—the lip thing is a typical expression for me, so it's interesting to see it on her. Like maybe it's genetic or something.

"This is great. I just... Thanks so much—again—for..."

Jodi waves a hand vaguely. "I've told you already. You don't need to thank me. Kristyl, I know we haven't been close, but we're still family. Your dad leaving doesn't make that any less true. I'm glad I can be here for you. I can't imagine what you're going through, but I want to do everything in my power to help you through it. Okay?"

I nod.

She starts back down the stairs and I follow. It would be rude to stay up in the room alone. Besides, all of my things are still in the front hallway.

Jodi leads me to the sitting room and settles down on an overstuffed couch. The only other piece of furniture in here is a red chaise lounge, which I perch on, my legs hanging off sideways. I feel strange sitting like this, but it would be even weirder to recline. I could sit on the couch, but after spending two and a half hours in the car together, I figure Jodi wants me out of her personal space.

"I've been in contact with the high school. They're expecting us tomorrow. We'll go in early and get you all set up. But if you think you need a few days before you start, just say the word. The secretary said they excuse bereavement time—and no one expects you to just jump right in—"

"No, it's fine. I'll start Monday." I take in a breath, relieved. Part of me had wondered if my suspension from my last school would follow me here. The last week has been a whirlwind of lawyers and funeral plans and packing. It's strange, but I'm actually looking forward to the monotony of school. "I think it'll be good for me."

Jodi's mouth twitches. "I talked with your last school. I'm a little surprised you're so eager to jump in here."

What do I say to that? For once, I would welcome the flashes of thoughts I'm able to pick up when I'm upset, but nothing comes to me. Does she think I'm a problem child? Does she think I'm responsible for all the things I was constantly being blamed for? I wait for a moment, wondering if she'll go on, but she doesn't. "I'm ready to make a fresh start."

Jodi nods. "I think we're all entitled to at least one of those in a lifetime."

"I didn't have a lot of friends at my old school. None, really. Everyone thought I was this weird kid and they all kind of kept their distance. Unless they were knocking into me—you know, accidentally-on-purpose." I sigh. "I don't want to be that girl anymore. I'm looking forward to being somewhere where no one knows me."

Jodi appraises me and I shift under her gaze. Does she already know those things about me? Is she judging me now? I can't fully articulate just how much I need to be somewhere new, how I need something different. I just wish it hadn't taken my mother's death to make that happen.

My stomach swoops and I take in a sharp breath. My mother is dead. Obviously I know that; I was at the funeral. Still, the thought stabs me just like it did when I first found out. It's like remembering something from a dream: One second, you are thinking about what to eat for lunch and then it hits you so hard you see stars. My heart races and I press my hand to my chest to keep it from busting through my ribcage.

Jodi stands and beckons for me to follow her. In the kitchen, she takes up a tea kettle and fills it with water from the tap. "Do you like tea?"

"Um, sure." I'm actually not sure whether I like tea. It's not something we drink regularly at my house.

Drank. This is my house now.

Jodi sets the kettle on the stove and lights the burner beneath it. I expect her to go to a cupboard to pick out a box, but she moves down the hall instead. After a moment, I follow.

"This is the greenhouse," Jodi says, opening a door at the end of the hall. "I grow all kinds of herbs in here. In the spring and summer, I have a garden in the backyard, but I've got this for when the weather's colder." She walks past the rows of plants to the back of the room, to the wall of windows overlooking the back yard. A curtain of plants hangs there, upside down, drying. She approaches a purple flower and shakes some dried petals into her palm before walking past me to exit the room. I close the door behind me and follow her back to the kitchen.

She searches through a drawer until she finds a device I've never seen before. She squeezes the metal arms together and a round mesh basket splits open at the middle like a mouth. She tips the purple petals into the mesh basket and closes it again. The tea kettle whistles and she removes it from the burner. She pours water into a cup, puts the metal device into the water, and hands it to me. After filling a glass with water for herself, she leads the way to the dining room.

I sit across from her at the table and look down at my mug, hesitant. "Is there a reason you're not having the tea?"

"I made it for you." She sips her water.

It's not exactly an answer. I want to press her for more, but I also don't want to seem ungrateful or rude. I put my lips to the mug, but the water is still too hot and I don't take a sip.

Jodi watches me. "I can't imagine how hard all this is for you, and I want to help you any way I can. I hope you get your fresh start here. But be careful. There's the kind of reinventing where you lose yourself and the kind of reinventing where you find yourself. Do you understand what I mean?"

I have no idea what she means. I attempt the tea again but it sears my upper lip. "Anything's better than who I've been."

"I don't believe that."

I want to tell her she has no idea what she's talking about, since she hasn't seen me in about five years, but I don't. If she gets mad at me, she might take back her guardianship and kick me out on the street. I blow on the tea, just for something to do. It smells earthy, more like a lawn than a beverage, and I hesitate before taking the first sip. The taste is sharp but not unpleasant. As the hot liquid trickles down my throat and coats my stomach, I take in a deep breath. The tense knot in my stomach loosens just a little and my shoulders relax. "Things have just been rough. And now..." I shake my head. I'm not even sure what else to say.

Jodi doesn't seem to expect me to go on. "It's getting late and you've had a long—well, a long run lately. You finish up your tea and I'll haul your stuff to your room."

"You don't have to—"

Jodi sets down her glass and walks toward the front door, ignoring my protests. I feel guilty for making her do the work for me, but she did offer.

For the first time in a week, I can breathe. The oppressive weight of change and uncertainty lifts. My mother is gone, and I'm living with a woman who is virtually a stranger to me. But Jodi dropped everything when I needed her and she's willing to haul my things up three flights of stairs. Tomorrow I'll start a new school where no one knows me, where I can be a new person.

All things considered, life could be much worse.

Chapter Three

I stand at the top of the stairs, surveying my new room. I'm struck anew by its size. The house I lived in before was an average-size ranch with three bedrooms and a basement. The suite that Jodi gave me is probably larger than all three bedrooms at my old house combined.

I lie down on the sleigh bed to test the mattress, pulling the yellow duvet around me. A wave of fatigue washes over me and I sit up reluctantly. I should unpack before I go to sleep.

I drag the garbage bags that contain my clothes over to the closet. My family never traveled much, and after my dad left, Mom and I didn't really have the extra money to take vacations. When it came time to pack up my belongings, Jodi and I shoved everything we could in garbage bags and the two odd boxes we found lying around the house. Everything I owned fit in the back seat and trunk of Jodi's car.

There are hangers inside the closet, but my tee-shirts don't seem like the kind of clothes one would normally hang up. Instead, I pull the clothes from the bag and arrange them on the shelves at the side of the closet. Out of the second bag, I pull out three pairs of Converse and toss them to the floor.

One of the shoes makes a strange hollow sound as it hits the wood. Curious, I bend down. One of the floorboards is warped, rising up above the level plane of the rest of the floor. I push it downward and it rocks under my hand. It's not just warped—it's loose.

Before I consciously make the decision to do so, my fingers pry at the board, wrenching it free of its place. Putting it aside, I peer into the hole it leaves behind.

The reveal is anticlimactic at best. Within the small space is one thing: an envelope, yellowing around the edges. It's clearly been there for some time. My fingers twitch as I reach toward it. The envelope bulges in the center. What could be in there?

Guilt sweeps over me as I pick it up. This isn't mine. I should take it down to Jodi. My muscles tense, ready to stand, but I freeze. I need to see what's in this envelope.

With a shake and a tilt, something slides out of the envelope into my waiting palm. A ring—a large, weighty one. It's silver and tarnished, set with a smoky dark gray stone about the size of my thumbnail. The stone is flat, but when I rub my thumb over it, I feel small bumps and ridges.

I bite my lower lip and, after a moment's hesitation, slide it onto my ring finger.

A flash of bright white light fills my vision, blotting out the room. I close my eyes and shield my face, but the light lingers. I blink and the light dissipates, replaced by a shadow that encroaches in my periphery.

I dig my fingernails into my palms and bite my lower lip, willing the darkness away, willing the pain to anchor me. It's been five years since a vision has overtaken me. I squeeze my eyes closed, taking a deep breath.

When I open my eyes, the darkness is gone. I look around the room. It's my room, but it's not my room. The bookshelf is stuffed full of mass market paperbacks and the sleigh bed is covered with a navy comforter. I'm not sure how, but I know I'm seeing the same place in a different time.

A young man in his early twenties with sandy brown hair and broad shoulders emerges from the stairwell and my heart hammers in my chest. He grumbles under his breath, clearly agitated by something. He turns toward me and I suck in air, afraid of what he'll say. What I could tell him to explain my presence in his space? But his eyes look through me and my body relaxes.

Until I look at his face. I recognize him. I've seen his face a thousand times, tucked away in the photo albums my mom kept in her closet. He's younger here than he is in any of her pictures, but there's no denying that the man standing at the top of the stairs is my father.

Shadows encroach on my periphery again and I panic, not ready to leave this vision just yet. Not ready to leave him. It's no use; the image of my father fades before my eyes. I come back to myself, to my room, my time, gasping for air. When I look around, I gasp again: my shoes, my clothes, the pillows on my bed are all hovering in midair. I crouch to the floor, covering my head. "I don't want this!"

A breeze washes over me and a chorus of dull thuds echoes through the room. I allow my eyelids to open a crack. My things are no longer floating. My shoes and clothes are scattered haphazardly over the floor of my closet, but I don't care. I press myself to standing and head for the stairs; I can't be alone in the room any longer.

The flash. I saw my father. He was standing in my room. It's been years since I had a flash like this—years since I even thought about them. It's been so long, I was able to convince myself they were all a figment of an overactive imagination—just like my mom always said. But this vision of my father didn't feel imaginary, and there is one way to find out if I'm right. I pull the ring from my finger and slip it into the pocket of my jeans before heading downstairs.

I find Jodi in the sitting room at the back of the house. She's on the couch with her legs tucked up under her, reading a book. She smiles when I enter the room and places a bookmark between the pages of her novel. "Settling in okay?"

I sit on the chaise lounge and force a nod. "Yeah, I'm getting my things put away."

She watches me. She's waiting for me to continue. I'm just not sure how to ask the question I want to have answered.

"This house," I begin. "Did you grow up here?"

She cocks her head to the side, her eyes crinkling just slightly at the corners. "Why do you ask?"

14

I open my mouth and close it again quickly. I don't want to tell her what I saw. What if she just writes it off the way my mom always used to? "I just... wondered."

She studies me for a moment, her face inscrutable, then smiles. "Yes, grew up here. When my folks died, the house went to me. It was supposed to go to your dad, but... he didn't want it."

My heartbeat speeds up at the mention of my father. "The room you put me in..."

She nods. "It was his. My room has been mine for my whole life. My folks had the room that's now the guest room. Actually, your dad's room was originally where the office is now. When he was a teenager, he decided he needed more space and he moved to the third floor."

I look around the sitting room, trying to imagine my father lounging on the couches and walking through the halls. I can't.

"If you change your mind about wanting to stay in that room, I completely understand. I just thought... Well, I thought it'd be the place you'd feel most comfortable. But I'm open to whatever you want."

"The room's fine," I say quickly. "When he moved out—my dad—did he leave anything behind?"

Jodi's face softens. "Not much. Some clothes, which went to Goodwill years ago. There might be some boxes in the garage, if you want me to check."

I shake my head. I want to know about the ring specifically. Maybe Jodi doesn't know anything about it. There is only one way to find out. Carefully, I pull the ring from my pocket and hold it out to her. "I wasn't snooping," I begin, "but this was in the closet—under a loose floorboard."

Jodi reaches for the ring. I don't want to give it to her, but it seems rude not to. She studies it for a moment, her eyes narrowing. "This was his," she says after a pause. "Well, really, it was our dad's. And his dad's before him. It's been passed down through several generations."

"Oh," I say. My fingers twitch. I have the urge to take the ring back, but Jodi is still scrutinizing it.

"I wondered what happened to it. I always figured your dad

took it when he moved out." She smiles. "It actually makes me happy to know it's safe." She holds it out to me. "Well, it's yours now."

"Really?" I didn't expect her to hand it over to me quite so easily.

"Of course. If you want, I could clean it up for you first. I'm sure I've got some silver polish kicking around here somewhere."

"I'd like that."

Jodi sets her novel on the coffee table and stands. I follow her into the dining room, where she opens the bottom cupboards of a heavy-looking hutch laden with white plates and cut crystal glasses. After a moment, she holds up a bottle triumphantly. "Aha!"

It doesn't take long for her to restore the ring's shining luster, but every second that passes feels like a geologic age. I need the ring back in my hands. It was my father's. I have so few connections to him that this new discovery is precious. It's like having a piece of him back.

She finishes wiping off the polish and my fingers twitch again, but before I can reach for it, she curls her fingers around it and darts from the room. "I'll be right back," she calls, and her footfalls thump on the stairs.

My body lunges forward involuntarily, and only with effort do I manage not to follow her. She'll bring it back. She said it's mine.

Seconds tick by, and after what feels like minutes, the stairs creak to herald Jodi's descent. When she reenters the room, she's smiling. She holds up her hand, and dangling from it is the ring, threaded through a fine chain of white gold. "It's probably a bit big for your fingers," she says, latching the clasp at the back of my neck.

I pick up the ring and look down into the stone. I stare for a long while before I realize what I'm doing: waiting. When I put it on my finger before, I saw something. Now I'm waiting for it to show me something else. But that is ridiculous, isn't it? "Thank you."

She nods, eyes crinkling again in the corners. She tilts her head to the side. "Is there something else?"

The cadence of my heartbeat picks up. I want to tell Jodi about what I saw, but fear stops the words in my throat. Adults don't generally respond positively to children who tell them they're seeing visions. I learned that years ago, the hard way.

I shake my head, but Jodi doesn't break eye contact. "You can talk to me about anything, you know," she says, and her words pierce me. The corners of her mouth upturn slightly. "You know, scientists say the linear progression of time is actually just an illusion?"

I blink, shaking my head. "What does that even mean?"

"Sorry, I'm kind of a PBS junky. I was watching a special a while back about how what we think about time might not actually be accurate. Apparently, even though we experience time minute by minute, second by second, it might not really exist that way. All time occurs right now. It's just we can only see it unfolding in one direction." She rubs her eyebrow. "It kind of makes my brain hurt to think about."

An empty feeling forms in the pit of my stomach. "Why are you telling me this?"

She shrugs. "Your dad grew up here. If all time is really happening right now, that means he's here with you. I just... I thought it might be a comforting thought." She smiles. "Or not. Don't worry—if you need to ignore your creepy aunt Jodi when she starts talking about space-time, feel free."

I force a smile, but her words don't calm me. Instead, I'm unsettled because I think I can see through the illusion.

Chapter Four

Though I spend all of breakfast assuring Jodi that I am both ready and excited to start school Monday morning, a knot of dread forms in my stomach as we drive to Clearwater High School. What if things are the same here as they were at my old school? The only thing that's changed is geography; I'm still the same person I've always been. What if the strange incidents that have plagued me for the last five years follow me here?

When we pull up in front of the building, I'm frozen, and it's not until Jodi opens my door for me that I actually make a move to get out of the car. The sandy brown brick edifice stretches three stories into the sky, its windows like blank, soulless eyes staring at me. My stomach sinks as I start toward the front door.

School doesn't officially begin for another half hour, so there aren't many people milling around as we make our way inside and to the principal's office. A woman with shoulder-length dark brown hair and a broad forehead stands just inside the main office, looking official in her heather gray suit and white blouse. She smiles at Jodi and the two hug and exchange pleasantries. Jodi mentioned at breakfast that she and my principal are old friends, but their greeting is still weird to me.

Mrs. Cole also smiles warmly at me, then ushers me into her office. This is such a sharp contrast to the last time I was in a principal's office, it's surreal. She settles behind her desk and Jodi and I take the seats across from her. On her desk is a manila folder. The tab reads *Kristyl Barnette* and an icy feeling washes over me. Has she looked at that file yet? She can't have if she's smiling at me like this.

"Well, Kristyl, are you excited to be starting school? I understand the circumstances surrounding your move to Clearwater are tragic, but let me just say how excited Jodi is to have you here with her. I'm sure she's told you that, but I want to assure you it's true. Family is very important to us here in Clearwater."

I fix my eyes on Mrs. Cole, unwilling to look over at Jodi to confirm what she's saying. "Have you read my file?" The words come out in a rush and I press my hand over my mouth as soon as I say them.

Mrs. Cole's eyes crinkle, her eyebrows furrowing. "Of course. Why?"

I put my hands in my lap. "Nothing... It's just... You're being so nice to me. I'm not used to that. If you read my file, you'd know how often I was in trouble."

Mrs. Cole smiles. "I'm sorry your experiences with administrators have been negative. I think a move to a smaller school—a smaller community—is just what you need. You'll get the attention you need here, Kristyl. I have no doubt the disciplinary issues from your past will remain there."

I nod enthusiastically. "That's what I want. I want to be able to start over here. Does anyone else know what's in my file?"

"Your teachers will have access to it, but I see no reason why any of them would come to check it. You'll have your fresh start here, Kristyl."

For the first time since pulling up in front of the building, I can breathe freely. "I'm glad for that."

Mrs. Cole goes over my schedule with me and explains some of the big rules in the student handbook. By the time we're done, the energy in the building has changed and I'm not surprised to hear a bell.

"You should get going so you're not late to your first hour."

In the hallway, dozens of students, most in groups, head off in different directions. I take in a deep breath. No one knows me here. I can be whoever I want to be. I don't have to be the freaky girl who's always in trouble. I can just be... me.

Jodi doesn't pull me into a hug before she leaves, even though her eyes say she wants to. Instead she presses a handful of bills into my palm for lunch money, squeezing my hand a beat too long before heading out the main door.

Part of me wants to follow her, but another part—the part that speaks with my mother's voice—urges me to grab this opportunity for a new beginning and make the most of it.

A prickling sensation builds in the corners of my eyes at the thought of my mom and I try to rub it away. I won't cry about my mom, not here. Taking in a breath, I start toward the nearest stairwell. I take no more than two steps before I collide with someone. Searing pain cascades down my chest and I cry out, my hands going to my abdomen to find my shirt soaked with hot liquid. A sniff tells me it's coffee.

A squeal emanates from the girl standing in front of me. She is tall—or at least taller than me—with long brown hair that hangs in loose spirals around her shoulders and the coldest blue eyes I have ever seen. Her eyes narrow and her mouth curls into a sneer.

"What the hell? Watch where you're going!"

"I'm sorry." The words escape my mouth instinctively. I've learned it's best to ask for forgiveness right away, no matter if something is actually my fault. It's a coping mechanism I've developed after years of getting into this kind of situation with this kind of girl.

So much for a fresh start.

"Not as sorry as you're gonna be if you got any of that on me." The girl examines her outfit—a tight-fitting green tunic top over leggings and knee-high boots—and turns in place so her companion can help her check. Her hands clutch at the necklace she wears around her neck—some kind of pendant with an ornate design that holds a clear, glass-like stone in place. "Bridget, how does it look?"

"It looks okay," Bridget pipes in after completing her inspection. "I think it all got on her."

After the brief reprieve, the girl turns her cold eyes back on me. "Do you have any idea how much that coffee cost?"

I don't look away from the girl, but I feel the eyes of other students on me. A crowd has gathered, the way one always does at the hint of drama. "Four dollars?" I venture tentatively. "I'll buy you another one. I can get you the money tomorrow, if you like—"

The girl's withering glare stops my tongue. "How is that supposed to help me *today*?"

I'm not sure whether the question is rhetorical.

A bell sounds in the hallway and the students who had gathered to watch our spectacle scatter. I want to scatter with them, but I remain rooted to my spot.

Bridget tugs on the girl's arm. "Crystal, we've gotta go. We've already been late once this week."

I'm stabbed by a pang of irony at the girl's name. Well, at least I won't forget it.

Crystal's eyes tell me she doesn't want to leave—she wants to dole out the appropriate punishment for my actions—but she relents. "Watch where you're going, new girl. You'll stay out of my way if you know what's good for you."

Duly noted, I think, but I keep my mouth shut. Crystal and Bridget strut off in the direction they had been heading and I scurry the opposite way, even though I'm not entirely sure where I should be going. Once safely enclosed in the stairwell, I look down at my coffee-stained schedule. A brown stain covers my stomach and the crotch of my pants and I lean against the wall, squeezing my eyes closed tight in an attempt to stop the prickling sensation gathering there. I can't cry. Not now—the school day hasn't even started yet. But how am I supposed to go through the entire day with a coffee stain covering so much of my body? That's all anyone will ever remember about me—the spaz of a girl who wore coffee-covered clothes her first day. It might be better than the way people at my other school thought of me, but not by much.

I could call Jodi, but she told me she was heading into work right after dropping me off. She was already off all last week on account of me, so I don't want to pull her away from it. I don't want to give her any reason to regret taking me in.

Another bell rings and a wave of dread sweeps over me. I'm late to class. Not a great way to make a good impression on my teacher.

21

I need to get moving, but I can't make myself go.

The stairwell door creaks open, but I refuse to look. Whoever it is can't make the day better. In fact, they could only make things worse. Maybe he'll continue on his way without noticing me.

"Hey, you okay?"

No such luck.

I take in a steadying breath before opening my eyes. Standing before me is a guy with the brightest, clearest blue eyes I've ever seen. They're such a contrast from that Crystal girl's eyes that for a moment, they're all I see.

His eyebrows furrow. "Do you need some help?"

"I'm okay." The words are an obvious lie, but I press on. "I just bumped into some girl and she spilled her coffee on me. That's all."

"It looks pretty bad. Do you have something to change into?"

I shake my head. "It's my first day. I don't have, like, a closet of clothes stashed in my locker or anything. I don't even know where my locker is. Or my class, for that matter." I press my lips together to keep from continuing; if I do, I'll spin out of control. Hysteria is rising in my chest. If only I could go back in time and redo this day.

"It'll be okay," the guy says. His face goes thoughtful and I take in the rest of his appearance. The amazing eyes are set in a handsome face with a jaw that is strong but not pronounced. His blond hair is short and gently spiked. He looks a little like he could be in a boy band, but in a good way. The curve of his lips is gentle and pleasant and he has a cleft in his chin. On his face is the barest hint of stubble.

A thrill of electricity courses through my brain. He meant to shave this morning. But he forgot to plug his phone in last night and it died before his alarm went off. That's why he's late.

He snaps his fingers, pulling me out of the flash. "Here, hold this," he says, handing me the folder he's been holding.

I take it without question and he pulls the dark blue hooded sweatshirt he wears up over his head. As he does, his tee-shirt rises up, revealing a stretch of taut stomach. There's a swooping sensation low in my belly.

"Here," he says, holding the sweatshirt out to me.

I stare at him. "You want me to hold this too?"

A smile stretches across his face, revealing a set of perfect teeth. My stomach swoops again. "Sure, that. Or you could wear it to cover up the coffee stain. It's long, so it should cover it all."

I shake my head. "I couldn't do that."

"What, you'd rather walk around with the coffee stains all day? Go on, I insist." He takes his folder from my hand and presses the hoodie closer to me. He's not going to give up, so I take it, turning it over in my hands. Emblazoned in white on the front of the shirt is the high school's name and two C's bisected by an arrow. On the back is the number seventeen, below the name MARSH. I pull it over my head. It's warm and smells spicy, like aftershave or body spray—something distinctly masculine but not overpowering. I tug the sweatshirt down so it comes to my mid-thigh. It's far too large for me, but the guy was right—it covers all the coffee stains.

"Thank you." My voice is small.

The corner of his mouth twitches upward, revealing a dimple in his cheek. "Of course. What kind of man would I be if I let a damsel remain in distress?" He winks.

I feel heat in my cheeks and look down at my schedule. Something about wearing his clothes makes me brave. "If you're still in the rescuing mood, maybe you could help me navigate to my first hour."

"Of course." Instead of taking the schedule from my hands, he moves to stand behind me, looking over my shoulder. His nearness overwhelms my senses. My stomach flutters. Warmth is radiating off his body and I think I might spontaneously combust.

"You've got Buchanan in two-fourteen. I'll take you." We walk up the stairs side by side. He watches me out of the corner of his eye. "What's your name, anyway?"

"Kristyl Barnette."

"Kristyl, huh?" He makes a face. "No offense. I'm not a huge fan of that name."

"Would it have anything to do with the raging bitch who spilled her coffee all over me?" The words come out before I can stop them and I slap my hand over my mouth, mortified. Wearing this stranger's sweatshirt, or maybe his kindness, is making me say things I normally wouldn't.

He laughs and I relax. "Ah, so you've already had the pleasure. I've known her my whole life and, well, I think you got it right. Raging bitch pretty much sums her up. Crystal Jamison is not one of my favorite people in the world. But you..." He studies me as we reach the top of the stairs and I feel self-conscious. "You, I like. So I think the name's gotta go."

"What? You're just gonna change my name? Start calling me Persephone or something?"

He laughs, holding open the door and allowing me to pass through. "While Persephone isn't bad, I was thinking of something a little less dramatic. A nickname, maybe." His lips press together as he thinks. "Krissy and Kristy are a little too pedestrian. Kris is too masculine." He snaps, a smile spreading across his face. "I got it. How about Krissa?"

"Krissa?" I've never heard the name before. It sounds unusual, but not too unusual. "I think I like it."

"Okay then. Krissa it is. New school, new name."

"New friend?" The assumption is bold, but I'm feeling bold. "I don't even know your name."

He holds his hand out formally and I take it. "Owen Marsh."

"Owen." I like the feeling of his name in my mouth. "It's nice to meet you, Owen."

"It's nice to meet you too. But I'm afraid it's time to say goodbye." He nods toward the door to our left. "This is Miss Buchanan's class."

"What about your sweatshirt?"

"Don't worry, I'll be back for that." With a grin, he starts off down the hall.

I knock on the door to the classroom and after a moment, the teacher opens it. "Ah. You must be the new student I saw on my roster today." She smiles and walks over to her desk. I close the door and follow her. She clicks the mouse on her computer a few times before looking at me again. "Kristyl Barnette, is it?"

"Actually, I go by Krissa."

Chapter Five

The first few classes of the day pass without incident. Owen is in my second hour and manages to convince the teacher to give me a seat near him. During third hour, I try to pay attention to the lesson, but my thoughts stray to Owen. I catch myself smelling his scent and smiling and try to tell myself not to harbor any delusions about Owen liking me, but I can't help it.

When the third hour bell rings, I head into the hallway. Owen is standing there, and his face lights up when he sees me.

I walk over to him. "Were you waiting for me?"

"I may have inadvertently memorized your schedule. You know, so I could keep an eye on my sweatshirt."

"Of course." I can't help smiling. Is this what it's like to flirt? I bite my lower lip. No, he's not flirting with me. He's just being nice.

"You've got lunch now, right?"

I check my schedule, although I know I do. "Would you look at that." I grin.

He starts down the hallway and I keep pace with him. "I thought you could sit with me and my friends. Unless you've already got lunch plans."

"No, no plans. Just a few dollars from my aunt. Maybe you can show me what's edible in the cafeteria."

We walk through the large foyer by the front office where I bumped into Crystal Jamison. So far I haven't seen her again and I can't say I'm sad about that. Owen leads me through a back hallway and we emerge in a large, open area with vending machines. "This is the commons. There are doors here that lead out into the courtyard. When it's warm, sometimes we'll eat out there. Back there is the lunch room. And here is the dreaded lunch line." He shudders dramatically. "Actually, all things considered, the food's not terrible. Was it bad at your old school?"

My gaze drops to the floor as we get into line. My mom always packed my lunches. Even when I was in high school and complained I was too old for it, even when I begged for her to let me buy lunch. She insisted it was too expensive. I probably could have qualified for reduced lunch, but my mom never filled out the paperwork. I think it was pride: She wanted to prove she could take care of me, even without my dad's help. She always made sure my needs were provided for and that my wants, which were few, were satisfied. A lump forms in my throat and I swallow hard. "The food at my old school was fine."

Owen's eyes narrow and he closes them for a moment, shaking his head. "Yeah, I think people always make it out to be way worse than it is."

When I'm three people away from the register, the hairs on the back of my neck stand up. Someone is watching me. I glance over my shoulder but see no one. Still, the feeling doesn't leave me as Owen and I walk to his usual lunch table. I take the seat across from him, but he immediately shakes his head. "Can't sit there."

My heart skips. Didn't he invite me to sit with him? "Why not?"

"Spot's taken." He points at the seat beside it. "You could sit there." A smile curls the edges of his mouth. "Or your could sit by me."

The tension that had formed in my stomach dissipates and I take the seat beside the first one. While the idea of sitting next to Owen is appealing, I'm not sure whether he's joking. Besides, I like to look at him, and that would be more difficult if I was directly beside him.

"So, who's the seat taken by? A ghost? Your invisible friend?"

He shakes his head. "Nah, just a friend who's a little territorial when it comes to seating arrangements."

"Really? What's his name?"

Before Owen can respond, someone nearly collapses into the seat beside me. To my surprise, it's not a guy; it's a girl with wavy red hair and a distinct sense of style. I recognize her from first period. She is wearing a bright orange tunic, heavily embellished with sequins across the bodice, over a pair of purple leggings with cat faces on the knees. Her boots come halfway up her calf and are covered in what looks like black fur. On her face is a harassed look. When she notices me, the look switches to confusion. She looks across the table at Owen, as if verifying she's at the right table. Then she looks back at me. "Who are you?"

I bite my lower lip. She seems annoyed by my presence and a thought passes through my mind: What if she's Owen's girlfriend? That would explain her irritation. Not only am I some strange girl sitting with him, but I'm also wearing his sweatshirt. Did she notice? I open my mouth to introduce myself, but Owen is already talking.

"Be nice, Lexie, she's new. Her name's Krissa and she's cool."

My heart swells at Owen's words. Really, he has no foundation on which to base his pronouncement, but it makes me feel good anyway.

"Krissa?" Lexie asks, turning the syllables over in her mouth. "What kind of name is that? Is it short for something?"

I nod. "Yeah. For Kristyl."

Lexie's head cocks to the side and she raises an eyebrow. Then her eyes widen and her mouth drops open. "Hey, I know you!"

I glance at Owen, who looks as confused as I feel. Lexie turns toward Owen and slams her hand on the lunch table between them. "Kristyl *Barnette*. She's Jodi Barnette's niece."

My confusion deepens as I look back and forth at the two of them. "Wait—you guys know my aunt?"

It's Lexie and Owen's turn to look at me with confusion.

"Of course we do," Lexie says, as if it should be obvious.

"Small town," Owen says. "She owns the homeopathic shop on Main. Everybody's been in there at least once."

I nod. It shouldn't surprise me that they know Jodi. She's lived here her entire life. Living in such a small community is going to take some getting used to. "And you guys know about me?"

"My mom said something about Jodi's shop being closed last week because she was out of town with her niece." Lexie picks up a french fry from her lunch tray and chews on it. "She didn't mention you'd be showing up here, though."

I take in a breath. Maybe because I never talked to anyone at my old school, I hadn't really planned how I would address my reason for moving to Clearwater. I also hadn't counted on people knowing who my aunt was. When new people started at my old school, it was just assumed they moved to town with their families. But how was I supposed to explain my being here? I cast a glance at Owen. "I... I'm living with Jodi now."

"Really?" Lexie asks. "Why?"

Owen lets out a little laugh. "Wow, Lexie. Let's save the twenty questions for later, how about?"

I mouth *Thank you* to Owen and he nods. I'm not sure if he can tell what I'm feeling or if he already knows something about why I'm here. Either way, I'm glad he intervened.

I start poking around at the food on my tray, no longer hungry. The back of my neck prickles and, once again, I'm sure I'm being watched. At my old school, people generally ignored me—unless they were really bored and needed a target. The feeling now is the same as the one I'd get right before someone at my old school would come up to do something to mess with me. Surreptitiously, I look over my shoulder, eyes scanning for anyone whose attention is directed my way.

"Why is Crystal Jamison watching you?" Lexie's neck is craned around in the direction I'm looking.

A knot ties itself in the pit of my stomach. "I think I'm already on her bad side." I turn my attention back to our lunch table.

Lexie stares at Crystal a moment longer before turning back as well. "She's only got a bad side."

"Really?"

She nods. "Think of crossing her as a rite of passage. You're officially initiated into Clearwater High."

I smile. "I guess that makes me feel a little better. I thought she just hated me because I spilled her coffee."

Lexie's eyes go wide. "Oh, *you're* the one who spilled her

coffee?" She holds up her hand and, after a moment, I bring my hand up to meet her high five.

"That's how Owen and I met, actually. Her coffee spilled all over my shirt and he offered me his hoodie to cover it up."

"Such a gentleman." A guy with artfully disheveled blond hair settles down in the seat beside Owen, placing his lunch tray down in front of him. He fixes his warm brown eyes on me and smiles. "Coffee Girl. Excellent."

Heat rises in my cheeks. "Coffee Girl? Is that what they're calling me?"

"West, this is Krissa," Owen says, nodding toward me. "Krissa Barnette, West Harmon."

West reaches across the table and I take his hand. The palm is warm and his grip is firm. His eyebrows are heavy, giving him a brooding look, even though he's smiling at me. "I think we're in first hour together. It's nice to officially meet you, Krissa. Anyone who pisses off Crystal Jamison so thoroughly is a friend of mine."

I force a smile. "Is she really that upset? I mean, it was an accident. I apologized."

West waves off my concern. "She'll get over it. She just loves the drama of it all."

A girl with black hair cut in a severe bob sits down on Lexie's other side. "Drama? Let me guess: We're talking about Crystal Jamison?"

West laughs. "How'd you know?" He gestures toward the girl. "Krissa, this is Bria Tate. Bria, this is Coffee Girl."

Bria fixes her gaze on me and I'm taken aback by the amount of eyeliner surrounding her eyes. It's heavy and dark, making her look almost menacing. But she smiles, revealing a dimple and a gap between her front teeth. She salutes me and, unsure of what else to do, I salute back. She laughs. "Good move with the coffee. She's been out of sorts all day."

I bite my lower lip. "It's not like I planned to do it."

"Still." Bria stabs her salad with a plastic fork.

The eyes are still prickling me, but I don't want to turn around. I look at Owen. "Is she still watching me?"

Owen nods.

"Probably trying to figure out how to exact her revenge," West says. "What do you think, Lexie? A little eye of newt, toe of hamster?"

Bria titters with laughter and Owen groans and shakes his head. I look at Lexie. "What does he mean?"

"Not this again," Owen mutters.

Lexie throws a fry at him. "Don't listen to Owen. He's an unbeliever."

Owen snorts. "Don't listen to Lexie. She's delusional."

"If by delusional you mean completely correct." Lexie turns to me. "Crystal Jamison is a witch."

It takes a moment for her words to register, and even when they do, it takes me a moment to process them. I watch Lexie's face, waiting for a tell that she's joking, but she appears entirely serious. "Wait. Witches?" A laugh escapes my lips. "Like, spells and magic and—like, witches?" Another laugh bubbles up within me and I smile hesitantly. "Yeah, right. You really had me going there for a second."

Lexie and West exchange glances. "What's so funny?"

I shake my head. "Witches aren't real. Not, like, *magic* witches."

But even as I say the words, something tugs at the back of my mind. What about what happened to me last night when I put on my dad's old ring? Or all the times when I get upset and things *happen*? Or when I know what someone's thinking? The thoughts bubble to the forefront of my mind, and I press my lips together to keep from speaking them aloud.

"She's not joking," Owen says. "She seriously thinks Crystal and her friends are witches."

I look at Bria for confirmation, but she just shrugs. This motion isn't lost on Lexie, who gives an exasperated sigh. "Come on, guys. Do we need to go over the evidence again?"

"Evidence?" I ask. "Does she usually wear a pointy hat?"

Lexie shakes her head. "Look, loathe as I am to admit it, I do have a little bit of special insight into Crystal."

I wait for her to go on, but her mouth puckers, like she's tasting something sour.

Owen leans across the table. "What Lexie's trying to say is that she used to be really close with Crystal."

"So, what? They used to be friends?"

"More than that," Owen says. "They're cousins."

Lexie's eyes narrow at the word but she doesn't deny it. "Summer before ninth grade, she started getting all weird. She got convinced there was something special about the descendants of the founding families—"

"The founding families?"

West nods. "Yeah—you know, the families that first settled here in Clearwater?"

I shake my head. "And I should know this... why?"

His eyes narrow in confusion. "Because you're from one of them."

I look to Owen, who nods. "Yeah—there's a handful of the founding families still around. Some have died out or moved away. You're from one. So is Lexie. Crystal, of course. Bridget Burke, Felix Wolfe. Mrs. Cole."

"Wait—Mrs. Cole? The principal?"

"Yeah." He shrugs. "It's not really a big deal—unless you're Lexie."

Lexie clears her throat. "Unless you're *Crystal.* I'm telling you, she's convinced being a member of a founding family is really important." For a moment, it looks like Lexie won't go on, but she finally turns to me, taking in a deep breath. "Summer before freshman year, she found some stuff that used to belong to our aunt, Crystal Taylor. The original Crystal. Like, an old diary and some jewelry or something. But after that, she started acting weird—you know, spending long hours at the library weird. She got joined at the hip with Bridget, even though the two barely spoke all through middle school."

I chew on my lower lip. Making a new friend hardly seems like cause for concern. "And how does this get you to her being a witch?"

Lexie sighs. "It's not just that. My dad's told me some stuff about his sister—Crystal Taylor. See, before she died, my dad's family was all one big happy, you know? Crystal was the kid sister both he and Crystal Jamison's mom doted on. But all that changed after my grandfather died. My aunt Crystal got all weird and started keeping to herself. She dumped a bunch of her friends and started hanging out with a new group. Apparently she got obsessed with the idea of the founding families. Is this sounding familiar? My dad thinks she got involved in something that was too much for her and it got her killed. He thinks that something might have been magic."

I suppress a shiver. Whether or not the words are true, Lexie is good at spinning the tale. "How'd she die?"

"A fire. My grandma was out of town visiting relatives. My dad says the official story is my aunt Crystal lit some candles and fell asleep and something caught fire. But he says he doesn't buy that. A couple months earlier, before he went off to college, he caught her trying out some incantations or something. He thinks she started messing with something she didn't understand."

A bell sounds and I jump. West and Bria laugh as they stand up, taking their empty lunch trays with them. They call goodbye to everyone—to me, too—before disappearing into the crowd to head for their next class. Neither Lexie nor Owen leaves and it strikes me that they're waiting for me so we can all go together. Something swells in my chest and I can't suppress a smile as I stand to discard my garbage.

Owen walks beside me as we join the surge of students. "So, what do you think about Lexie's story?"

I shrug. "It's interesting, I guess. But I'm not sure how much I believe."

Lexie appears on my other side, shaking her head. "With the kind of store your aunt runs, I didn't think you'd be this close-minded."

Owen bumps my shoulder with his, nodding in Lexie's direction. "I bet you didn't think Lexie'd be this crazy."

I force a smile, but something in Lexie's words strikes me. Am I being close-minded? After the things that have been happening around me, the things I've done, can I really rule out the idea of witches so quickly?

Another thought enters my mind so fast it takes my breath

away: What if Crystal and her friends can do the things I can do? What if *I* am a witch?

I shake my head to dispel the notion. It's ridiculous.

Isn't it?

Chapter Six

Eyes follow me for the rest of the day, but if Crystal Jamison is thinking of getting back at me for the coffee incident, her revenge plans are still in the conception phase. After the final bell, I go to my locker. Owen is already there.

"You really are stalking me, aren't you?" I duck my head as I spin the dial, hoping to hide the smile pulling at the corners of my mouth.

Owen leans against the locker beside mine, a grin stretched across his face. "I'm just looking out for my sweatshirt."

My fingers go to the hem of the shirt, but I'm reluctant to remove it. In addition to still being coffee-stained underneath, I like the feeling of the material on my skin. Biting my lower lip, I return my hands to the business of collecting the night's necessities. I slam the locker and turn to Owen. He's still smiling.

"So, you got plans this afternoon?" he asks as we start down the hall.

My stomach twists, but the feeling is not unpleasant. Why does he want to know? Does he want to invite me to do something? Or is he just making polite small talk? "I'm not sure. Jodi's picking me up and I think we're going to hang out at the shop for a bit." I almost tag *Why?* to the end of my statement, but the word sticks in my throat.

We head down the stairs. "So, are you gonna be helping Jodi at the shop now? Every day?" Owen asks.

I shrug. "We haven't really discussed it."

"Because I drive by there on my way home. I could drop you off—you know, so Jodi doesn't have to leave to get you."

He holds the door open for me and we step out into the crisp October air. I lead the way to the street in front of the school, where Jodi parked this morning. Her silver Ford Focus is nowhere in sight.

Owen shifts beside me—I haven't responded to his offer. "It'd be nice for you to drop me off. I'll talk with Jodi about it, okay?"

Relief sweeps over his features and it strikes me that he's been tense during this whole exchange. A jolt of energy courses through me.

A horn honks and Jodi's car pulls up in front of me. The passenger window rolls down and Jodi leans over to it. "Hey, Kristyl. Does your friend need a ride?"

Owen touches my elbow. "I'll see you tomorrow." He nods in Jodi's direction and heads for the parking lot.

I watch him go until he disappears into the crowd of people swarming the lot. When I slide into the passenger seat, Jodi's eyes are on me, her eyebrows raised. I click my seatbelt in place, heat rising in my cheeks.

Jodi puts the car in gear and pulls away from the curb. "Were you wearing that sweatshirt this morning?"

I clap my hand to my forehead. "No—it's Owen's. I forgot to give it back to him."

"Something tells me he won't mind." Jodi smiles as she turns a corner. "That was Owen Marsh, wasn't it?"

Does everyone know everyone in this town? "Yeah. He lent me his sweatshirt after I got coffee all over my shirt—long story."

Jodi takes my cue and doesn't ask me to elaborate. In minutes, we drive over a small river and arrive at what Jodi refers to as "downtown," which looks like three blocks' worth of small stores, plus a gas station. The storefronts are all painted muted, natural tones—sea green, pale blue, storm gray. There are a couple pairs of women pushing strollers, and a few people walking leashed dogs. A few knots of high school students lounge outside the coffee shop. A restaurant's outside dining area spills onto the sidewalk and the tables are populated with people ranging in age from early twenties to late seventies. I try to imagine myself walking down the street, belonging here. The image feels hollow until I add in the friends I made today—Owen, Lexie, Bria, West. Might I be one of the people laughing outside the coffee shop or eating at the restaurant one day?

Jodi turns onto a side street and pulls into a small parking lot behind a block-long stretch of buildings that all share walls. She gets out of the car and leads me toward a glass door with a white decal of flowery-looking letters that spell out a name.

"Hannah's Herbs?" I ask as Jodi unlocks the door and pushes it open.

Jodi pulls a sign that reads "Back in 15 Minutes" from the door as she enters. "This is my store. Well, mine now. It was my parents' store—your grandparents. When they passed, it passed to me. One day, if you want it, it'll pass to you."

How do I respond to this information? I look around the store. The place isn't large, and it's nearly twice as deep as it is wide. Banks of tall shelves running perpendicular to the long walls maximize the space for displaying wares. Jodi walks to the front of the store to unlock the other door, but I don't follow her. There is too much to look at, from the dried plants bundled and bunched in decorative aluminum planters to the books with titles like *Homeopathic Healing* and *Herbs that Help, Herbs that Harm*, to the shelves stacked with crystals and other stones. There are dozens of brown paper bags full of different blends of tea. On one shelf is a long line of bracelets. Some have different colored gemstones on them, others appear to be made of magnets.

"So, what do you think?" Jodi asks, moving to the register.

I tuck my hair behind my ears. "This is... an interesting place."

Jodi laughs, her head tipping backward. "That's a diplomatic way to say 'strange,' isn't it?"

I shake my head and open my mouth to apologize, but Jodi is smiling at me.

"Don't worry, I'm not offended. It's nothing I haven't heard before, believe me."

I nod, approaching a shelf full of vials of liquids with names I can't even begin to pronounce and little blue tubes filled with tiny white pellets. "What is all this stuff?"

"Medicine. A lot of it, anyway. There are homeopathic remedies along that wall, reference books on the shelf there. Herbs here, of course. And then gemstones."

"What are the stones for?" I move to the shelves that hold the gems and study them. They come in all shapes, textures, and colors.

"Some people believe they have therapeutic qualities. Some people use them as paper weights." She grins at me.

"You said this was your parents' store?"

She nods. "It's been in the family for generations. After her husband died, to make ends meet, my great-grandmother, your great-great-grandmother, started selling herbs out of her house. Our house. This storefront is relatively new. Your dad was supposed to take it over, but he went down a different path. So, here I am."

"Are you okay with that?"

She shrugs. "I could always sell the place. But it doesn't seem right. Besides, I like it. It's like a second home, really. The hours I spent here growing up." She smiles. "I can't imagine doing anything else with my life, you know?"

I keep my eyes on the stones in front of me as I ask the next question. "Did my dad spend a lot of time in here?"

"Yeah, he did. It was a pretty big scandal when he decided to go to college for engineering instead of a sensible business degree. I remember he was so nervous to tell our dad, but when he did, Dad took it well."

Longing swells within me. Besides last night's discussion, it's been years since I've talked about my dad. Mom always tensed up and frowned when I asked questions about him, so I learned not to ask. "What was he like?"

Jodi's shoulders sag and her eyes soften. "He was good," she says quietly. "A really good big brother. He's eight years older, and he always kind of doted on me. I could get him to do anything. I remember going through a phase where I wanted him to be my horsey all the time. I'd make him give me rides on his back from the kitchen to the living room to the dining room—everywhere.

And he never complained."

I pick up a smoky pink quartz from the shelf and rub the pad of my thumb over its rough edges. "Have you... heard from him?"

She bites her lower lip and shakes her head. "Not in years. He called me once after he left you guys. I tried to get him to tell me where he was, why he left, but..." She sniffs and rubs her nose. "Damn, I miss him."

I nod. I know exactly what she means. An ache builds in my chest and I hold the stone in my hand out to her, eager to change the subject. "So, what does this do?"

Relief flickers across her face and she smiles. "It doesn't really do anything. Not on its own. It's more like a conduit."

"For what?"

"Energy. It can amplify energy, direct it. Store it, if you know what you're doing. Quartz is particularly versatile. That's a rose quartz that you're holding. It's usually associated with love and affection. So, a person might wear or carry it if they're wanting to focus that kind of energy on themselves."

I raise an eyebrow at her. "Seriously? You believe that?"

She shrugs. "Everything's energy, right? Why is it so strange to think that certain objects can't help direct energy in a certain way?"

I don't say anything, but Jodi doesn't seem to expect a response. She moves to the counter on the left side of the store and ducks behind the cash register. When she emerges, she's holding a clipboard and a pencil.

"Why don't you make yourself useful? The bracelets need to be inventoried."

I set down the rose quartz and cross the room to take the clipboard. I can't argue with her—counting bracelets seems like the least I can do to repay her for taking me in. She tells me how to match up the numbers on the list and the tags on the bracelets and I get to work.

I lose count twice when customers come into the store. The first is an older woman, stylishly dressed in knit slacks and a blue blouse. She selects a few bunches of herbs and a couple bottles of dark-colored liquid. I try to figure out what she's buying, but I don't want to appear like I'm snooping. The woman and Jodi have a long conversation at the register before she leaves. The second customer is a man who is probably Jodi's age. He selects several blue vials of pellets and pays, not bothering to engage in conversation like the woman did.

I decide piling the bracelets into groups of ten might be my best course of action. I glance up at Jodi as I make piles on the floor around me, waiting for an admonishment, but it doesn't come.

I'm on the last page of the list when the bell over the door chimes for the third time. I ignore the patron who passes me, intent on finishing my task. I smile triumphantly when I get to the end of the list and start replacing the bracelets on their stand. When I do so, the newest customer finally catches my eye. He appears to be about my age, tall, with dark hair. If he goes to school with me, he must have been absent today. The long lines of his body move with the elegant grace of a cat. Even in a crowded hallway, I would have noticed him.

He doesn't look in my direction. His eyes scan the bundles of herbs, but the set of his jaw tells me he isn't seeing what he wants.

Jodi doesn't approach the guy, but her eyes don't leave him. Maybe he's been in here before, and she doesn't trust him for some reason. Is he a shoplifter? Seeing as there is no one else in the store, it seems unlikely—there isn't nearly enough distraction. Besides, are herbs and crystals really worthwhile targets for theft?

He scans the rows of herbs twice before turning his attention to Jodi. "Have you got any lavender? In back or something?"

Jodi raises her eyebrows. "*More* lavender?"

"Give me a break, okay? My grandma likes using it in tea and lemonade and potpourri—I think she's got a problem, truth be told." An easy smile stretches across his face as he looks at Jodi. "Could you look for me?"

Jodi's mouth twitches. Her eyes dart to me briefly before she responds. "I've got some lavender in my greenhouse, but it's not ready yet. I can give your grandma a call when it's ready, if you like."

He shakes his head. "No need."

I figure that since Jodi doesn't have what he's looking for, he'll leave, but he doesn't make a move toward the door. Instead, he wanders over to the shelves of gems and stones and passes his hand over them. After a moment, he picks up the same piece of rose quartz I held earlier. Slowly, he turns to face me, his head tilting to the side. He is intensely attractive. Before, I just caught glimpses of his profile and the way he moved, but now, with him staring right at me, I find it hard to draw breath. There's something in the intensity of his cool gray eyes, maybe, or the shape of his lips. I can't put my finger on exactly what it is, but I also can't ignore the effect he has on me.

"Jodi," he calls, his eyes not leaving me, "who's your friend?"

I stand and open my mouth to introduce myself, but my name sticks in my throat, so I close my mouth and swallow. The guy raises his chin, exposing his smooth neck.

"This is Kristyl," Jodi says, coming to my rescue. "I'm a little surprised you don't know. She was at school today."

"I wasn't there. But I wish I would've been." He takes a moment to look me up and down before closing the distance between us and offering his hand. "Any friend of Jodi's is a friend of mine. I'm Fox Holloway."

I take his hand and a thrill courses through my arm as our skin touches. I shiver involuntarily.

"She's my niece," Jodi adds, and there's an edge of warning in her tone.

Fox grins and looks into my eyes. I can feel him searching me out and for once, I don't want to shy away. I want him to see me, to know me. "Jodi's niece, huh? That makes you exceptionally interesting."

Jodi clears her throat but I barely hear her. It's not until she moves to my side that I release Fox's hand, feeling dazed. I glance at Jodi. She wears an expression I can't identify.

Something tugs at the back of my mind. I'm not behaving like myself, not in the least. What is it about Fox that's making me feel so different? Yes, he's good-looking, with his broad shoulders, strong jaw, and stormy eyes. But he isn't the first or only good-looking guy I've ever encountered. Owen is incredibly cute and I talked with him all day without a problem. So why is Fox affecting me like this?

"Besides the lavender, is there anything else I can help you find today, Fox?" Jodi asks pleasantly, but I detect a hardness underneath.

Fox's eyes don't leave mine. "I think I'm good. For now. It was nice meeting you, Kristyl. I'll see you at school tomorrow, okay?"

Heat spreads over my cheeks and I manage a smile. "I look forward to it."

Fox winks before turning and exiting the store. Once he's gone, I watch his figure through the glass of the door until he's out of sight. A pressure squeezes my chest momentarily and I turn to my aunt, feeling suddenly disoriented. "Wow."

Jodi is watching me with interest.

"He seemed nice," I say when it's clear she's not going to speak.

"He's certainly... charming." The way she says it, it doesn't sound like a compliment.

I shake my head, the fog in my mind clearing. "I don't know what came over me. I'm not usually like that around guys."

"Really? What are you usually like?"

"I dunno." I don't mention that before today, I haven't had a real conversation with a guy my age in years. Instead, I recall today's interactions with Owen and West. "Normal, I guess. But with him... I felt a little overwhelmed."

She considers this for a moment before nodding. "It seems like that's the consensus lately."

I arch an eyebrow at her. For a woman in her thirties, that seems like an odd insight into the lives of teenagers. "How do you know that? Do you secretly stalk the hallways of the high school or something?"

She smiles. "No. It's just a small town. Fox is in here pretty regularly and I'm also friends with your principal, remember? Shelly mentioned there've been a couple times so far this year where girls have gotten into fights over him."

Somehow it doesn't surprise me that girls would fight for his attention. But why doesn't it surprise me? I conjure the image of his face in my mind, the color of his eyes, the shape of his face. Sure, he's good-looking, but now that he's not standing in front of me, it's difficult to remember exactly why I'd felt so overwhelmed by his presence. When I compare Fox and Owen now, I find Owen more appealing.

Jodi clears her throat as she crosses to the shelves lined with bags of loose tea. She pulls open a cupboard at the bottom of the shelves and starts filling in the empty areas. "Speaking of school, did you have a good day? You didn't say much about it earlier."

In the past, talking about school would have brought a knot of tension to my stomach; today it brings a smile to my lips. "It was actually really good. I mean, it started off rough, but then I met Owen and he introduced me to all his friends."

She straightens the rows of bags. "The rough start, I assume, is where the spilled coffee and Owen's sweatshirt come in?"

I nod. "Yeah, I bumped into a girl and she spilled her coffee all over me. And, get this—apparently she's the school's head witch and now I'm mortal enemies with her." I roll my eyes for effect.

Jodi raises an eyebrow. "Witch, huh?"

I laugh. "Yeah. Lexie says she's going to plot revenge against me. West seems to think it'll be revenge of a magical variety. Crazy, right?"

But as I say the words, I look around the store and press my lips together in a tight line. "No offense or anything."

"None taken." Jodi smiles at me and walks to the shelf of quartz crystals. "So, who's this mortal enemy?"

I sigh, grateful I haven't offended her. "That's the best part: her name's Crystal, like me. Only..." A bubble of happiness swells in my chest. "I've got a nickname. Well, two, I guess. Some kids are calling me 'Coffee Girl' since I spilled Crystal's coffee. But Owen started calling me Krissa." A smile tugs at the corner of my mouth as I say it. "I like it."

"It's nice," Jodi agrees. "Now, this girl whose coffee you spilled? Is her last name Jamison?"

I nod. "Yeah, how'd you know?"

"She's the only other Crystal I know." She selects a murky stone from the shelf. "You know, if you're worried this girl's gonna cast a spell on you, smoky quartz is known for its protective qualities."

I reach for the quartz for a moment before stopping and pulling the ring out from under my shirt. I study its stone before holding it out for Jodi. "Is this smoky quartz?"

She steps toward me and squints at it. "Could be."

I smile and tuck it back in its place. Even if it's not, having the ring around my neck makes me feel protected, like somehow my dad is watching out for me. It's a good thought.

A woman enters the store and Jodi moves toward the door to greet her. I watch as my aunt tips her head back and laughs at something the woman says. A few weeks ago, I wouldn't have known the last time she crossed my mind. Now I'm glad Jodi is in my life, and not just because without her, I'd probably be in foster care. She's not afraid to talk about my dad. In a small measure, it's like having a piece of him with me again. With Jodi around, I can almost forget I've lost both of my parents.

Almost.

Chapter Seven

For the first time in a long time, I wake up excited for school. My first day at Clearwater High started out rocky, but it definitely only got better from there. I can't wait to see my new friends, to sit with them in class, to eat lunch with them. I can't wait to have a regular high school experience. Every time I think of Lexie's laugh or Bria's dry humor, my anticipation for the day increases. And when I think about Owen's eyes, his smile, my stomach flips. I can't believe I let Fox affect me like that yesterday, not when I have a real friend like Owen.

I take care selecting today's outfit. I own almost exclusively tee-shirts and jeans, but after some digging I locate the tunic and leggings my mom bought me for Christmas last year in an attempt to get some variety into my wardrobe. The tunic is deep jade green and comes to my mid-thigh. The leggings are simple and black, but they look good with the green. When I study my reflection in the mirror, it's easy for me to believe I'm a new person here. I even pull my hair back in a low half pony-tail. For the first time in years, I don't think I'll need it to hide behind.

Jodi lets out a whistle when I walk into the kitchen and I duck my head, hoping to hide the blush I'm sure has painted my cheeks. Her eyes follow me as I pour cereal and milk into the bowl she's set out on the counter for me.

"I thought all you owned was tee-shirts and jeans." Jodi surveys me over her steaming mug of tea.

I put the milk into the refrigerator and take my breakfast into the dining room. Jodi follows me. "That's pretty much all I have," I admit, settling at the table. "But I... wanted to try something different today."

She sips her tea. "You know, I've got some boxes of clothes I keep meaning to donate to Goodwill. When I hit thirty, I figured there were some clothes it was no longer socially acceptable for me to wear." She grins. "You're welcome to poke through them, if you want. No pressure or anything. I won't be offended if you don't like any of my old stuff."

Today Jodi wears a gently shimmering gray tank top under a long, draped cardigan, skinny jeans, and knee-high black leather boots with three-inch heels. If this is something she deems appropriate for a thirty-something, the idea of what she may have marked as inappropriate is pretty appealing. "That'd be nice. I'd like to look through the boxes."

"I'll bring them in later. Or, better yet, you can help me bring them in when we get home from the shop." She winks.

My conversation with Owen about working at the shop comes back to me. "Speaking of that—is it going to be an everyday thing, me coming to the shop after school? I mean, I'm more than happy to help out. But, if you like, Owen said he could drop me off so you wouldn't have to leave every day to get me."

Jodi's face scrunches as she considers it. "That sounds fine. It's nice of him to offer."

I nod. "He says it's no big deal because the shop's on his way home."

Jodi's mouth twitches at this, but she says nothing.

I finish my breakfast and we head out to Jodi's car. I hum as we drive toward the school, my pale fingers drumming against Owen's sweatshirt, which sits folded in my lap. The navy color of the sweatshirt brings out the blue of my veins. My mom always described my skin color as *translucent*. It used to bother me, but now I hold onto the description, tucking it away in my mind along with all the other things I want to remember about her.

I don't notice Owen on my way into the building and wonder, as I head up the stairs, whether he's going to be late again today.

I spin the dial on my locker, a smile on my lips. When someone approaches in my periphery, I'm so convinced it's Owen that I turn with the smile still firmly in place.

But it's not Owen. Crystal Jamison stands before me, as perfectly put together as she was yesterday. Her brown hair falls in gentle spiral curls around her shoulders and her makeup accentuates her blue eyes. Beside her is Bridget, nearly an exact copy, except her hair, eyes, and complexion are darker and her curves a bit more ample. The bubble of joy that has been swelling in my chest all morning deflates at the sight of them, and my mind returns to every reason I've ever had to hate school.

Crystal crosses her arms over her chest and, after a beat, Bridget follows suit. "You're Jodi Barnette's niece." There's no question in Crystal's tone, but she doesn't speak the words like a condemnation, either.

I take in a breath. "Yes."

Her cool blue eyes survey me and I bite the insides of my cheeks. The urge to turn and look down the hall for Owen or Lexie or Bria or West is strong, but I resist. To look away shows weakness; I know that.

Crystal's hand goes to the pendant she wears around her neck as her eyes continue to scan me. I wish she would say whatever it is she's come to say and be done with me, but she seems to be in no hurry to let me get on my way. The seconds tick by and I wait, agitation growing within me. Behind me, the lock on my locker begins to rattle gently. I dig my fingernails into the palms of my hands, hoping the sharp pain will anchor me to the moment and keep something unexpected from happening. It can't happen here. This is my new start: a new place where nobody knows my history. I'm not alone anymore. I have friends here.

I have friends here.

The panic building within me ebbs. The rattling of the lock ceases. I square my shoulders, feeling much braver than I have in a long time. "If you've got something to say, say it. If not, get out of my way so I can get to class."

Crystal's eyes flash and without warning, she grabs my wrist. Her hold is firm and her nails bite into my flesh. I try to wrench my hand away, but I can't. The swirl of emotion that was just beginning to recede flows back in full force and heat builds in my stomach. I stare into Crystal's cold blue eyes, pleading with my own for her to let go. My lips part, but a flash overtakes my sight, stealing the words from my mouth.

Eyes. Green eyes. Strong jaw covered in dark stubble. A man's face. But who is he? And why am I seeing him?

"Hey, what's going on here?"

The words snap me out of my vision. Crystal tenses and turns toward the voice. After a beat, she releases my wrist. I step away from her. Mrs. Cole is stalking down the hallway toward us as fast as her high heels will allow. I take in a breath, waiting for her to release a stream of vitriol in my direction, but her eyes are fixed on Crystal.

"I asked you a question," Mrs. Cole says as she approaches. "Crystal, why were your hands on Miss Barnette?"

A spasm crosses Crystal's face. "I... I thought she had something of mine. I was trying to make her let me see what was in her hand."

I stare at her, too shocked by her blatant lie to react.

Mrs. Cole's eyes flit from Crystal's face to Bridget's and finally to mine. There's an expression on her face I can't quite read. "May I see what's in your hand, Kristyl?"

I open both my hands and hold them out to her. Her gaze merely brushes my empty palms before returning to Crystal, whose face tightened.

"And what was it you believe she had?"

I recognize the tone of Mrs. Cole's voice: It's the same tone teachers and administrators used on me time and time again. Mrs. Cole doesn't believe Crystal's story. Mrs. Cole is on my side. The thought of someone—an adult—standing up for me almost makes me want to cry.

Crystal's gaze doesn't falter as she looks at Mrs. Cole. "I thought she had my lip gloss. It's not in my purse and some freshman said they thought she had it."

"Well, as this isn't kindergarten, I shouldn't have to remind you that we should keep our hands to ourselves. I recommend if there are any further problems, you come see me."

Mrs. Cole's eyes slide to me for the briefest of moments and I understand her meaning: If Crystal Jamison bothers me again, I should come see her.

A bell sounds overhead and Mrs. Cole's attention turns from us to the rest of the students in the hallway. I quickly hang Owen's sweatshirt on one of the hooks in my locker and grab what I need for first hour before heading down the hall, not wanting to be in Crystal's presence anymore. I'm halfway to Miss Buchanan's class when I hear someone behind me calling out my nickname.

Owen.

He jogs down the hall to catch up with me, concern creasing his eyes. "What was going on with you and Crystal and Bridget? When I got to my locker, I saw Mrs. Cole standing there. I would've gone to check it out, but Cole would've just sent me away."

I shake my head. "It's nothing. Crystal just asked me if I was Jodi's niece, then she grabbed me."

"Grabbed you?" His blue eyes widen with alarm.

I wave away his concern. "She just grabbed my wrist. She told Mrs. Cole she thought I had her lip gloss. It's fine."

"It's not fine." He stops in the center of the hall and turns me by the shoulders to face him. A stream of students jostle past us, but he remains unmoved. "I may not believe Lexie's witch theory, but that doesn't mean I want you on Crystal's hit list. If she bothers you again, you tell us, okay?" Another bell rings and Owen sighs. "I'll see you second hour."

I nod. The corners of his mouth upturn slightly as he makes his way back down the hall toward his class. I walk into first hour and make my way to my desk, tugging at my ear. As Miss Buchanan begins class, I pull out a notebook and pretend to pay attention, but my thoughts keep circling back to Crystal and the man's face.

Why did I see it? What could it mean? Owen was so concerned about Crystal, and I want to tell him it's not Crystal I'm worried about. I want to tell him about the flash I saw when she touched me. But I know I can't do it. It sounds crazy, even to me, and I'm well-versed in strange occurrences.

Chapter Eight

The rest of the week passes and I'm able to forget about the face I saw when Crystal touched me. Though she's continued to stare at me whenever we're in the same room, I've been able to ignore her. I'm finding it's much easier not to pay attention to something like that when my time is filled by my new friends.

True to his word, Owen started taking me to Jodi's shop after school every day, and I look forward to the time alone with him. He asks me about my day, and about Jodi's shop and what I'm learning there. And he tells me about himself: He has an older brother who's in college and a younger sister who's still in middle school, he wanted to be a veterinarian when he was younger, he's been on the track team since middle school, and his favorite movie is *It's a Wonderful Life*.

It's Owen I'm thinking about on Friday during history class. History is the only class I have without one of my new friends, and it's also the only one I share with both Crystal and Bridget. Owen, Lexie, Bria, and West invited me to hang out tonight, and although I still haven't asked Jodi if I can go, my mind is already there. It's a movie night at West's house, something the group of them do regularly—and they decided to include me. If Crystal is staring at me the way she has been all week, I don't notice it. I'm too happy.

The hair at the back of my head prickles, as if brushed by a breeze, and I rub my hand over it to smooth it. None of the windows are open and the only heating vent is on the other side of the room. I turn to my textbook and start reading the chapter. Mr.

Martin assigned the reading five minutes ago and I still haven't read past the first paragraph because I'm so preoccupied. I take in a breath, pushing my excitement about tonight to the back of my mind. Jodi might not let me go if I have homework, so I should get the assignment done.

No more than three sentences into the paragraph, I feel the breeze again, this time more tightly aimed, shifting the hair by my left ear. I close my eyes and take in a slow breath, trying to convince myself I'm imagining things. But when another blast comes, I bang my fist against my textbook and turn around. "Will you knock it off already?"

The boy seated behind me looks up from his book, his eyes wide. He's mousy, with curly dark blond hair and a sprinkle of acne across his cheeks. In short, he's nothing like the kind of kid who would go out of his way to bother a person. He looks like the kind of kid who's usually on the other side of that equation.

"I'm sorry," he says automatically. "Did I kick your desk? I won't do it again."

My breath catches. How many times did I say those same kinds of things to people when I hadn't done anything? Guilt presses down on me and I shake my head. "I'm sorry. I think I was imagining things." I offer him a smile before I turn back to my desk.

Except I'm not imagining things. Another gust of air ruffles my hair as soon as I look at my textbook. Who could be doing it? If it's not the boy behind me, who is close enough to do it without me noticing?

Surreptitiously, I knock my pencil from my desk to give myself an excuse to turn. When I reach for the pencil, I cast a quick glance in Crystal and Bridget's direction. They're seated in their usual spot at the back corner on the opposite side of the room, but their eyes are on me.

I grab the pencil and return to facing forward. Why are they staring at me? It had to be due to my outburst a moment ago, didn't it? They couldn't be blowing at my hair from all the way over there; it's impossible.

The pages of my textbook begin to rustle and before I can do anything, several pages turn. It's suddenly in the middle of the last chapter. I flip back to where I was and start reading again. Air whispers past me again and I gather my hair up and pull it over my right shoulder. My pencil slides off my desk and rolls toward the front of the room.

I tap the shoulder of the girl in front of me. "Would you mind handing me my pencil?"

She rolls her eyes at me before acquiescing, and I thank her. I set the pencil in the groove at the top of desk and turn my attention back to my reading. As I turn the page, my pencil falls again, clattering as it hits the floor. Mr. Martin looks up from his desk, his eyes scanning the room. "Let's keep our belongings on our desks, please."

I grit my teeth. I consider asking the girl in front of me for my pencil again, but I'm sure she wouldn't be particularly amused by a second request. Instead, I get up from my desk and move two people ahead of where I sit. My pencil has rolled that far. I smile apologetically at the boy whose desk the pencil is under and reach down by his feet to pick it up.

On my way back to my desk, the pages of my book rustle again. I reach forward and slam my hand on the book.

The noise is louder than I anticipate and Mr. Martin clears his throat. "Is there a problem, Miss Barnette?"

I bite the inside of my cheek as I sit down. "No, sir."

"Then I recommend you sit down and finish your assignment."

"Yes, sir." I tuck the pencil behind my ear and put my hands on either side of the book to keep the pages from moving.

I manage to read the rest of the chapter without incident. When I get to the questions at the end of the chapter, I reach for the pencil, but before I touch it, it slips from behind my ear and clatters to the floor.

"Miss Barnette, are you having some sort of seizure?" Mr. Martin quips from the front of the room.

The class erupts in laughter and my face burns. It's one thing to be harassed by students; it's an entirely different sort of embarrassment when the teacher turns me into a joke. My fingers tremble as I reach for my pencil and I bite my lower lip. Pressure builds in me, starting in my stomach and pressing outward.

The book on my desk begins to tremble and I press my hand down on it to make it stop moving, but it doesn't. It shakes so violently, my desk begins to bang against the floor. The boy behind me looks up, horrified, and jumps from his desk. Several other students are on their feet as their desks begin to rattle against the floor. A girl in the front of the room screams.

The entire room is quivering and my classmates curse as textbooks slip off desks and fall to the ground. The only people who seem unfazed are Crystal and Bridget, whose eyes remain fixed on me.

The shaking stops as abruptly as it started. My wide-eyed classmates look around the room, dazed.

Mr. Martin, his complexion ashen, clears his throat at the front of the room. "Is everyone okay? Is anyone hurt?"

Voices swell in an indistinct murmur as people hold out their arms and legs for inspection, as if expecting to find unfelt pieces of shrapnel lodged in their skin.

Three beeps echo through the room and four girls jump, clutching at their chests.

"Attention teachers." Mrs. Cole's voice is controlled over the PA. "We appear to have experienced a small earthquake. If any of your students have been injured, please have them report to the office. If your classrooms have sustained any damage, please e-mail me."

Mrs. Cole's voice seems to have broken most of my classmates from their shocked states. When the announcement ends, conversation erupts.

"Mr. Martin," calls the boy behind me, "was that really an earthquake?"

Mr. Martin pushes some papers back onto his desk, his fingers trembling. He looks up at the boy, some of the color returning to his cheeks. He straightens, resuming teacher-mode. "It's not outside the realm of possibility. There aren't any faults here in Clearwater, but it's not uncommon for us to feel a quake centered in Canada." He sits down in his chair, his eyes on the computer monitor. "I wonder if the USGS has a report up yet..."

I gulp in breaths as the room erupts around me. The girl next to me pulls her cell phone out and taps out a text under her desk. The boy two desks ahead of me stands and shakes his body violently, illustrating, perhaps, what it feels like to be in a larger earthquake.

The class has dissolved into chaos. Mr. Martin calls for us to get back to work, but he doesn't actually look at us. A crease forms between his eyebrows as he clicks through web pages.

A prickling sensation crosses the back of my neck and I turn. Crystal and Bridget are still watching me with inscrutable expressions on their faces. I turn away quickly. I look down at my textbook but don't see it. It was an earthquake, I try to convince myself. I didn't do that. I couldn't do that.

But what if I'm wrong?

Chapter Nine

The crowded hallway buzzes louder than usual at the end of the hour. I've taken to lingering by Mr. Martin's door, waiting for Owen to emerge from his class, but today I dart into the stream of people passing me. I don't want to wait until Crystal and Bridget catch up to me.

I've taken only a few steps when someone grabs my arm and spins me around. Fox's gray eyes greet me, open and wide. My first instinct is to pull away from his grip, but his fingers squeeze tighter the more I struggle. Over his shoulder, Crystal and Bridget approach. The sight of them makes my heart rate increase, and I'm so keyed up by what just happened that even the wave of peace that envelops me at Fox's nearness is not enough to calm me. He opens his mouth, but I don't want to hear whatever he has to say. I shove the heel of my hand into the center of Fox's chest, and the movement is enough to knock him off balance so he loosens his grip. I don't stop at my locker. I run down the hall to the stairs and don't stop running until I reach Owen's car. He and I usually walk out together, so I tap out a quick text telling him where I am.

After I click "send," I lean against the hood of his white Grand Prix, closing my eyes. I try to tune out the voices of others as they filter past me to their cars, but certain things lodge themselves in my ears: shaking, earthquake, scared—*Can you believe it?*

I press my hands over my face. It can't have been me. It was just a coincidence.

Even as these thoughts surface in my mind, others appear to

rebut them. It can't be a coincidence that every time I'm upset these strange things occur around me. I'm not trying to make them happen, but is it possible I'm somehow causing them? And if that's the case, what does that say about me, about who—or what— I really am?

Hands settle on my upper arms and I uncover my face, afraid of who I might find in front of me. But it's not Crystal or Fox; it's Owen, and his eyes are narrowed.

"Are you okay?"

I try to force a smile, but my mouth doesn't want to move. "I'm fine. I just…"

He nods. "Earthquake really freaked you out, huh?"

"Yeah," I agree, thankful for the easy explanation. "You felt it too?"

"I think the whole school felt it." He unlocks my door before heading to the driver's side. "Mrs. Wertz said she remembers feeling one back in the eighties or something. She thought a truck hit the building. I guess it's something that happens from time to time." His voice is soothing and I can tell he's trying to make it sound like what happened wasn't a big deal. He's trying to make me feel better.

I slide onto the seat and latch my seatbelt, wishing what happened to me in class could be explained away so easily.

We don't talk much on the way to Jodi's shop, but he makes sure to remind me to ask about the movie night. I promise to text him as soon as I get a response from Jodi.

"Perfect timing," Jodi says as I walk into the shop. "I'm in major need of a caffeine fix."

I make my way to the back room and drop off my backpack on the worn couch.

Jodi picks up a clipboard and holds it out to me. "You want a latte?"

I shake my head, relieving her of the clipboard. "Inventory?"

"Nope," she says, a smile playing at the corners of her mouth as she turns and heads toward the door. "I'll be back soon."

I stare at the clipboard in my hands. It takes me a few seconds before I realize what she's given me. It's a list of herbs with descriptions of each one. Along the top of the page she's written one word: *Memorize*. Beside the name of each herb is a list of uses, along with a blank column labeled *Your Thoughts*.

I stare at the list. I had no idea there were so many herbs in the world. Some of them are familiar to me: lavender, sage, thyme, basil. But there are others I've never heard of before: blood root, slippery elm, motherwort. I have no idea how I'm ever going to remember all of these, but if Jodi's asking me to do it, I know I have to give it a try.

I pick up the first herb on my list: oregano. It smells hearty and robust, like Italian food. One use is to relieve a nervous headache. I study the small round leaves and inhale the scent again, trying to commit both to memory.

The bell above the door tinkles, but I don't turn, figuring it's Jodi returning from the coffee run.

"Hey, I don't think I'm going about this in the most effective way," I call, setting the bunch of oregano back in its place. "What's the easiest way to memorize all these herbs?"

"I find experience is always the best teacher."

The voice isn't Jodi's and I jump, clutching the clipboard to my chest. Fox stands in the middle of the store. My breath catches and my hand goes to the ring around my neck. I pinch it through the material of my shirt. My heart thuds against my chest and I can feel the ghost of Fox's fingers pressed against my upper arm. Why did Jodi leave me alone? "What are you doing here?"

Fox takes a step nearer to me and my worry begins to ebb. His gray eyes are fixed on my face and there is no malice in them. "I wanted to check on you. You ran off so fast after school I didn't get a chance to ask how you are."

My cheeks flush with pleasure at his concern for me. "Why would you care?"

He shrugs. "An earthquake is pretty out of the ordinary for Michigan. I wanted to see how... how you felt about it. If you have anything to say about what happened."

A giggle escapes my lips and I look up at him through my eyelashes. Part of me questions my behavior—just a second ago I was nervous at his appearance and now I'm giggling? But the concerned part of my mind is so small I'm easily able to ignore it. "What would I possibly have to say about it? Everything started shaking. It was pretty scary."

"Well, Crystal and Bridget seemed to think you might know something about it."

I bristle at the sound of their names and take a step away from him. "So that's the only reason you're here? Because of them?"

He shakes his head. "It's not what you think. Actually, I'm here to apologize for the way those girls've been treating you. All the creepy staring—I told them it's gotta stop."

A flutter builds in my stomach. The anger I felt a moment ago is completely gone, replaced by a gentle fuzziness, a pleasant warmth. I smile. "What, are you their ambassador?"

"Unfortunately, they didn't send me. They're kind of bitches, you know? But I wanted you to know we're not all like that."

Fox steps closer, an arm's length away from me. I have the urge to reach forward and run my hand through his dark hair. So clearly can I imagine the feeling of the silky strands against my fingers that it sends a thread of cold through my system. I manage to turn away from him, rubbing my hands together to keep them from reaching for him. This is ridiculous. Never in my life has a guy affected me like this. Why do I feel so out of control around Fox? I take a few steps away, toward the end of the herb rack. "I know you're not all like this. If you haven't noticed, I've found some friends." In my mind's eye I see the faces of Lexie and Bria, West and Owen.

Owen. The image of his eyes cuts through the fog enveloping my mind.

Fox has a gentle smile on his face. "I've noticed. Quite the group you've fallen in with."

Irritation flares within me. "I'm not sure why you care who my friends are."

"I care because you're a fascinating creature, Kristyl Barnette. I don't think you realize just how amazing you are. And I just want to be around you."

Part of me melts. I want to run into Fox's arms, to bury my face in his chest. The urge surprises me so much, I shake my head to clear it away. This isn't right. I don't want this—I don't want *Fox*. I haven't even spoken to him since the last time he was here in the shop. Then why can I see myself with him so clearly? I take a few steps backward. "It's Krissa."

A tinkling sounds and I almost jump. Jodi's face creases with concern when her eyes take in the scene.

"Alright, Krissa?" She walks into the shop until she's next to Fox, her eyes on him. "More lavender?"

Fox shakes his head. "I was just leaving. Jodi, a pleasure, as always." He inclines his head toward me briefly before heading out the door.

Jodi watches him go. "What did he want?"

I shrug. I could tell Jodi the truth, but I'm not exactly sure what to say. She hasn't said anything about the earthquake, and if she didn't feel it, I don't want to bring it up. What would I tell her about it, anyway? I may or may not have made the entire high school shake today when I got upset? It sounds insane. "More lavender, I guess."

Jodi's eyes are still on the door. "There's something about that boy."

I bite my lower lip. I can't agree more. When he's not around, the thought of him doesn't affect me. Even now, my earlier desire for him leaves me. It's not like that with Owen: Whether I'm with him or just thinking about him, I still get butterflies in my stomach. But as soon as Fox is near me, it's like he's the only guy in the world. I don't understand it. I consider mentioning it to Jodi, but what could she possibly say? Probably that it's just the work of hormones in my body or something like that. No, whatever it is about Fox, it's better I keep it to myself. Instead, I focus on something simple. "Um, do you think it'd be okay for me to go out tonight?"

She shakes her head slightly, as if clearing it of its last train of thought. "Depends. Who, what, when, where?"

"Movie night at West Harmon's house. I think Lexie said they usually meet around eight." I bite the inside of my cheek. It's Friday, but eight o'clock, plus a two-hour movie, puts me out until after ten. Since I had no friends at my last school, I never went anywhere and never had a curfew; I don't even know what is reasonable for a sixteen-year-old on a weekend.

Jodi eyes me closely. "So, it's going to be West, Lexie... Owen?" She waggles her eyebrows at me.

Heat rises in my cheeks. "Yes, Owen. And Bria. Maybe some other people. I'm not sure."

She studies me for a beat longer before shrugging. "Sure. I don't see why not." As she moves toward the employees-only room, she pauses to look at me again. "I'm glad you're making friends here."

I can't express how glad I am, too.

Chapter Ten

West Harmon's house is a large Victorian just a few blocks away from Jodi's place. Though I insist I can walk there, Jodi and Owen both decide it's best I get a ride.

By the time Owen and I arrive, Lexie and Bria are already settled on the couch, on either side of Felix Wolfe, a guy who sat with us at lunch earlier in the week. He is broad in the chest with brown hair that brushes against his shoulders.

The three of them call out greetings as we enter. Owen settles on the couch adjacent to the one Lexie, Bria, and Felix sit on, and although there's a recliner on the other side of the room, I decide to take the spot beside him. He raises an eyebrow at me when I sit and I bump his shoulder with mine. When he bumps mine in return, I smile.

Once we're settled, Lexie and Bria turn back to each other and continue their previous discussion.

"I'm telling you, it's not a good idea," Lexie says, tugging at Felix's arm. "Tell her it's not a good idea."

Before Felix can get a word in, Bria is talking.

"I'm telling *you*, I don't care."

I look at Lexie. "What's going on?"

Lexie rolls her eyes. "Just dance talk."

A thrill courses through me. "Dance?"

"Yeah. The annual Halloween dance? You haven't noticed the posters plastered all over the school?"

"Harvest dance," Lexie mutters.

Bria snorts. "Everyone knows they only call it a harvest dance to be politically correct."

"It's a whole week before Halloween," Lexi counters.

I lean forward on the couch. "So, what's the problem?"

"Attire." Lexie says it as though it should be obvious. Owen grins.

"What about it?"

"Well," Bria says, sounding like she's been waiting for just such an opening, "I said I'm going as a wraith. You know—gauzy black dress, pale face, the works."

I nod. "Okay. So, what's the issue?"

Lexie snorts. "It's not a costume party."

"Who's gonna know it's a costume?" Owen asks.

Bria pelts him with a throw pillow. "Come on!"

"Hey, no offense." Owen holds his hands up in front of him. "You know I appreciate your stylistic choices. But, let's be fair: If you show up at a school dance dressed in a wraith costume, do you really think anyone's gonna bat an eye? Anyone who knows you?"

I have to admit Owen has a point. For our movie-watching evening, Bria is wearing a black jean jacket artfully ripped and held together with an abundance of safety pins. Her shirt is blood red with a black cartoon cat face crossing her abdomen. She wears a tight striped skirt that inches up her ample thighs as she bounces on the couch.

Bria bites her lower lip, a look of contemplation crossing her face. "I suppose you've got a point."

I lean toward Lexie. "So, tell me about this dance."

She shrugs. "I dunno. It's like any other dance, I guess. They decorate the cafeteria with streamers and play lame music. Just imagine the dances at your old school, except subtract for extra lameness factor here."

I press my lips together. I don't want to admit I've never been to a school dance before. I considered it once, back in middle school. I even bought a ticket. But the day before the dance, I realized there was nothing magical about the event. People wouldn't suddenly accept me just because we were all dressed in pretty clothes. A school dance would just be an extension of the rest of my school life, and I didn't want to spend any more time around those people than was necessary. But here, things are different. I actually have friends here. And the idea of a dance delights me.

"You wanna go?" Owen asks, bumping my shoulder again.

My insides flutter and I swallow hard. Is Owen actually asking me what I think he's asking? I want to tell him yes, I'd love to go to the dance with him, but before I get a chance, Bria is talking.

"My mom's letting me take the car, and I can fit five people. West just told me he's taking Dana Crawford and that skank is *not* riding in my car, so we've got room for you."

Reality washes over me. Of course Owen wasn't asking *me* *specifically* to the dance: he was asking me to join them, the group. I squash the growing bubble of disappointment. This isn't a bad thing. I'm still invited. I'm part of this group. That has to count for something.

"I'd love to come. When is it?"

"Friday," Bria says.

I stare at her. "Friday? You mean like a week from today Friday?"

"Do you have a dress?" Lexie asks. "I mean, any old dress will do. It can be the dress you wore to your last dance. The beauty of being new is no one's seen your clothes before."

I shake my head. "I don't really have anything." I've long outgrown the dress I bought for the middle school dance.

A smile stretches across her mouth. "Even better. Plan B: We'll go shopping tomorrow afternoon. There's a really cool boutique in town."

I shift on the couch. Lexie volunteering to take me shopping is incredibly nice. I don't want to turn her down. But... "I think I've got to work at the shop tomorrow. Besides," I say, looking down at my hands, "I don't have much to spend."

Lexie waves away my concern with her hand. "No worries. The boutique's just down the street from Jodi's store. It shouldn't take us too long to find you something. And I bet I can swing a discount for you."

Bria snickers and I get the distinct impression I'm missing

something. Before I can ask about it, West enters the room carrying a large bowl full of popcorn and two bags of licorice. "Drinks are in the kitchen. Go help yourselves while I get the movie going."

The five of us get to our feet and head to the kitchen. Lexie and Bria are the first to the counter and as they pour themselves some pop, Owen touches the back of my arm.

"You're gonna come, right?" His eyes lock on mine.

I shrug. "I'm not sure. I have to ask Jodi first, and I still don't know if I can afford a dress."

"Ah, come on. You've gotta come."

"Really? Why's that?"

Lexie and Bria move away from the counter and Felix steps into their place, but Owen doesn't move forward. "You've gotta be there so you can save a dance for me."

His blue eyes don't leave mine and my insides do a flip. So, he doesn't just want me to come as part of the group. He wants *me* there. I take in a breath. "I'll ask her tomorrow. I'm sure she'll let me come."

My words are more confident than I am, but my assertion seems good enough for Owen, who finally breaks eye contact and moves to the counter to pour himself some pop.

By the time I make it back out to the living room, the opening credits to the movie are running. I settle back in my spot beside Owen and fix my attention on the screen, but I seem to be the only one who does so. Felix and Owen are discussing how West managed to convince Dana Crawford to agree to go to the dance with him. I think I know who she is—there's a girl named Dana in my first hour. She's late every day and is always wearing ridiculously high heels. After throwing out a few aspersions on Dana's character, Lexie and Bria launch back into wardrobe conversation. Soon, I'm not watching the movie at all; I'm watching everyone as they talk and laugh. And while the atmosphere of the room is light and cheerful, a cloud descends over me. Though I'm here, in the middle of everything, I still feel like a spectator.

I turn my attention back to the TV and try to focus on the

movie. The plot appears to have something to do with flying sharks, but I'm not really following it.

Bria and Lexie cross between me and the TV and sit beside me on the couch. There's really not enough room, and I squeeze closer to Owen in an attempt to accommodate them. The length of my body presses against his. He gives no indication that he minds.

"You're quiet over here," Lexie says.

I force a smile. "I guess."

"You're not actually interested in the movie, are you?" Bria asks.

I shake my head.

She sighs. "Good. West always chooses the most ridiculous stuff. But it's his house, so we have to let him choose every once in a while, you know?"

Lexie leans across Bria so she's close to me. "So, you survived your first week. How are you adjusting to life here? Probably boring compared to where you used to live, huh?"

"Not really."

Lexie and Bria exchange glances, like they're sure I'm lying.

"Truly," I press. I haven't mentioned how bad things were for me at my old school, and I don't want to bring it up now. I'm afraid if I tell them about my previously friendless existence, they'll look at me differently. At the very least, they'll want to know why I was such a social outcast, and I'm not sure I can even begin to explain it to them. "I'm liking how close-knit things seem to be here. How friendly people are."

"Yeah, like how Crystal and Bridget have rolled out the welcome wagon for you." Lexie rolls her eyes.

"Please. Their attempts at mean-girling are weak at best. Believe me." I bite the inside of my cheek as soon as the words are out of my mouth. Lexie's eyebrows cinch together and Bria's lips part like she's going to ask me what I mean. I step over her unsaid words. "Besides, what do I care about those two when I've got you guys? You're clearly superior to them in every way." I force a big grin, hoping my compliment will be enough to distract them from my last statement.

Owen shifts so he's looking at me, his arm moving so it rests behind my back. "Come on, now. Don't say things like that to Lexie. Her opinion of herself is swollen enough without you adding fuel to the fire."

Lexie lunges across Bria and me to swat at Owen, who fends her off easily. "Come on, Owen, admit it. I'm the coolest person you know!"

"Speaking of cool," Bria says as the two of us press ourselves backward into the cushions of the couch to avoid Lexie's flailing arms. "How is it living with Jodi?"

My stomach sinks at the mention of my living arrangements. After Lexie asked me why I moved in with Jodi on my first day, no one else has brought it up, and I haven't volunteered the information. I don't know why, but the idea of telling them about my mom scares me. I don't know how I'll handle it if they start looking at me with pity. One of the main reasons I'm not a wreck is because I'm not constantly reminded of my loss. If I have to see it in their eyes each time they look at me, I won't be able to deal with it.

If Bria notices anything odd in my expression, she ignores it. "I mean, it's not like I really know your aunt or anything, but she just seems like she's a pretty awesome person."

Owen's hand twitches, sandwiched between my back and the couch, distracting me from Bria's question and my own thoughts. Lexie finally gives up on her attack and Owen turns his attention back to the guys, but he doesn't attempt to move his hand from behind me. "Yeah, she's pretty cool, I guess." I indicate tonight's outfit: a dark blue cap-sleeve shirt overlaid with black lace and a pair of black skinny jeans that have a matte shine to them. "She helped me pick this out. It was in some boxes of clothes she was gonna give away."

Lexie gives a low whistle. "I've always appreciated your aunt's sense of style. That shirt is totally hot on you, by the way—I meant to say something earlier. Hey, if there's anything left after you go through those boxes, do you think she'd let me poke around through them?"

The look on Lexie's face is so eager I can't help smiling. "I'm sure she wouldn't mind."

"Ooh! Me too!" Bria tugs at the hem of her skirt, which is riding up again. "Not that she and I are the same size. But maybe there's something I can use."

Bria leans forward as she launches into a description of how she once altered a dress she found at a thrift store. I lean forward too, reluctant to move away from Owen's warm hand. It feels unnatural for me to be resting against the back cushions when no one else is. I expect Owen to pull his hand away immediately; his body is angled toward Felix and West, who are sitting on the adjacent couch, and I'm sure it's been annoying to have his arm twisted behind him. But when Owen finally does move his hand, he rests it on the outer edge of his thigh and it brushes gently against my leg any time one of us shifts. I try to pay attention to Bria, who is now talking about her forays into sewing her own clothes, but I'm distracted by the tiny fireworks that ignite my belly whenever Owen's pinky rubs against the material of my jeans. And later, after Bria gets up to get more pop and settles on the other couch between West and Felix, I don't scoot over into the space she vacated. And Owen doesn't complain.

Chapter Eleven

I resolve to ask Jodi about the dance first thing in the morning. I don't get home until around midnight, so I set my alarm for eight so I won't oversleep. The shop opens at nine on Saturdays, and Jodi likes to get in half an hour early.

In the morning, I dress in jeans and one of Jodi's cast-off shirts that's somewhat more low-cut than I was expecting, and head downstairs to eat a quick breakfast. Jodi's voice reaches me before I enter the kitchen and my stomach sinks. She's on the phone and she doesn't sound happy.

She barely acknowledges me as I dart around her to grab something to eat. Her brow is furrowed and her lips pursed. I take my bowl of cereal into the dining room, keeping my ears attuned to her conversation. I'm not sure, but after a few minutes, it seems like there may have been a problem with a delivery she was expecting.

Jodi looks frustrated by the time she's off the phone and I decide to postpone asking about the dance. I'm afraid she might take her irritation out on me.

The car ride to the shop is silent. Jodi doesn't even turn on the radio. At one point, I almost ask what's going on, but I stop myself. If she wanted to tell me, she would say something.

When we arrive at the shop, Jodi immediately goes to the back room, perhaps to check stock. She doesn't give me a task, so I find a feather duster and start dusting the shelves. Jodi doesn't emerge from the stock room until it's time to open the store. To my surprise, there are people waiting to be let in. In the time I've spent here so far, I've never seen more than one customer in the shop at a time.

It's a little after nine when my cell vibrates. I pull it from my pocket to see that Lexie has sent a text: *What did Jodi say?*

I bite the inside of my cheek as I type my reply: *Haven't asked yet.*

"Krissa," Jodi calls as I hit "send." I quickly shove the phone back into my pocket. "Could you help Mrs. Houston with the teas?"

I nod and approach the person Jodi is indicating, a small woman with straight white hair and narrow shoulders. "What can I help you find?"

It takes an eon to help Mrs. Houston identify a half dozen teas to help her with various ailments, and when she goes to the register to pay, another customer calls me over to help choose the right bracelet for his niece's birthday. It seems every time there is a brief lull, Jodi is on the phone with her distributor again, trying to work out a solution to the shipping error.

It's eleven when my cell vibrates again. The only customer in the store at the moment is at the register, paying, so I don't feel too bad about checking the message.

It's from Lexie again. *Have you asked her yet? I'll be there in five.*

My stomach clenches. She's on her way here? I can't very well tell her not to come if she's already en route, but between the delivery problem and all the customers, I haven't had an opportunity to ask Jodi yet. It's not that I think she'll say no; I'm sure she'll let me go. She didn't bat an eye when I asked about going to West's house for movie night. She didn't even ask if his parents would be home—which they weren't. The thing I'm afraid to ask about is cash for a dress. Jodi is already doing so much for me by just taking me in. She shut down the shop for the whole week when she helped me get things sorted after my mom died, but she hasn't mentioned it once. She gives me a few dollars every morning to buy lunch at school. What if I ask for money and she thinks I'm ungrateful for everything she's already doing for me?

I glance back down at the text. I've run out of time. Taking in a deep breath, I square my shoulders and walk toward the counter. I wait until the customer has said his goodbyes before approaching Jodi. She presses her hand against her forehead and sighs, and a wave of guilt flows through me. The store's been so busy today. I'm supposed to be helping, not leaving to go shopping with Lexie. I almost chicken out and walk away, but before I can, she looks up and meets my eyes.

"Before you say no," I blurt out.

Jodi rubs the spot over her right eyebrow. "I already don't like the sound of this."

The words tumble out of my mouth before I can stop them. "I got invited to go to the harvest dance and I've never been to a dance before and I really want to go, but that means I need a dress. Which means I need money. And a couple hours off. Well, maybe not a whole couple hours, but at least a little while."

Jodi's eyebrow hitches upward. "Who invited you?"

"It came up at West's house last night and Owen invited me." I catch myself. "He invited me to come along with the group."

A smile plays about the corners of Jodi's mouth and heat rises in my cheeks. "You want to go to the harvest dance with Owen and Lexie and the rest of your friends? Okay."

"Okay?"

She laughs, heading out from behind the counter and toward the employees-only area. "Yeah, okay. What did you expect me to say?"

Relief washes over me. But her letting me go isn't the bit I'm worried about. I take in a breath to steel myself before venturing further on the topic that concerns me. "Lexie's gonna be here in a couple minutes to get me so we can shop for a dress."

Jodi returns, her purse in her hands. She sets it on the counter and rifles through it. "You're probably going to Enchanted Evenings Boutique." She pulls out her wallet and counts out some bills. "This will probably cover a dress. If it's not enough, you can run back here and I'll give you some more. Or, better yet, tell Bonnie she still owes me some cash from the last time we went out to dinner." She grins, dropping her wallet back in her purse.

I stare down at the money in my hands. I don't think I've ever held this much at one time. My mom and I didn't live like paupers, but we weren't exactly queens either. And I'd never had the occasion to purchase anything particularly expensive. Part of me wants to push the money back at my aunt—it's too much, and she's already doing so much just by letting me live with her—but the look on Jodi's face is so expectant that I push the money into my back pocket instead. "Thank you," I say, my eyes on the countertop.

Jodi reaches across the counter and touches my arm. "It's my pleasure." She pauses, catching my eye. She holds my gaze, letting her words settle into my mind. "Think of it as an advance on your paycheck, okay?"

"Paycheck?"

Jodi laughs. "Yeah, paycheck. What do you think you are, slave labor? I think there are laws against not paying your employees."

I smile. "Employee?"

She shakes her head. "You're silly."

I look around the shop. *Employee*. I suppose I thought I was just helping around here so Jodi could keep an eye on me. Pride swells within me, followed immediately by guilt. "It's been so busy here today. I shouldn't just leave you—"

She waves away my concern. "Devin's coming in at noon. I think I can manage things until then."

My shoulders relax. I'd met Devin earlier in the week. She has pink hair and a nose ring. She only works part time because she's taking classes at the local community college.

The bells tinkle and Lexie walks into the store. "Hey, Miss Barnette," she says, waving at Jodi. "Krissa, you ready to go?"

Jodi winks at me and I start at a jog for the door. Lexie bounces as she walks beside me. "I'm so excited."

I raise an eyebrow at her. "Why are you excited?"

She looks at me like it's a ridiculous question. "I've had my dress picked out for a month. It'll be fun to pick one out for you. Especially since Bria won't let me help. That girl..." She sighs.

Four doors down, Lexie guides me into a store. I laugh. "I didn't realize you meant this place was *right* down the street."

"It's not like downtown is that big."

I gasp when we enter the store. There are racks filled with the most colorful garments I've ever seen. Some glitter, some shimmer, some are subtle, and some are bold. There's so much to look at that I can't focus on anything for more than a few seconds. I have no idea where to start.

Lexie tugs at my arm and pulls me toward a rack in the middle of the store. She begins pawing through the dresses, muttering to herself. I let my hands skim over the fabric, enjoying the sensuous feeling of the silky material as it glides under my fingers.

"I'm thinking blue for you," Lexie says. "Or maybe a purple or green. You're a cool."

"I'm a what?"

"A cool. It means cool colors look better with your skin tone." She looks at me, eyebrows furrowed. "How do you not know this?"

I'm not sure how to respond. She doesn't say it like an accusation, more like she's unsure how I could have reached the age of sixteen without this information. I consider telling her that my general shopping tendencies have me grab the first few tee-shirts that fit, but I figure she'll just look at me like I've grown another head, so I keep the comment to myself.

She pulls out a dress in shimmery silver and grins. "This is pretty. Here, hold it."

Before long, my arms are piled high with dresses ranging from the gentle shimmer of the silver to a dark forest green. By the time Lexie shoves me into the dressing room, I begin to wonder whether I'll make it back to the shop before Jodi closes up for the night.

"Try on the blue one," Lexie calls through the door.

After hanging up the different dresses, I search for the blue one she wants me to try on. There are three dresses I would consider blue, and I choose the one that's easiest to get off the hanger. I pull off my shirt and kick off my shoes and jeans. I'll also need appropriate footwear, I realize. Does this store also sell shoes? I don't think I've owned a pair of dress shoes since before my dad left. I even wore tennis shoes to my mom's funeral.

Out of nowhere, I'm hit by the memory of my mother's

presence. Perhaps it's because Clearwater is so different than home, but I've been able to avoid thinking about her much. Somehow I've been able to convince myself I'm on an extended vacation, or I've been sent away to live with my aunt because I've caused too much trouble at home. Deep down, I know it's not the case; I just usually ignore it. I look at my reflection, at the way the dress stretches across my abdomen and hugs at my hips. It's just the kind of dress my mom would've loved for me to put on, but I was always fighting her about it. My style has always been more tomboy than glam-girl, and it bothered her. And now here I am, trying on a dress she will never see.

I press my hands to my eyes, attempting to rub away the burning sensation. I can't cry, not here. Not with Lexie humming happily on the other side of the door, waiting for me to come out and show her how I look in the dress she selected.

"Hey, you coming out? Do you need help with the zipper?"

I take in a deep, steadying breath. I can cry later. "Yeah, that would be nice."

"Come out and I'll get it."

I touch the latch and pause for a moment before opening the door. Lexie's eyes go wide when she sees me and a smile crosses her face.

"Turn around, let me zip it up."

I turn, and when I do, I'm facing a three-way mirror. I'd seen my reflection in the changing room, but it was nothing compared to the view I have now. With the dress zipped up, it hugs me in a way that usually makes me uncomfortable. I tend to gravitate toward clothes with a bit of breathing room—nothing that shows off too much of my shape. But this is different. It makes me look sophisticated. It makes me look beautiful.

I hear someone clapping and turn to see a woman with dark brown hair approaching, a smile on her lips. "Wow, that is stunning."

I smile, shifting a little at the stranger's praise. "Thanks."

"Alexis, who's your friend?" the woman asks, her eyes on Lexie.

Lexie pulls her gaze from me and shakes her head, smiling. "Oh, Mom. Yeah, this is the new girl I've been telling you about.

Krissa Barnette."

Lexie's mom stretches her hand out toward me and I shake it. "Jodi's niece. It's nice to finally meet you."

I nod. "It's nice to meet you, too." I glance at Lexie, wondering if she'll explain what her mother is doing here. Did Lexie have to get a ride to the store from her mom? Or did she just happen past and see her daughter inside?

"I'm not sure if Alexis told you, but I extend a discount to friends of hers." Mrs. Taylor smiles at me.

"Oh, this is your store?" Suddenly things make more sense. Of course Lexie would know things like what colors look best on me—her mother sells dresses for a living. Then I remember Jodi's words as I left. "Is your first name Bonnie?"

Mrs. Taylor nods. "Has Jodi mentioned me? We try to get together for lunch at least once a month. She's a fabulous woman, your aunt."

My heart swells at her words. "Yeah, she is," I agree, and I mean it.

Her eyes linger on me a moment longer. "I'll leave the two of you to it, then. I know if I stay much longer Lexie will just shoo me away anyway. Let me know if you need anything." She turns and heads toward a curtained-off area with the word "Alterations" stenciled above it.

Even though I'm completely sold on the blue dress, Lexie presses me to try on each of the ones she's picked out, just to be sure. At first I find the exercise tiresome, but by the end I find I'm having fun. When Lexie declares that I was right about the blue dress and I pay for it, I'm sad the fun is all over.

Lexie follows me back to Jodi's shop and I'm surprised—and relieved—to see it's not as busy as it was earlier. When Jodi and Devin see that I'm carrying a garment bag, they descend on me, insisting I show them what I got. I reveal the dress to them and they *ooh* and *aah*. Jodi seems to be in a better mood. She follows me when I go into the employees-only room to hang the dress.

"Lexie's mom gave me a discount," I say, pulling the leftover money from my pocket.

Jodi shakes her head. "Keep it. I told you, it's an advance on your paycheck."

I want to disagree with her, but the look in her eyes tells me I won't win the argument. "Speaking of work, I'm ready to get back to it."

"Devin's here. Why don't you and Lexie go out for lunch or coffee or something?"

When I don't agree right away, Jodi takes me by the shoulders and spins me toward the door. "I insist," she says, pushing me gently toward the shop's main room. "Go, have fun."

I laugh. "Okay, okay, I'm going." I find Lexie perusing the bracelets and link my arm through hers. "Wanna go get a coffee? Apparently I'm not wanted here."

She grins. "Sure." She selects a bracelet from the rack and slips it onto her wrist. "Think your aunt would give me a friends and family discount?"

I shrug. "Wouldn't hurt to ask."

Chapter Twelve

Jodi does give Lexie a discount, and Lexie stares at the way the different crystals glisten in the sunlight as we walk down the block to the coffee shop. "So, what does this bracelet do?" she asks, holding her wrist out to me.

I laugh. "Shouldn't you have figured that out before you bought it?"

"I bought it because I like the colors." She pulls open the door to the coffee shop and lets me walk in before her.

There are three people already in line and while we wait, I inspect Lexie's bracelet. There are alternating semitransparent light blue stones and opaque dark gray ones. "I'm pretty sure this bracelet wards off flatulence."

She giggles. "Are you serious?"

"No," I say, smiling. "Jodi's been having me learn about herbs. I don't really know anything about the stones yet."

She sighs. "Oh, well. It's pretty, anyway. And that's what matters."

We order our drinks and settle at a small, high table near the front window. I ask Lexie what her dress looks like, which launches her into a description not only of the dress for Friday's dance, but of every dress she's worn to every dance. I try my best to pay attention, but everything begins to blur after the third or fourth description. My thoughts drift back to my own dress and excitement about the upcoming dance bubbles inside me.

I drum my fingers on the tabletop, feeling foolish; I can't wipe the smile off my face. I've found the perfect dress, I'm going to my very first dance with my friends, and I have the promise of a dance with Owen. I can't keep my mind from conjuring scenes of the moment Owen first sees me in my dress. I know I'm stealing material from every movie I've ever seen, recasting Owen in the role of the heroine's love interest, but I can't help myself. Maybe my life is finally going to take the turn to normalcy. Maybe I'll finally get to enjoy what people usually call *the best years*.

Lexie's voice trails off and I press my lips together, embarrassed, figuring she's noticed I'm not really paying attention. But her gaze slides over my shoulder.

I turn, and my stomach drops as Crystal Jamison's eyes clasp mine. A smile curls at the corners of her mouth as she starts toward me, Bridget close behind. The memory of history class yesterday, of the trembling ground, of Crystal and Bridget staring at me floods my mind and I grip the edge of the table.

"What do you want, Crystal?" Lexie asks, her voice cold.

Crystal holds her hands up innocently. "Wow, hostility. We just want to say hi."

Lexie crosses her arms over her chest. "Hi. Bye."

Rolling her eyes, Crystal turns her attention to me. "I tried to catch you after history yesterday, but you ran out of the building so quickly. You looked so scared during that earthquake. I wanted to make sure you were okay."

Bridget presses her lips together in a tight line, but she's not entirely able to suppress a smile.

Fear swells within me. They can't know, can they? They can't know I think I might have been the cause of shaking. But if they don't suspect anything, why are they making a point of asking me? I dig my nails into my palms. "I'm fine."

"You hear that? She's fine." Lexie's tone indicates her irritation. "I don't see why you care anyway."

Crystal turns her cool blue eyes on her cousin. "Jealous much? But I guess I shouldn't really be surprised. You've always had an issue with jealousy."

Lexie's eyes flick from Crystal to Bridget for an instant before she snorts. "Yeah, right."

"Then you won't mind if I have a word with Kristyl. Privately." Crystal's tone is sickly sweet, but there is an edge of challenge underneath.

A muscle in Lexie's jaw jumps. She wants to say yes, she would mind—I can see it written clearly on her face. She takes a slow, deliberate breath before shaking her head. "If *Krissa* wants to talk to you," she says, putting deliberate emphasis on my nickname, "she can feel free to. I'll be outside."

Crystal waits until Lexie exits the building before settling in the seat she vacated. Bridget stands between us, her forearms resting on the round tabletop.

Silence stretches out for a beat and then two. I don't know exactly what their game is, but I want them to know they don't intimidate me. I stare unblinkingly at Crystal, willing her to speak first.

"So," Crystal says at last, drawing out the word. "What do you know about... earthquakes?"

Bridget titters at the word and I get the impression I'm missing something. "Not much. I can't say they really interest me."

Crystal nods. "I understand that. But if you don't really know much about them, how can you judge whether or not they'd be interesting to you?"

I shift in my chair. She's talking in code. She has to be. There's no way she really wants to have a conversation about geologic activity. Part of me wants to shake her and demand she tell me exactly what she's going on about, but the other part doesn't want to know at all.

She watches me for another few seconds before standing. "If you ever want to learn more, you know where to find me."

I don't respond. When I walk out the door, Lexie is standing there, staring across the street, waiting. "Hey," I say, stepping beside her.

"Hey," she returns. "You wanna go for a walk?"

I nod and Lexie starts down the street toward the river. We don't talk. I'm not sure whether she wants to know about my conversation with Crystal, and I don't want to volunteer the information. What if she starts asking about why Crystal's so interested in the earthquake? How can I explain I might have caused it without sounding crazy?

We cross over the river and Lexie leads the way to a playground. There's a large play structure where four small children climb, and Lexie and I walk past it to a set of four swings. We each sit down on one and stare out at the water.

"We used to be best friends, you know?" Lexie says the words as if they're a continuation of a conversation we'd been having. "Even though our folks don't really get along, they dealt with it so the two of us could have a relationship. But when she started getting all obsessed with our aunt Crystal..." She sighs. "I don't know. Maybe it's my fault. I refused to get caught up in it like her. My dad never really spoke badly of his sister, but I always knew he thought she was responsible for her own death. So I just couldn't get excited about learning about her, you know? She was reckless. I didn't want to be like her. I didn't want to end up dead. But when I told that to Crystal, she just got pissed. Like I was dishonoring our aunt's memory by saying she got herself killed—even if it's the truth." She shakes her head. "And then she found Bridget, and she didn't need me anymore."

"I'm sorry," I say. And I mean it. I know what it's like to blotted out of existence and replaced. I know what it's like for people who used to be your friends to suddenly turn into your worst enemies.

The two of us sit in silence for a long time, swinging back and forth, our feet never quite leaving the ground. I work up the nerve to ask the question buzzing around in my mind. "Do you really think it's true? That she's a witch?"

Lexie digs her feet into the earth below her. "I don't know. All I know is she changed. Maybe it's just easiest to blame it on witchcraft."

I stare off at the thicket of trees across the water. Does Crystal really know something about what happened in history class? Could magic or witchcraft really be the cause of the strange occurrences that plague me? And if that's the case, should I look into it if what I learn has the power to change me?

Chapter Thirteen

"Do you think I'm strict enough?"

Jodi watches me as I eat my breakfast on Tuesday morning, and I sputter a little on the bite I'm chewing. "What?" I ask, my mouth still full of scrambled eggs.

She spears a strawberry with her fork and picks it up but doesn't bring it to her mouth. "I had a dream last night about your dad."

My heart speeds up at the mention of my father. Though the topic is not taboo here like it was with my mom, we don't speak about him often. I swallow my eggs, coughing a little as they stick in my throat. "What about him?"

She waves her hand, the fork and strawberry swaying gently with the motion. "Well, I misspoke—it wasn't actually about your dad. It was about giant pandas attacking Clearwater. But your dad showed up at one point, and I was all like, 'Yeah! You're here to save me!' but all he did was ask me about you. He accused me of not being strict enough."

"Hence the question."

She nods. "I mean, this is all new to me. I've never had a kid before, and here you are, almost grown. I think I've been doing alright, but maybe my subconscious doesn't."

Some of the tension drains from my body. Of course she doesn't think my father really came to her in a dream. I sigh. It was silly of me to think she was actually talking about him. "I never really had a reason to leave the house before, so my mom never had to institute rules about me hanging out with friends or curfew or anything like that. I don't really have anything to compare your strictness to."

Jodi finally puts the strawberry in her mouth and chews it thoughtfully.

She's different from my mom in so many ways. I would never wear my mother's hand-me-downs, and Jodi laughs more easily than she did. I interact with Jodi more like a friend or how I imagine I would with an older sister, but I still respect her. I want to please her. I don't want to lose her. I finish my last bite and stand to take the plate into the kitchen. On impulse, I set my hand on my aunt's shoulder as I pass. "I think you're doing a great job."

At school, the atmosphere is already buzzing with excitement about the upcoming dance. It's the topic of conversation throughout the day. In health during fifth hour, Lexie, Owen, and Felix weigh the pros and cons of going out to dinner before the dance.

"All I'm saying is that if we eat too much, we won't want to dance," Lexie says. Her health book is open, but she's not even pretending to answer the questions.

Felix flicks a small wad of paper across the table at her. "So? Don't eat too much."

Owen snorts. "Have you never watched Lexie eat?"

Lexie winds up like she's going to hit him in the arm and leans over me to reach him just as Mrs. Stanton walks by. Dropping her hand and painting on a large, fake smile, Lexie nods at the teacher, who raises an eyebrow as she passes.

I smile as I write out the answer to the next question on the worksheet.

"Krissa, you're too quiet," Felix says, tapping my text book with his pencil. "What do you think? Should we do dinner or not?"

I'm taken aback, as I always am, at being asked my opinion on something. I've spent so much time just listening in on the lives of others, I'm still surprised to be part of the plan here. Heat rises in my cheeks as I try to formulate my response. "I... I'm not sure."

"Look," Owen says, drawing Felix's attention away from me. "I get that going out to eat in a big group can be fun, but it just doesn't seem right for a dance. I mean, if I'm going out to eat before a dance, it's gonna be with a date, not just my friends."

I think I see Owen's eyes flick to me for the briefest of seconds as he says the word *date*, but it's entirely possible I just imagined it. Either way, his argument resonates with me. "I agree with Owen."

He smiles at me as Mrs. Stanton announces there are only five minutes left of class. Lexie leans toward me and begins feverishly copying down my answers to the questions. When the bell rings, Owen walks me to history before heading off to his English class.

Mr. Martin assigns group work and I stifle a groan. Group work was the bane of my existence in my last school. But here, I remind myself, I'm not a social leper. I sigh as I glance around the room. Unfortunately, this is the one class that none of my friends are in. I think of the mousy boy who sits behind me and wonder if he'll need a partner, but before I can turn around, Crystal and Bridget appear at my desk. Both of them are smiling.

"Work with us, Kristyl," Crystal says. It's not an order, but it's not a request either.

I shift, uncomfortable. So far this week, I've been able to avoid talking to either of them. After Crystal's weird coded words at the coffee shop on Saturday, I've done my best not to even make eye contact with her. I look at the boy behind me, but he's already turned around to work with two kids behind him. A quick survey of the rest of the class tells me everyone else has already found a group to work with. Steeling myself, I nod.

The desks nearest to me have been vacated and Crystal and Bridget drag them so they're by mine. I look down at the assignment sheet Mr. Martin passed out and open up my textbook. Crystal and Bridget do not mirror me. They watch me.

Irritation flares in the pit of my stomach. Do they expect me to do all the work by myself? It's one thing when Lexie copies my answers in health, but this is entirely different. "Why are you staring at me?"

"You look different," Crystal says, tilting her head thoughtfully. "Doesn't she, Bridge?"

Bridget squints. "Definitely."

I wait for the other shoe to drop. What is it about my appearance they're going to make fun of? What flaw have they detected?

Crystal leans toward me. "Did you do something different with your hair?"

Self-consciously, I run my fingers over my hair. Nothing seems out of place.

"Maybe it's your makeup," Bridget suggests.

I haven't got any makeup on, but I refuse to tell them that. "Can we just get started on the assignment, please?"

Crystal sighs. "I'm just saying, you look nice today. You don't need to get all snippy."

Both Crystal's and Bridget's expressions seem genuine, but years of experience tell me that it doesn't mean they're truly sincere. I look down at the assignment. "It looks like we're supposed to read section three and make a chart..."

"Do you like history?" Bridget asks.

I don't look up. I'm not sure what her angle is.

A few beats pass before Crystal speaks. "I think history can be pretty interesting. I mean, not like textbook history. But there's some fascinating stuff you can learn from the past. Especially here in Clearwater. Do you know much about Clearwater's history?"

Their eyes bore into me so steadily that I can't concentrate on the worksheet on my desk. "No, not really. But that's not what the assignment's about—"

"Did you know your ancestors were some of the founders of the town?" Crystal presses, talking over me. "Mine and Bridget's, too. I guess that means we're connected."

"Yeah," Bridget adds. "I bet we've got lots in common."

Crystal exchanges a glance with Bridget and smiles as her eyes flick in my direction. "Yeah, I bet we do, Kristyl."

My stomach clenches at the sound of my name. I had my suspicions this weekend, and this conversation is only solidifying them: They think it was me who caused the whole school to tremble. I bite the inside of my cheek, feeling ridiculous for even thinking it. But it has to be true, doesn't it? It can't really be a coincidence that the whole building shook when I got upset and embarrassed, not when strange things always happened at my old school when I was in those states.

But even if it is true, Crystal and Bridget are two of the last people I would want to confide in. Sure, they're being passably nice to me at the moment, but who's to say how long it will last? What if they only want to know so they can use my secret as ammunition? What if they use it to turn Owen and Lexie against me?

My pencil rolls away from its position against my text book, toward the edge of the desk. I catch it before it falls off, my heart thudding in my chest. When I look up at Crystal and Bridget, I see smiles playing at the corners of their mouths. "Maybe there's something wrong with the building. The foundation or something. In any case, I'm not really concerned about it. We should get to work."

"Don't worry about it," Crystal says, waving her hand. "The work'll get done."

"By who? Do you have magical little mice in your purse who love doing history projects or something?"

Crystal and Bridget exchange a loaded glance at the word *magical*. A shiver courses through me. It can't actually be true, can it? They can't really use magic, can they?

I could just ask. The simplicity of the idea surprises me. If I really want to know, I can just ask them.

But do I really *want* to know?

Mr. Martin heaves himself up from his desk. Though he's not an incredibly tall man, he's thick around the middle and moves like he's in his sixties rather than his forties. He's checking in with the groups, which means there isn't much time left in the hour. My stomach twists as I look down at my empty assignment sheet. I haven't even written my name yet. I pick up my pencil and begin filling in the chart with whatever random information I can find.

Crystal reaches across our desks toward my hand, but I pull away before she can make contact with my skin. "Calm down," she says. "I've got this under control."

Her hand rests on my book, obscuring the information below. Mr. Martin is only two groups away from us. "Move your hand.

Someone has to do the assignment. I don't want to get a zero."

Bridget chuckles softly. "We don't *get* zeroes."

Before I can respond, Mr. Martin is upon us. "I'm interested to see what this group has come up with, seeing as I haven't seen any of you writing anything all hour."

My eyes drop to my worksheet, heat rising in my cheeks. Mr. Martin is the kind of teacher who holds students up as bad examples, who pokes fun at their shortcomings under the guise of "teachable moments." I can't handle the eyes of all my classmates on me, judging me.

But Crystal doesn't seem worried. She presses her hand to her worksheet and takes in a deep breath before holding it out to the teacher. "We did it all on one sheet. I hope that's okay."

Mr. Martin's dubious expression turns to confusion, then to curiosity as his eyes scan the sheet Crystal gave him. He flips it over twice before looking up at us. "Well, I guess you were getting your work done after all. It looks thorough."

Crystal smiles as she and Bridget exchange glances. I gape openly at both of them. Like Mr. Martin, I didn't see either of them pick up a pencil since they sat down. How, then, was Crystal able to turn in such a "thorough" assignment?

The bell rings and I'm torn between wanting to linger back to ask how Crystal pulled it off and the desire to put distance between myself and these girls. Flight wins out and I gather my belongings and dart into the hallway before Crystal or Bridget can say anything else.

I can feel Crystal's eyes on me as I twist the dial on my locker. I try to ignore her as I take my history book out of my backpack and replace it with my math and science books. Inhaling the scent of Owen's sweatshirt—which, despite my best efforts, I have yet to return to him—I try to calm down. I just want to leave the building and forget what happened last hour.

As I stand and slam the locker closed, I scan the hall for Owen. But the masculine form my eyes land on belongs to Fox. His back is to me, but I can tell it's him. Forgetting their mission, my eyes follow his progress down the hall.

Crystal sees him and waves him over. When he approaches,

Bridget sidles up next to him and a flash of jealousy overtakes me. I close my eyes and shake my head. I have no reason to be jealous, I remind myself.

When I open my eyes, Fox is watching me. He smiles as our eyes connect. I want to look away but can't. He glances at Crystal and Bridget for a second before breaking away from them and heading back down the hallway toward me.

Bridget looks put out but I can't make myself care. My stomach flutters as he approaches and I shift in my spot.

"Hey," Fox says, stopping in front of me.

"Hey," I return, smiling.

"You going to the dance?"

My mind is fuzzy. Am I going to the dance? Yes. And I've been excited about it since last week. But why? It's because I promised a dance to someone. But who? "Yeah, I'll be there."

I lean toward him and inhale his scent. It's spicy but understated, but there's something else. I take in another breath and detect a distinct floral note. It's familiar; I know I've smelled it before at Jodi's store, but I can't recall the name.

A black cord circles his neck, disappearing under the collar of his shirt. I reach up and brush my fingers against a small lump under his shirt. "You're wearing a necklace."

His hand pushes mine gently away from the hidden pendant. "Yeah. It's a special necklace."

I bite my lower lip. "Can I see it?" Unbidden, an image flashes in my mind: a small rose quartz pendant resting against Fox's bare chest. I shake my head to rid myself of the image. "Rose quartz," I murmur. Jodi told me something about that particular stone once, but I can't recall what.

Fox's eyes widen in surprise. "How do you—"

"Hey, Krissa."

Owen's voice cuts off whatever question Fox was about to ask. He appears at my side and cups his hand around my elbow. My head clears and I take a step away from Fox. When I look up at Owen, his expression is concerned. Confused.

"Owen." Guilt sweeps through me, although I'm not entirely sure why. "Fox and I were just talking."

"About quartz crystals." Fox winks at me.

"Fascinating," Owen says dryly. He tugs gently at my elbow. "You ready to head out?"

I nod. "Yeah, let's go."

I allow Owen to lead me down the hall toward the stairwell. It's not until we exit the building that he speaks.

"Was Fox bothering you?"

I shake my head. Why is such a simple question so difficult for me to answer? "I don't think so."

A muscle in Owen's jaw twitches. He opens and closes his mouth twice before managing to speak. "He's not a good guy, Krissa. For some reason, the girls all seem to like him. And he seems to like all the girls, if you know what I mean. I just don't want to see you get hurt."

His words pierce me. He sounds protective—jealous, even. We arrive at his car and I'm spared having to respond right away. I open the door and slide into the seat. I take my time putting on the seatbelt. "Thank you."

Owen starts the car. "For what?"

"Looking out for me. I've never really had someone do that before."

He offers a lopsided grin as he puts the car into gear. "Well, get used to it."

My heart swells at his words. Owen is a good friend. I'm overcome by the desire to tell him about what happened with Crystal and Bridget last hour, from their talk about the founding families to the strangeness of our assignment completing itself. But what can I really say? Crystal and Bridget might really be witches and, by the way, I might be one too? It's best if I keep it to myself. Will Owen's promise of looking out for me extend to a place where he might have to protect himself *from* me—from the things I can do?

Chapter Fourteen

In science on Wednesday, Mrs. Bates drones on about the flowers and plants in the courtyard by the commons. I'm not paying attention. The lesson for today is over and I'm two questions away from being done with tonight's homework. But when I hear her say something about sixth hour today, my ears perk up.

"I only had a handful of students who were going to do the work out in the garden, and half of them are out sick today. I'm just worried about what will happen to the plants if we wait much longer to take care of them." Mrs. Bates is addressing the four girls at the front of the room, the ones too close to politely ignore her. "The weather's already getting colder, and it always seems to rain about this time of year."

I tap my pencil against Owen's desk. "What's she talking about?"

He looks up from his textbook. "I think she was going to have a group of kids do some gardening during sixth hour today, but a bunch of them are absent."

Excitement courses through me. Is it possible I could get out of going to sixth hour today? I really don't want to face Crystal and Bridget and their obscure questions and vague accusations again. "We should volunteer."

He raises an eyebrow at me. "Yeah?"

I nod enthusiastically.

"Okay then." He raises his hand. It takes a moment for Mrs. Bates to notice him. "If you need some volunteers, Krissa and I would love to help you in the garden today."

Mrs. Bates's eyes light up and she clasps her hands together. "Owen, that would be marvelous. Thank you so much for so selflessly volunteering to help beautify our campus. I'll make sure to e-mail your sixth hour teachers to excuse you from class today."

At this, a handful of other students regain their hearing and utter a chorus of "me too"s. Apparently everyone thinks gardening is a worthwhile endeavor now that they can get out of class to do it. By the time the bell rings, Mrs. Bates is at her desk scribbling down the names of the dozen students she selected to assist her.

Owen and I head into the hallway together. "So, is gardening a secret passion of yours or something?"

"Not exactly," I admit. "Is it terrible that I just kind of wanted to get out of sixth hour?"

"Nah. I'm actually a little excited to miss sixth hour, too. It's precalc." He makes a face. "I'll probably regret it tomorrow, but I think it'll be worth it."

A smile tugs at the corners of his mouth as he says the last part and my stomach flip-flops. Based on the look on his face, he means spending the time with me will make missing class worthwhile—but maybe I'm reading into it.

We reach my third hour Spanish class and Owen pulls me into a brief hug before heading for his own class. The act is so casual, so natural, like we've done it a thousand times before. Only we haven't. As I walk to my seat, I tingle in all the places his body brushed mine.

When I sit down, West eyes me suspiciously. "What's up, smiley?"

I press my lips together. "Am I smiling?"

West laughs. "Like a lunatic. What's going on?"

"Nothing," I say automatically. The last thing I want to do is to make a big deal about the hug to West. He's Owen's friend and I don't want him reporting back to Owen about how silly I'm being, especially since Owen probably didn't mean anything by the hug. I'm sure I've seen him hug Lexie or Bria before, even if I can't call a specific instance to mind. "I'm just in a good mood is all."

I'm spared having to answer any more questions by the arrival of Felix, who takes his seat behind us. West turns and engages him in conversation as the bell rings and Mrs. Ortiz takes attendance.

The rest of the day speeds by. Instead of dreading sixth hour, I'm looking forward to it. Not only do I not have to deal with Crystal and Bridget, I get to spend extra time with Owen. So what if it means digging around in the dirt?

After health fifth hour, Owen and I make our way down to the commons. Lexie walks with us, pouting the entire way about how we couldn't volunteer her as well.

"I've got gym this hour. *Gym.*" She emphasizes the word like it's the worst of all possible fates. "The class is almost entirely freshmen."

Owen snorts. "It's your own fault. You're the one who failed gym freshman year. I told you you'd regret it."

I raise an eyebrow at Lexie. "How do you *fail* gym?"

"She never dressed out, barely participated. Even when the teacher refused to let her sit out, she'd just kind of stand in the middle of whatever game we were playing. Got hit in the back of the head with a basketball several times, if I remember correctly." Owen wiggles a finger at her face and she smacks it away.

"It was first hour," Lexie says by way of explanation. "These people can't honestly expect me to run around and get all sweaty first hour and then go through the rest of the day like a hot mess."

Owen shrugs. "I did."

She rolls her eyes. "Well, you're a *boy*. No one expects you to be clean."

When we arrive at the courtyard door, Mrs. Bates is standing in front of it with a clipboard and a harassed look on her face. From what I can tell, several students are hoping to get added to the work detail last minute and Mrs. Bates seems to have finally gotten wise to the real reason so many people in second hour volunteered to help.

The minute bell sounds overhead.

"You'd better get going, Lex," Owen says. "Don't wanna fail gym again, do you?"

She makes a scathing noise at him before the two exchange a one-armed hug. She waves at me, pouting, as she heads out of the commons.

Despite the fact I've been trying to explain away Owen's earlier hug as no big deal, a wave of disappointment overtakes me as he and I approach Mrs. Bates to get checked off her list. Part of me really wanted for him to give Lexie as simple nod of his head or a wave—something to prove that his hug meant he thought of me as more than just a friend. I was silly to get so worked up. Clearly, a quick goodbye hug is just something he does.

Despite my disappointment, my spirits remain high as we begin our gardening work. Owen and I are assigned to the same task—pulling some annual flowers from a bed along the cafeteria wall—and as much as I try to ignore it, a thrill courses through me each time our hands brush. I know it's a dangerous road to travel, but I can't help it that I'm developing a crush on Owen. It's hard not to—he's kind, friendly, and attractive. And is it really so crazy to think he might have more-than-friendly feelings for me too?

We're nearly done with our task by the time the final bell of the day rings, and while about half of the volunteers disappear through the doors into the swell of students moving through the cafeteria and commons, Owen and I agree to stay and help Mrs. Bates cover the beds with compost. Mrs. Bates gives us each a bag and shows us where and how to spread it.

As I gather the rich, black material in my hand, the promise, the potential within it is tangible. I cover my assigned area as evenly and thoroughly as I can, imagining the flowers that will grow there in the spring. In that moment, I understand why Jodi spends so much time out in her greenhouse. It's both relaxing and invigorating to work with the earth.

By the time Owen and I leave, nearly half an hour later, the hallways are void of students.

Owen nods toward the bathrooms by the stairs at the far end of the commons. "Let's get washed up."

"Sounds good," I say and head into the girls' bathroom. It's strange to see it empty; during the day, it seems like there's someone in every bathroom at any given moment. I turn on the tap and fill my hand with soap from the dispenser as I wait for the water to warm. I gaze absently into the mirror over the sink as I lather my hands, picking at the dirt under my nails. When I'm almost done washing, something sparkly catches my eye. I quickly rinse and dry my hands and turn around to locate the source: On the floor of the center stall is a necklace.

I look around the bathroom again. I know I'm alone, but suddenly it feels like I'm not. I shake my head to dispel the feeling. There's no one else in the room.

I move to where the necklace lies. It's an odd spot, for sure, and I'm positive whoever it belongs to is missing it. I pick it up. A clear crystal shard dangles from a thin silver chain. I know I've seen it before, but where?

I leave the bathroom, and Owen is already standing in the commons, waiting. His eyebrows cinch together when he sees me.

"What have you got there?" He moves close to me, so close that his shirt brushes against my elbow. I shiver.

"I don't know. I just found it in there." I hold it out toward him. "Does it look familiar to you?"

"No. Maybe we should take it to the lost and found. Someone's probably looking for it."

I nod, but my eyes don't leave the pendant. There's something that's familiar about it. Not just the way it looks, but the feel of it. I let the crystal settle into the palm of my hand and a shock shoots through me, like a bolt of electricity. I gasp and close my eyes to collect myself. An image flashes in my mind.

Green eyes.

My eyes snap open and I shake my head. There's something about this necklace. Something strange. I look at Owen, but he doesn't seem to feel what I'm feeling.

"This is so weird," I murmur. "It's like déjà vu or something."

"What? You remember finding this before or something?"

I shake my head. It's not that—not exactly. "No. It's like... It's like I know this necklace or something. Does that make any sense?"

He smiles. "Not one bit. Come on, let's get it to the office." He starts for the nearest hallway.

As I walk, I look down at the pendant. Something about it *is* familiar. "Owen, touch this."

He raises an eyebrow at me. "Do what?"

I grab his hand and press the pendant into his palm. "Do you feel anything?"

"Besides this cold rock being shoved into my flesh? No." He laughs, shaking his head. "Come on, let's go."

I hesitate for a moment. I don't want to relinquish the necklace. It feels like it's supposed to be mine—like I used to own it but lost it and forgot about it. I can't explain the feeling. But I try to shake it off. Owen's right. The best thing to do is to turn it in to the office. Someone out there is probably actually missing this.

We enter the front foyer of the school, across from the office. The distinct click of high heels echoes through the open area. From the hallway to the right, Crystal emerges, walking as fast as her shoes will take her, followed closely by Mrs. Cole.

"You can check the lost and found tomorrow," Mrs. Cole says, sounding both harassed and tired. "You can't just wander the halls after school."

"I'm not *wandering*." Crystal's voice is equally irritated. "I'm *looking*."

Mrs. Cole sighs. "Are you sure you wore it to school today?"

"Of course I'm sure. I wear it every day." Crystal's eyes zero in on me, a smile playing about her lips. "Look," she says, pointing in my direction.

Mrs. Cole closes the distance between us. "Krissa, what's that in your hand?"

I look down and, reluctantly, hold the crystal pendant out toward her. "I found it in the commons bathroom."

"We were just heading to the office to turn it in to the lost and found," Owen says, moving to my side.

An eager look spreads across Crystal's face. "Can I have it back, please?"

Mrs. Cole reaches forward and takes the pendant from my hand. When her skin makes contact with the crystal, a gentle shudder passes over her face. It's so quick, I'm almost sure I imagined it. Except I know exactly how she's feeling right now—or near enough. There's something strange about that necklace.

Mrs. Cole's eyes go to Crystal, who reaches out to snatch the necklace, her hand closing over the principal's. Mrs. Cole wrenches her hand from Crystal's grip. "Where did you get this?"

"Does it matter? It's mine."

"It's true," I say, a memory floating to the surface of my thoughts. The day I met Crystal—the day of the coffee spill—she had been wearing it. "I've seen it on her."

Crystal looks mildly gratified and reaches for the necklace again.

Mrs. Cole holds the pendant in a closed fist close to her chest, an odd look crossing her face. "Crystal, will you accompany me to the office, please? I'd like to talk to you for a moment."

Crystal crosses her arms over her chest. "Will you give me my necklace back?"

A spasm crosses Mrs. Cole's face, and for a moment I think she's going to tell Crystal no. "Yes," she murmurs finally, holding the necklace out so she can look down at it. "But first I'd like to talk to you."

I glance at Owen, and the look on his face tells me I'm not the only one who thinks Mrs. Cole is acting strange. Why isn't she just giving Crystal the necklace back and calling it a day? Unless I'm right, and she saw something when she touched the pendant too. Does she know something about the man with green eyes I've glimpsed twice now? I want to ask her, but I know how it will sound. And I don't want Owen to think I sound crazy, to look at me the way the kids at my old school did.

Mrs. Cole sways on her feet and takes a quick step forward to regain her balance. Owen moves to her side and grabs her by the arm. "Are you okay?"

She presses the hand holding the necklace to her forehead. "I'm fine. I just... Just a dizzy spell."

Owen doesn't release her. "Let me walk you to your office."

Mrs. Cole smiles at him, shaking her head. "That's not necessary."

"I insist," Owen says. "Ma'am."

Mrs. Cole doesn't refuse him a second time and they begin walking toward the office. Crystal and I follow.

"It's a nice necklace," I say as we walk.

Crystal appraises me out of the corner of her eye. "Thanks. It was my aunt's."

"The original Crystal." The words are out of my mouth before I make the conscious decision to say them.

She arches an eyebrow at me. "Yeah. I never knew her, but wearing it makes me feel close to her." She shakes her head. "You wouldn't understand."

My fingers go to my father's ring hidden under my tee-shirt.

We arrive at the main office and Owen takes Mrs. Cole inside. Crystal follows, but I linger in the hall until Owen returns.

"That was weird," Owen murmurs, placing his hand on the small of my back and pressing gently as we start toward the parking lot.

"Yeah." There's something strange about that crystal pendant. I felt it, and so did Mrs. Cole. I'm not sure why Owen couldn't sense it.

I shake my head. *Sense it.* How silly. I must be imagining things. I saw the necklace on Crystal's neck the first day of school; that's why it was so familiar to me.

Still, that doesn't explain the fact that it felt like it was mine, like something long forgotten. It doesn't explain the shock that coursed through my body when I touched it or the vision of green eyes that flashed in my mind.

Jodi said crystals could sometimes store energy. Maybe I just experienced the release of some kind of stored energy. Or was it something else entirely?

Chapter Fifteen

I wake up before my alarm Friday morning and can't fall back asleep: Tonight is the dance.

At breakfast, I drum my fingers against the table. It seems to me Jodi is eating in slow motion, savoring each bite of her banana nut muffin and her apple slices, taking painfully tiny sips from her mug of tea.

"Are you even going to eat?" she asks, surveying me.

I look down at my own plate, but food doesn't appeal to me. My stomach is too full of butterflies. "I'm not hungry."

She presses her lips together. "At least stick the muffin in your backpack in case you get hungry later."

I nod, eager for something to do to work off my nervous energy. I go to the kitchen and try three drawers before I find the one with sandwich bags. As I move to the living room to put it in my backpack, I hum.

"What's with you today?" Jodi is standing in the archway between the dining room and the main hallway. "You're all keyed up about something." She snaps her fingers. "Oh, I know what it is. You're really looking forward to the overnight inventory at the shop. I can't blame you: Eight at night to six in the morning spent counting every single thing in the store makes for a pretty fun night. Devin and I usually order pizza and play music really loud. Around three, we really start getting loopy, and last year, we may or may not have danced on the counter by the register while singing karaoke."

I freeze. Inventory? Is this the first time she's mentioned it? There can't be inventory tonight—I'm supposed to go to the dance. She knows that. She gave me permission.

Jodi claps her hands together, laughing. "Oh, my gosh, the look on your face right now is priceless. I wish I thought to have my phone ready to take a picture!"

I gape at her. "You're not serious about inventory?"

She shakes her head. "Of course not. Even if I was, do you think I'd be so mean as to make you miss a fun night with your friends to come hang out with me?"

She laughs again and I'm finally able to take in a deep breath. A second later, I laugh too. "You're evil."

"Eh, maybe a little."

At school, the excitement in the air is palpable. In first and second hour, people are buzzing about their plans for the evening. Miss Buchanan and Mrs. Bates even play along, spending the first part of the hour asking girls about their dresses and asking boys if they remembered to buy corsages for their dates.

But by third hour, something changes. As I try to make sense of the translations Mrs. Ortiz assigned for homework, my attention wanders. The girls sitting behind me are engaged in a whispered conversation and my ears perk up when I hear Mrs. Cole's name.

"Yeah, she's not here today," says Jayne, a girl with a sheet of black hair that tickles the desktop as she speaks.

Her friend Haley taps her pencil on her textbook. "That's weird. Mrs. Cole's, like, never absent. Especially not when there's a school event."

I bite my lower lip. Mrs. Cole is absent? I saw her just the other day. She seemed fine then.

But even as the thought enters my mind, a memory floats to the surface to combat it. Mrs. Cole hadn't been fine when I'd last seen her: She was dizzy. Owen had to walk her to her office. If she's sick, I wonder if there's something Jodi could give her to make her feel better.

When the bell rings to end class, I pull out my cell and tap out a quick text to Jodi to ask just that. When I'm finished at my locker, my phone vibrates.

Thanks for the info. I'll check on her. Shouldn't you be learning or something?

I smile and fight the urge to tell her it's lunchtime and I'm not disrupting my learning by texting.

The cafeteria is more boisterous than usual. Mrs. Cole's absence is measurable in decibels. When I settle down at the table, West is already there, along with Felix and another guy I recognize but have never formally met. The three pause in their conversation when I sit, regarding me as if determining whether I'm trustworthy. I pass the test and they begin talking again as I pick up a chicken tender.

"I bet we could do it. No way the chaperones are chilling by the punch bowl all night," says Felix. His hazel eyes are alight with mischief.

"I get what you're saying," says the guy I don't know. He wears a black leather jacket over the white tee-shirt stretched across his chest. His hair swoops down into his eyes and curls slightly at the back of his neck. Everything about him projects a bad-boy image and I wonder why he's talking with West, who is much more slacker than bad-boy. "I just think if we've got it, why waste it? So a couple people complain that the punch tastes funny?"

"Parts per million, my friend," Felix says. "If we've got enough, it'll only take a few sips."

"And if we don't have enough, it's all a waste," says West, running a hand through his blond hair, causing the front to stick up more than usual. "I think we need an outside opinion."

West turns his deep-set eyes on me. I struggle to swallow the food in my mouth as the other two guys look my way. The guy in the leather jacket smirks.

"So, here's the conundrum, Krissa," West says, ignoring the fact that I'm chewing like a madwoman. "Let's see if you can help us. Rumor is Mrs. Cole will *not* be in attendance at tonight's festivities, so we're trying to make the most of her absence. Tucker is pretty sure he can get his hands on some vodka, and the question is whether we should spike the punchbowl and spread the love or keep it all to ourselves. Felix wants to spread the love, but Tucker's against it. I'm undecided."

"Um." I bite my lower lip, considering the options. Having spent more than my fair share of time in trouble with the powers that be, going out of the way to break a rule seems foolish to me. However, I know these guys won't share that opinion. "Maybe keep it to yourselves?"

Tucker snaps his fingers and points at me, a smile spreading across his face. "Finally, someone with some sense." He looks at Felix. "The fewer people who get some, the more for each one. Supply and demand." He stands and begins backing up. "Later."

Lexie and Owen arrive at the table, but Owen doesn't immediately sit. His eyes follow Tucker's progress through the cafeteria for several beats before he settles in his usual spot.

A dull thrum of energy courses through me. Owen doesn't like when Tucker hangs around West and Felix. Felix is far too easily led astray, and astray is Tucker's perpetual direction.

I shake my head, dispelling Owen's thoughts from my mind. Having these flashes is nothing new—it's been happening for just about as long as I can remember. But usually, they only occur when I'm highly emotional—upset or scared. I'm not sure what it is about Owen, but I don't seem to need the emotional trigger with him.

"What does Tucker want?" Owen asks, dipping a couple of fries in ketchup.

"Give him a break," West says easily. "We're just making plans for the dance."

"He can't come with us," Lexie says. "Bria's car is full. He'll have to hitch a ride with you and the hussy you're bringing."

West holds a finger up. "One, you say 'hussy' like it's a bad thing." He puts up a second finger. "Two, he doesn't need a ride to the dance."

"Three," Felix says, leaning across the table toward Lexie, "I'm hitching a ride with Tucker, so you guys don't need to pick me up."

He makes a move to stand up, but Owen catches his arm. "Just... don't do anything stupid, alright?"

Felix snorts. "Come on. You know me."

Owen nods. "Yeah, I do. Don't do anything stupid."

Chapter Sixteen

Jodi lets me have the afternoon off work to prepare for the dance, but I have no idea what to do with the time. Lexie and Bria announced at lunch that the three of us would be getting ready at my place, but they didn't plan to come over until five. That gives me two solid hours to fill from the time Owen drops me off.

I head up to my room. Even though Jodi is doing everything she can to make me feel like this house is my home, my room is the only place I feel is really mine. I lie on my bed and pull the ring from under my shirt. Maybe that's why I like this room more than any other: I feel connected to my dad here. I've spent countless hours over the last five years wondering where he could be and why he might have left. Somehow, being here in the room that used to be his makes me feel the closest to him I've felt since he's been gone.

Letting the ring slide onto my index finger, I close my eyes, my head sinking into my pillow. I haven't had a flash from putting on the ring since the first time, but I like the feeling of the ring on my hand. It's too large for any of my fingers or I would just wear it, despite the fact that it's gigantic and clearly meant for a man.

Sleep overtakes me so gently, I barely notice. Images float through my mind from the day: Lexie's smiling face, the way Owen's hair spikes up in the front. Fox's gray eyes and the feeling of his chest under my palm. Crystal Jamison's face as she approached me in history class.

Crystal's face floats before me. Not her body—just her face. Her lips move, but I can't make out what she's saying. I move toward her. She's telling me something important and I need to hear it. Thick white fog surrounds me and I can't see more than a few feet ahead. Crystal is moving away from me and I run toward her. If only I could hear her words...

Crystal disappears and my pace increases to a sprint. Suddenly, the fog dissipates and I find myself standing on the edge of a river. There's something familiar about it and after a moment I realize what: This is the river that runs through town. I peer along the banks of the river but there's no sign of Crystal. I turn around and see a dense patch of woods. Movement flickers along the tree line and I head for it.

I hear voices as I near the woods, but the words are garbled and indistinct, like they're coming through a wall. I edge around a thick tree trunk and see Crystal standing in a clearing, talking to a man whose back is to me. He's tall and broad-shouldered, with brown hair that dangles just past his shoulders. I don't recognize him, but he seems familiar. I strain my ears to understand what they're saying, but the words are still unclear.

I take a step forward and my foot comes down on a twig, snapping it. The sound echoes like a gunshot through the clearing and Crystal's eyes widen in horror as the man she's talking to turns to face me. But I don't see his face, all I see are his green eyes—

A thunderous pounding draws my attention and I turn. My body lurches and my feet collide with something solid.

The floor. My bedroom floor. I'm in my room, on my bed—well, half on. I push my hands into the mattress, pressing myself to standing, just as Lexie and Bria appear at the top of my stairs. They raise their eyebrows at me before exchanging glances with each other.

"Did we catch you in the middle of afternoon prayer time?" Bria asks, crossing to my bed and heaving a tan canvas shopping bag onto it.

I shake my head. "No, I just..."

"Holy bedroom, Batman!" Lexie lets out a low whistle as she surveys the space.

I force a smile, somewhat embarrassed by the awe in her voice. "I know—it's big, right? Why don't we get set up in the bathroom?" I point to the far corner of the room.

"Holy crap—you've got a bathroom up here?" Bria asks.

"Dibs!" Lexie yells, taking off at a run.

Bria shrieks and starts after her. "Is that a freaking *couch*?"

Their lighthearted banter cuts through the shadowy remnants of my dream. By the time I reach the bathroom, Lexie and Bria are jockeying for the spot in front of the mirror, giggling. My heart swells. I'm so thankful to have these girls as friends.

"Fine, Bria, you take the mirror first," Lexie says, exiting the bathroom. "I'm gonna put my dress on first anyway, otherwise I'll just mess up my hair later."

"There's another bathroom downstairs. I'm sure Jodi won't mind if you use it to change."

Lexie picks up her garment bag and salutes me. "Lead the way."

We walk to the second floor and I point out Jodi's bathroom. Lexie directs me to wait outside the door to help her with the zipper.

When she emerges, I gasp. She bought her dress weeks ago, and this is the first time I've seen it. The deep emerald color complements her red hair and coloring perfectly. The bodice is fitted and the skirt billows out from her waist, aided by crinoline underneath. The whole thing has a vintage feel that suits Lexie.

"Do you like it?" she asks, spinning.

"It's perfect." I beckon her toward me so I can pull up the zipper before the two of us head back upstairs.

Lexie digs into one of the bags she brought and pulls out two curling irons and a hair appliance I've never seen before, along with three bottles of styling product. "Okay, I need to start on my hair."

I point at the long, low dresser behind her. The mirror above it, coupled with the fact that I have nothing on top of the dresser, makes it the perfect place for all her tools. She nods a thank you before setting up shop.

After checking to make sure Bria doesn't need anything, I grab my dress and head down to Jodi's bathroom to put it on.

It takes a bit of work, but I'm able to zip the back up myself. I stand in front of the full-length mirror on the back of the bathroom door and finger the beaded bodice. The pattern of black, white, and blue beads seems to twist and swell like water. The gentle sprinkling of sequins on the gauzy skirt catches the light as I twist from side to side. Before moving here, I would never have imagined myself wearing a dress like this, but now it seems like it was made for me.

The only thing that doesn't fit the look is the ring around my neck. I hesitate before taking it off, wishing there were a way to incorporate it into the ensemble. Since I found it, I've only taken the ring off while I shower. Somehow, not having it on makes me feel naked and vulnerable.

I shake off the feeling and look at myself in the mirror again. My long, blond hair hangs loosely around my shoulders and I wonder if I'll be able to pull it up somehow. I spend a few minutes pulling it back and posing in the mirror. I can't help smiling as I make my way back up to my room, wondering what Owen will think of me in this dress.

After Lexie finishes with her hair, she insists on doing mine. I protest, but she won't hear it. When she's finished, I'm glad she didn't let me talk her out of it. My usually pin-straight hair falls in soft spirals around my face, the blond color somehow accentuated by the shape.

Bria takes a turn next, applying my makeup. I watch her the whole time, taking in the dark eyeliner and cat-eye makeup, the ultra-red tint of her lips. My stomach knots when I think of what she'll do to my face. It's not that her makeup looks bad on her— quite the contrary. The heavy hand she used to apply her makeup is the perfect complement to her gauzy black dress. But that look will not work for me.

When Bria finally allows me to look in the mirror, I'm amazed. My makeup looks nothing like hers: It looks the way I might do it myself, if I had any idea how. The eyeshadow she used is silvery and there's a light blush on my cheeks. My lips are their regular color only intensified, shinier. I stand in front of the full-length mirror on my bathroom door and swish back and forth in my dress.

"This is... amazing." I turn to Lexie and Bria. "Thanks."

Lexie snorts. "Don't get sappy. If you get sappy, you'll start crying, and then Bria will cry, and then I'll feel too guilty not to cry, and we'll all mess up our makeup."

I laugh and nod. "Okay, no sappiness," I promise.

Bria checks the time on her phone. "Okay, Owen said he'd be here at seven, and it's almost seven. We should head down."

The three of us carry our heels when we walk down the stairs and pause in the living room to put them on. Jodi emerges from the sitting room with a camera, her face alight.

"You three look so beautiful! Here, squish together in front of the stairs. Let me get a picture."

Lexie rolls her eyes good-naturedly as the three of us pose. Jodi snaps five pictures before she's satisfied.

Bria checks the time again and shakes her head. "I knew we should've just picked him up. That boy is always late."

Jodi motions for me to follow her into the living room. She picks up a small box on the coffee table and hands it to me.

"What is it?"

"Open it, silly."

My fingers tremble as I untie the ribbon around the box and pull off the top. Sitting atop a bed of cotton fluff is a large bracelet with circular beads in black and blue.

"It's an anklet," Jodi says, picking it up and unclasping it. "Would you wear it?"

"Sure," I say quickly. "I mean, of course. It's really pretty."

She smiles and kneels in front of me, affixing the piece around my ankle. "It's more than pretty."

She doesn't elaborate, but it looks suspiciously like some of the jewelry at her shop. I wonder if these particular stones serve a special purpose. I open my mouth to ask her about it when a knock sounds at the front door.

"I think your boyfriend's here."

I bite my lower lip, my cheeks flushing with embarrassment. I look toward where Lexie and Bria stand but neither of them gives any indication of having heard her. "He's not my boyfriend, Jodi,"

I say under my breath.

Lexie squeals and opens the door to reveal Owen. My breath catches in my throat as he steps into the house. He wears black dress pants that fit him well and a blue button-down shirt that amplifies the color of his eyes. A jacket is slung casually over his shoulder. He accepts a hug from Lexie and instructs Bria to spin to show off her costume. When his gaze lands on me, his eyes widen and a smile tugs at the corner of his mouth. My stomach flutters.

Jodi touches her hand to my shoulder and leans close to my ear. "Yeah, I believe that."

I turn to her to protest but she's already corralling us toward the stairs for another round of pictures before she lets us be on our way. Before I step over the threshold, she pulls me into a hug. "Have fun tonight. You deserve it."

I smile. "Thanks, Jodi."

Chapter Seventeen

While Bria and Lexie sing along with the radio and bounce in the front seats of Bria's mom's car, I sneak glances at Owen out the corner of my eye. He and I are sitting in the back. Once or twice I notice he's doing the same thing. My stomach flips and I bite my lower lip each time our eyes meet.

Bria finds a parking space in the school lot and the four of us walk toward the door. There are a few other groups heading in at the same time. As soon as we enter the school, I can hear the music echoing through the hallway. I resist the urge to giggle, but I'm not quite able to suppress my desire to bounce, and Owen casts a sidelong glance at me.

"Excited?"

I grin. "Can you tell?"

He shrugs. "Maybe just a little."

I press my lips together but can't quite hide my smile. "Aren't you excited?"

"Me?" He reaches out his arms, sliding one around my waist and the other along Lexie's and Bria's backs. "I'm here with the three prettiest girls at Clearwater High. Of course I'm excited."

Lexie elbows him in the chest. "Women," she corrects.

Bria nudges Lexie with her shoulder. "Take a compliment, will you?"

We approach a long table set up just outside the commons and Owen, who is the only one of us with pockets, pulls out our tickets. When the group ahead of us steps away from the table, I'm shocked to see Mrs. Cole sitting there.

"Are you feeling better?" I ask as Owen hands over our tickets. When she reaches out to take them, I see a dark patch on her palm, like a smear of strawberry jam. Could it be some kind of birthmark? Whatever it is, I've never noticed it before.

She smiles at me, but it doesn't reach her eyes. She looks tired. "I'm well enough to collect tickets."

Lexie tugs at my arm and I allow myself to be led into the commons. The main lighting is off, and there are streaks of colored light spilling into the far end of the commons from the cafeteria. There are a few groups of people lingering in the area, but no one is dancing. Part of me deflates. This isn't what I was expecting at all.

Bria moves to the head of our group and leads us into the cafeteria proper, and my chest swells again: This is more like it. At the far end of the room, the DJ is set up, and in front of him is a mob of dancers. Refreshments—cookies and punch—are set out where lunch is usually served, and there are a couple dozen small tables with chairs set up around that area. The energy of the room is infectious and my smile returns, my concern for Mrs. Cole forgotten.

Owen points at us. "Punch?"

Lexie and Bria shake their heads but I nod, and Owen heads off toward the refreshments. I watch him go as Lexie and Bria start discussing the attire of the people in attendance. Owen is almost to the front of the punch line when Lexie sighs.

"Incoming."

I don't have to turn to know who Lexie is talking about: The look on her face gives me all the information I need. I steel myself, hoping Crystal will pass by without engaging me in conversation. I feel a tap on my shoulder and stifle a groan as I turn to face her.

"Can I help you?" I try to keep my voice and expression impassive.

To my surprise, Crystal's mouth curves in a genuine smile. Lexie raises an eyebrow at me. "I just wanted to tell you your dress is a great color. It looks really good on you."

I cross my arms over my chest, suddenly self-conscious. I

suppress the urge to look above my head for a bucket of pig's blood. "Thanks."

She's still smiling broadly and I'm almost convinced she means it. Her mouth twitches like she wants to say something more, but before she does, her eyes flash downward. "Well, have a great night. I'll see you later, okay?"

My eyes follow Crystal as she sashays through the crowd to join Bridget and a small knot of people on the other side of the room.

Bria touches my elbow gently. "Is it just me, or is nice Crystal even creepier than mean Crystal?"

"Right?" I force a laugh as I turn to Bria, attempting to ignore the shadowy sense of foreboding lurking at the back of my mind. "Any ideas on that one, Lexie?"

She puts her hands up. "Don't ask me to ascribe logic to her. What, you think because we're related I have some kind of special insight into the way her mind works? No, I don't, thank you very much. But whatever she's up to, I don't like it. I don't like it at all."

Owen appears at my side and presents me with a cup of punch. When I take it, he slides his arm around my shoulder and gives me a squeeze. "What did I miss?"

Heat rises in my cheeks and I say a silent thank you for the mood lighting. Lexie raises an eyebrow and I press my lips together in a tight line, ignoring the butterflies taking flight in my stomach.

Owen removes his arm. If he's noticed anything strange about me, he doesn't mention it. A group of people moves off the dance floor, led by Felix, who calls Owen's name and waves him over.

Owen tenses, sighing. "Idiot," he murmurs.

I raise an eyebrow at him. "I thought you liked Felix?"

"I do. It's who he's hanging out with I'm not too fond of." He nods in the direction of the group.

The longish, wild hair of one guy in the group catches my eye. Tucker. But he's not the only one who stands out. When I look at another guy, the tallest in the group with close-cropped dark brown hair and heavy, dark eyebrows, an unpleasant twinge passes through me.

"I figured with Mrs. Cole here, they might not try anything

stupid, but Tucker Ingram *plus* Zane Ross can only mean those idiots actually did bring alcohol." He shakes his head. "I'm gonna go check on the situation." He offers a brief half smile before heading off toward the group.

The DJ spins a song I'm not familiar with, but some other people seem to be enjoying it. As I sip my punch, I let my eyes roam over the scene. So, this is a school dance. I suppose it's about what I expected it to be from television and movies. Still, I was hoping for... more. Now that I'm here, I guess I thought I'd feel like I belonged. But, as usual, I feel more like an outsider looking in.

The song changes and Lexie and Bria squeal and run off onto the dance floor. I look down at the plastic cup in my hands. I could join them, but where was I supposed to set this down? Besides, they didn't invite me out. I take another sip of punch and watch the two of them dancing, laughing, grins on their faces. Owen still stands with the guys. I could go over there, but, again, I wasn't invited. I look away.

Off against the windows by the courtyard, a familiar form catches my eye. Fox stands near a girl with golden blond hair whose pink dress is so short and tight I'm not sure it qualifies as much more than a tube top. He leans in close to her ear and she giggles, touching his arm gently.

Lexie tugs on my arm and pulls me toward the dance floor, her cheeks flushed. "Why aren't you dancing?"

I open my mouth, but my plastic punch cup no longer seems like a reasonable excuse. She grabs the cup from my hand and sets it on a table on our way to the makeshift dance floor.

Bria squeals when she sees me and I can't help but laugh. She's so much different from usual, more open and alive. I like this change in her. I'm not exactly sure how to dance, so I try to mimic the movements Bria and Lexie are making. After an entire song's worth of struggling to copy their motions exactly, it occurs to me that neither of them is a particularly gifted dancer. Plus, it doesn't matter that none of us are dancing well, because—I realize with a start—I'm actually enjoying myself. I can't remember the last time I've had this much fun.

After another song, Owen, Felix, and a couple other guys I don't recognize join our little group and we accept them, widening the circle. Felix, it turns out, is actually a pretty good dancer, and while the other guys make do with simple shuffle steps, Felix moves to the center of the circle, inviting Lexie to dance with him. As they move, their eyes lock, and an almost palpable intensity builds between them.

Bria claps her hands together and leans toward me. "Man, I wish the two of them would get over themselves and admit they like each other already."

I raise my eyebrows at her.

She rolls her eyes. "Please, they've been doing this weird mating dance for the last year." She casts an obvious glance in Owen's direction. "Tell me you don't know a little about that."

I look away, refusing to confirm her suspicions. In another corner of the dance floor, I spot West dancing dangerously close to his date, the infamous Dana. Her dark gold dress is only slightly longer than the one Fox's date was wearing.

My eyes scan the room for Fox. He's one of the taller guys and I find him almost immediately, dancing near the center of the makeshift dance floor with a busty brunette in a deep purple dress. I'm confused, but before I can ask Bria whether she noticed Fox with someone else earlier, the blond approaches Fox and the brunette and grabs the brunette by the hair. A scream pierces the air and before anyone can react, the two girls are locked in a brawl, ripping at each other's clothes and clawing at any exposed skin. Fox leaps back, his eyes wide. He seems too startled to do anything but watch the fight unfold.

The music stops. Miss Buchanan and a female teacher I don't recognize push through the wall of students that immediately formed around the fighting girls. After a couple failed attempts, they manage to pull the girls apart and drag them off the dance floor. Mr. Martin leads Fox off to a corner of the cafeteria.

The DJ says something into the microphone, but it's difficult to understand over the buzzing voices. A new song starts up and, after a few beats, people begin dancing again.

Lexie grabs Bria and me by the wrists, pulling us behind her as she walks toward the refreshment table. "I'm parched," she calls over the music.

I allow Lexie to press a drink into my hand and follow Bria to an empty table littered with the debris from its last inhabitants. I collapse into the chair, suddenly aware of just how tired I am. It didn't occur to me while I was dancing, but I doubt I've engaged in this much physical exertion... ever.

"Wow, can you believe that?" Lexie asks, leaning over the table toward me and Bria. "That's not even the first fight over Fox this year. I just don't understand it."

Bria snorts. "Really? You're telling me you're immune?"

I lean forward, wondering if she's talking about what I think she's talking about. "What do you mean?"

Bria rolls her eyes. "Like you haven't noticed. He just has this effect on people. Girls get all swoony around him."

Lexie clears her throat and Bria holds her hands up innocently.

"Hey, I'm not excluding myself in this. I don't know what happened. I've known him forever and then suddenly at the end of last school year it was like I was seeing him for the first time. I don't know if he hit a growth spurt or pulled out of an awkward phase or what."

I take a deep breath. "So, you're telling me that everyone feels... attracted to him?"

Lexie shrugs. "I haven't, like, taken a survey or anything, but... yeah. Are you telling me you haven't noticed it?"

I shake my head. "I'm not saying that. It's just... strange."

"That it is," Bria agrees.

The song changes and Lexie claps her hands. "Okay, I'm refreshed. Let's go dance some more!"

Chapter Eighteen

"I need a break," I call over the music. I can't remember how many songs have passed since our second foray onto the dance floor.

"What?" Lexie yells back, her body still in motion.

"I need a break!" I fan my face for effect.

Lexie waves me away before throwing herself back into the music at full force. I laugh as I weave through the throngs of dancing students and head for the refreshment table. I grab a bottle of water and leave the cafeteria to walk through the commons—where there are far fewer dancers—and into the far hallway. It's darker here, and quieter. My hair is sticking to the back of my neck and it's a million degrees in here, but I'm also having the time of my life.

"You looked great out there."

I turn to see Fox, his dress shirt unbuttoned to reveal a patch of his chest. A smile spreads across his face as he moves closer to me.

I ready myself for the strange swooping sensations that always accompany Fox's nearness, but nothing overtakes me. He's clearly attractive, but tonight he doesn't affect me the same way he usually does. "Fox. I thought you got kicked out after the fight between your girlfriends."

He shrugs. "Hey, I'm not with either of those girls. I convinced Miss Buchanan it wasn't my fault they got all worked up over me. I mean, honestly, can you blame them?"

His remark chafes and I cross my arms over my chest. "Are you here for a reason?"

"I just noticed you heading out here and I wanted to make sure you were okay." He reaches forward to stroke my arm, but I pull away. His eyebrows draw together slightly and his mouth twitches.

"I'm fine. I just needed a breather. Thanks for checking up on me."

Fox's brow wrinkles in confusion. "What's going on with you?"

His words are quiet and I'm not entirely sure he meant the question for me. "Nothing's going on with me—I just wanted a few seconds to myself. Is there a problem with that?"

A beat passes before he shakes his head. "Of course not," he says, but he doesn't sound convinced. He takes a step closer to me, a smile stretching itself across his lips. "I just thought you liked me, is all. And all of a sudden you're acting decidedly unfriendly."

He caresses my arm with his fingertips and my stomach clenches. The commons is sparsely populated and no one out here seems particularly concerned with what's happening in my little corner.

"Look, Fox, will you just leave me alone, please?" I take another step backward and find myself against a wall. Fox doesn't advance on me, but he doesn't back away either. His eyes run down the length of my body and the cadence of my heart speeds up.

"What's going on here?"

My eyes slide past Fox to see Owen approaching, his eyes narrowed and his features dark.

Fox holds his hands up innocently as Owen places himself between us. "Just a friendly conversation. No need to get all territorial."

Owen looks to me for verification. I release a breath. "He's just being annoying. No worries."

Fox looks at me like he's seeing me for the first time. "Sorry to annoy you," he murmurs, though his tone is more confused than apologetic. "Enjoy your night." He pivots on his heel and leaves.

Owen takes a step closer to me and touches my upper arm. His palm is warm and slightly damp against my skin. "You're sure you're okay?"

I nod, watching as Fox crosses the commons and disappears into the dancing crowd in the cafeteria. "Yeah. It's just... I'm glad you came along."

He smiles. "I didn't just happen by, you know. The dance is gonna be over soon and Bria's already talking about heading out so we don't get stuck in the parking lot."

I bite my lower lip. I'm not quite ready for the night to end, but I can't very well tell my ride she can't leave yet. "Oh. Okay." I start toward the cafeteria as the music changes from an upbeat dance number to a ballad. Owen catches my hand, pulling me to a stop.

"I told her I didn't want to leave yet," he says, taking a step toward me. "You promised you'd save me a dance." He guides my hand up to his shoulder and rests his free hand on my waist. Before I'm sure exactly what's happened, my fingers are laced behind his neck and we're swaying back and forth. His body brushes against mine each time we step with the music. I'm aware of each place where our bodies intersect, and I focus on my breathing, trying to keep it steady. My heart beats so hard and so fast I'm afraid Owen can hear it. I stare at his chest, not sure where else to look. I step on his toes and pull away.

"I'm sorry," I say, looking down at my feet.

"It's okay." Owen closes the distance between us. "You're doing fine."

I step closer as he places his hands on my hips again. "I've never danced like this before." It comes out as a whisper and I regret the words as soon as I say them. Owen stops moving, and his right hand leaves my hip. I glance up at him, sure I've said something wrong, but the look on his face tells me otherwise. He's looking down at me with an intensity in his eyes I've never seen. His fingertips brush against my right cheek and he leans toward me. I close my eyes.

I can't see him, but I can feel warmth radiating off him as he moves closer to me. His breath tickles my lips.

Then the radiating warmth is gone. Owen's hand drops from my cheek to my shoulder. I open my eyes—what did I do wrong?— but Owen isn't looking at me; his face is turned away, his attention fixed on the commons. I open my mouth, but I don't get the chance to speak.

A scream rips through the commons, reverberating off the

corridor we're in. I take a step back from Owen—the spell is broken. A girl in a lavender dress stands in the center of the commons, a ring of people staring at her. "Mrs. Cole!" she yells. "Mrs. Cole!"

I look around the faces in the commons, waiting for Mrs. Cole to appear. Other chaperones look around at each other, and it's clear none of them know where she is. Miss Buchanan approaches the girl, but she just keeps screaming. She points to the hallway at the far end of the commons and a couple of the chaperones move in that direction.

Owen starts toward the far hallway too. He takes hold of my hand, pulling me along with him, and my confusion about what's going on is quelled as a new sensation overtakes me. Owen's hand is warm in mine, his pressure firm, sure. Like I'm supposed to be at his side, like he doesn't want to leave me behind. The feeling of his warm body pressed against mine washes over me again, the heat radiating from him to me as he leaned in closer and closer...

Whatever this girl is going on about, it had better be good.

Owen pushes through the doors and joins a crowd already gathering in the hall. Someone shrieks. A chorus of murmurs shoots through the group. I shiver, suddenly cold. Something in the air here is different. It's not just cooler here than in the commons—there's a sense of dread hovering over us.

Owen stops at the edge of the group, but I have to know what's going on. I tug on his hand as I begin pushing past people, making my way to the center of the tight knot.

Mrs. Cole lies on the linoleum floor of the hallway, her eyes slightly open but unfocused. Mr. Martin kneels at her side, alternately performing chest compressions and blowing air into her mouth with his.

"Is she dead?" someone whispers.

"Who found her?"

"How long has she been here?"

Miss Buchanan pushes into the clearing. "I called nine-one-one. The ambulance is on its way. Is she...?"

The man doing CPR pauses to look at the other chaperone. He shakes his head just slightly before returning to his work.

Someone lets out a wail.

I look around. A couple girls appear to be crying into their dates' chests. One group of girls stands holding hands. A few guys stand around, looking both shocked and in awe.

Standing directly across from me is Crystal Jamison. Our eyes lock on each other's for an instant. She wears an expression I can't read. Breaking off eye contact, she turns, disappearing into the crowd.

Owen's arm slides around my shoulders. "We should go to the main entrance. I don't know if anyone is there and someone needs to tell them where Mrs. Cole is."

I allow him to lead me back through the throng. More people have arrived. A couple chaperones keep calling out something about giving Mrs. Cole some air, but I know she doesn't need it. I don't say anything to Owen, but I know it doesn't matter whether or not we bring the paramedics to the principal. It doesn't matter how long Mr. Martin does CPR. Mrs. Cole is dead.

Chapter Nineteen

I wake up early Saturday morning and for a moment, I'm able to convince myself that last night's events were just a nightmare. But even without leaving my bed, I know Jodi is awake. Her grief is contagious, moving through the house like a fog and covering me like a blanket. Mrs. Cole died last night. It wasn't a nightmare.

What happened after we saw Mrs. Cole lying on the floor is jumbled in my mind. Owen and I waited for the paramedics and led them to her body. The chaperones forced everyone out of the hallway, back into the commons. The DJ stopped playing music and slowly, everyone filtered out of the school. When I got home, Jodi was sitting in the living room, waiting for me to tell her all about my exciting and enchanting night. But I only told her one thing.

The air feels thin and I struggle to take a deep breath. I didn't know her well, but Mrs. Cole was nice to me. She gave me a chance. It seems impossible that I'll never see her again.

On my nightstand, my phone buzzes. I pick it up and see a text message from Owen. *There's a diner two blocks from Jodi's store. Can you be there in 20 min?*

My stomach flutters, remembering his fingers on my cheek last night, but a swoop of guilt blots the memory out. How can I think about that moment with Owen in light of the tragedy that followed? Still, my fingers tremble as I hit the reply button. *Maybe. Why?*

Mere seconds pass before my phone buzzes again. *I'll explain when you get here.*

A knot of apprehension twists in my stomach. Does he want to talk about what almost happened between us last night? Or did I completely misread the entire situation? Maybe he wants to talk about something entirely different. I won't know till I get there, so I dress quickly, pulling on a sweater and a pair of jeans, before heading to the second floor and approaching Jodi's room. I hesitate at the door; she's sobbing softly inside. I don't want to intrude on her grief, and, more selfishly, I don't want her to need me and insist I can't go. Stomach clenching, I turn from her door and head downstairs as silently as I can.

The air outside is crisp and my breath forms white clouds as I exhale. I've never walked to Jodi's shop before, but it only takes a few minutes when Jodi drives us there, so I figure it can't be much more than a mile away. I check the time on my phone. Owen wants to meet fifteen minutes from now. I pick up my pace.

By the time I reach the diner, I'm rubbing my arms, wishing I'd worn my jacket. Owen sits in a booth near the back of the diner and I go to him. I scan the room for Lexie, Bria, West—someone—but I don't recognize anyone else.

"Thanks for coming," Owen says when I sit across from him. "Did you walk here? I'm sorry—I should've picked you up. I'm just... I'm not thinking straight right now."

"Yeah, I understand," I say. "I still can't believe she's gone."

Owen shakes his head. "No, it's not that. I mean, yeah, Mrs. Cole is part of it. But something else happened last night. And I need to talk to someone about it."

The first question that floats to my mind escapes through my lips before I can stop it. "What about Lexie?"

The corners of his mouth upturn for an instant and he runs his fingers through his hair. "No way. I can't tell her this. I'd never hear the end of it."

A waitress bustles up to the table and asks whether I want coffee. Though I don't normally drink it, I need something to warm me up so I accept the offer. After she pours it, I wrap my hands around the mug, allowing the warmth to seep into my skin.

"So, what's going on?" I ask.

Owen takes in a breath and releases it slowly. "This is gonna sound crazy, but stay with me, okay?"

"Of course."

He takes a sip from his coffee mug, pulls a face, and adds two creamers. "Felix was in an accident last night after the dance."

"Oh, no! Is he okay?"

Owen nods. "He's fine. His car's a little worse off than he is, but it's not totaled or anything. He was on his way home from Tucker's house and he says a cat was in the road or something and he ended up hitting a telephone pole."

Felix was drinking last night at the dance. I knew that. And while it is certainly scary that he was in an accident, it doesn't sound crazy. I wait for Owen to continue.

"He called me right after it happened. But I was already on my way there. Somehow, I *knew* it happened. I knew right where he was." He looks up, but he doesn't meet my eyes. "I knew it because I saw it. I saw it yesterday at lunch."

My breath catches in my throat. "You saw it?"

Owen rubs his forehead with his hand. "I know, it sounds nuts. And I'd just write it off as a coincidence, except... When we were dancing, I knew something was wrong before that girl started yelling about Mrs. Cole. I felt this..." He shakes his head. "I don't know. It's crazy, right?"

He wants me to agree with him, to soothe him, to give him a plausible explanation for what's happening. But I can't do that. Instead of feeling the fear and doubt I see in his eyes, I feel a kind of elation.

I'm not the only one.

"How... how long has it been happening?" I ask, my voice shaking ever so slightly.

His mouth twitches and he shakes his head. "You don't believe me. Not that I blame you—"

I reach toward him, my hand resting on the tabletop in the space between us. "No, no—I do. I do believe you."

He offers a half smile. "It's okay. You don't have to be nice to me about this. I just... I needed to tell someone. I know it sounds crazy. Even to me, it sounds crazy."

I bite my lower lip. How can I make him understand that I do believe him? If I tell him I have flashes too, he might think I'm making it up to make him feel better. Or, worse, he might think I'm as crazy as he thinks he is. He wraps his hands around his coffee mug and on impulse, I cover them with mine.

The flash overtakes me immediately and I gasp. In my mind's eye, I see Owen and me standing at the bank of the river. We're holding hands, and while the energy between us is intense, it isn't romantic. As we stand there, the river stills, appearing frozen, even though the wind around us picks up, encircling us, catching my hair up in the swirling vortex. Then, just as abruptly as it began, the wind dies and the river starts moving again.

The vision fades and Owen comes into focus. His chest heaves as his breath comes in heavy pants. His blue eyes are wide as they fix on mine. "Did you see that?"

No words come when I try to speak, so I nod my head.

"What was it?"

I cast my eyes around the diner to see if anyone is watching us. At the counter is a man reading the paper, and there's a family of four in a booth by the door. No one looks in our direction. I lean over the table. "I'm not sure what they are, but I've had flashes like that for... years."

"Really?"

I nod. "The first time I can remember having one like that was five years ago. And I had one the day I got to Jodi's house." I pull the ring out from under my shirt and stretch it toward him as far as the chain will allow. "I put on this ring and I saw my dad. But it was the past—back when he lived in my house. I can't explain it." I think back to that day and what Jodi told me. "Apparently some scientists think time doesn't really exist the way we experience it—that instead, all things happen at all times. Maybe... maybe we're just able to see those things sometimes."

He shakes his head. "That's ridiculous. Things begin and things end. Actions have consequences. That's how time works. I mean, that's why we can remember the past, right? Because it already happened. If the future already happened too, then we'd be able to remember the future."

"I don't know how to explain it. But I also don't know how to explain how we could possibly know what's going to happen in the future—or see what's happened in the past."

"You said this has happened to you before. Do you know what causes it? Or how to control it?"

I look down at my hands. His tone is desperate, but I can't give him the answer he wants. "No. I don't know how to control any of it."

I regret the words as soon as they leave my mouth. Owen leans toward me. "Any of it? What else can you do?"

He makes it sound like a trick or a skill, and he sounds so hopeful, like I can help him. I want to tell him to forget I said anything, but the eagerness in his eyes prompts me to go on. "Sometimes it's not the past or the future—sometimes it's the present I get impressions about. Sometimes I know what people are thinking."

Owen's jaw actually drops. He nods encouragingly. "Okay, what am I thinking?"

I shake my head. "It doesn't work like that. I told you, I can't control it. Usually it happens when I'm upset or scared. But even then, there's no guarantee I'll be able to tell what's on someone's mind. Sometimes something else happens."

"What?"

I bite my lower lip. "Things tend to... break... around me. Or sometimes they fall down. Or explode."

A grin flashes across Owen's face. "That's so cool."

Relief swells like a bubble in my chest. I've never once considered any of the things I can do *cool*, but when Owen says it, I can almost convince myself it's true. "Believe me, it's not as great as you think it is." I press my lips together, hesitant to go on. But I've already shared things with him I haven't said aloud for years. I can't stop now. "When I was younger, I told some of my friends about the things I saw or the thoughts I overheard. At first, I think they all thought it was funny—like I was just making it up. But when I started getting impressions about them, about their secrets, they all turned on me. I was a freak, and everyone knew it. And as the years passed, no one remembered why anymore, they just remembered the label. No one wanted anything to do with me. Like I was toxic or something. They were... They were awful to me. And when I'd get all worked up, things would happen. I used to get into trouble all the time at my last school for vandalism and things like that." I look down at the table as I say it, afraid of what I'll see in Owen's face. He's quiet for a beat longer than is comfortable and I look up at him. His eyes are soft, thoughtful. A smile touches his lips as he shakes his head and sighs.

"I'm gonna owe Lexie the biggest apology in the history of the world."

This is not the reaction I expected. I just told him one of my most shameful secrets and his comment is about Lexie. Anger flares up in me momentarily, until I look into his eyes again. My story hasn't changed the way he looks at me. I accepted his secret and he accepts mine. I take a breath. "Why do you owe her an apology?"

"I've spent the past couple years scoffing at her Crystal-is-a-witch theory. But now... Do you think that's what it is? Do you think that's what we are? Well, you. Me... What do you call a guy witch?"

I shrug. "A wizard? I don't know."

"I wish there was someone we could talk to about this. I mean, if Lexie's right, then there's Crystal, but..."

I nod, understanding what he means. She isn't my first choice of person to talk to either.

"What about... I mean, do you think... Jodi?"

I consider this. Based on the kinds of things she sells at her shop, it seems logical that if she's not a witch herself, she would at least know a little about them. "There's only one way to find out."

I pull a handful of bills out of my back pocket and toss them on the table before scooting out of the booth. Owen follows me, pressing past me to get to the door first so he can hold it open.

"You didn't have to pay," he murmurs as he leads the way to his car.

"It's no problem. You can get next time."

He smiles as he pulls open the driver side door. "Count on it."

Chapter Twenty

I push open the front door of my house cautiously. Maybe it wasn't such a good idea to bring Owen home—not today. What if Jodi is still in bed? I can't say I would blame her if she was: Her best friend died yesterday.

But as I cross the threshold, the teakettle begins to whistle and I know Jodi is up. Still, I hold a hand up toward Owen, motioning for him to stay by the door while I move toward the kitchen. If Jodi's in pajamas and a mud mask, she might not want a visitor.

Jodi is pouring hot water into a big blue mug when I round the corner and she is, to my surprise, dressed in jeans and a sweater.

"How are you?"

Jodi jumps, hot water sloshing onto the counter. She turns to me, hand pressed to her chest. "Krissa. You scared the life out of me." She squeezes her eyes shut, shaking her head. "Not literally, of course." She opens her eyes and sets the kettle back on the stove. "There's more water, if you want some tea."

"Maybe later." I step into the kitchen, studying Jodi's face. Her eyes are puffy; she's been crying. I bite my lower lip. Perhaps this isn't the best time to ask her the questions buzzing around in my head.

A floorboard creaks and Jodi looks in the direction of the front door. "Is someone here?"

I nod. "Yeah. It's Owen. We actually... We wanted to ask you some things. We thought you might know about..." I can't make my mouth form the words. "If it's not a good time, we can maybe

122

do it later. In a few days or..."

Jodi's narrows her eyes, revealing the slightest wrinkles crinkling the delicate skin around them. After a moment, her shoulders relax and she picks up her mug, cradling it between both hands. "Let's sit in the dining room."

I walk to the dining room and wave Owen over. He settles in the chair beside me. Jodi sits at the head of the table and takes a long sip of her tea before nodding at me. "What is it?"

I look to Owen, hoping he's come up with the right thing to ask without making both of us sound crazy. The look on his face tells me he assumed I would be the one asking questions. I sigh, turning back to Jodi. "We have a theory," I begin. "Well, Lexie has a theory—and Owen didn't really believe it until last night." Jodi shifts and I silently curse myself before pressing on. "We think you might know something—because of your store and the Barnettes being one of the founding families and all. But if you don't know anything, that's fine too. Because we're just curious, really, and..."

Owen puts his hand on my forearm and leans close to me, toward Jodi. "Jodi, do you know anything about witches?"

Jodi takes another sip of her tea. The movement is so slow and deliberate I wonder if she's doing it to stall for time. Is she trying to think of something kind to say to keep us from feeling like complete idiots for asking such a question, for thinking such a thing even exists? She takes so long surveying us that when she finally answers, I'm not sure I've heard her right.

"What do you want to know?"

Owen and I exchange glances. The short answer is *everything*, but I figure such a broad response won't help. "Lexie thinks Crystal Jamison is a witch. She says some of her friends are witches too."

Jodi shrugs. "She's not the first to think there's something special about the founding families."

I sigh. It wasn't really the kind of response I'd been hoping for. Then again, I didn't really ask a question.

"But I'm not from a founding family," Owen blurts out. "My grandparents are the ones who moved here before my dad was born."

Jodi's face softens. "Is there something you want to tell me?"

Owen's hand finds mine and he squeezes it. Taking this as a cue, I tell Jodi about what he told me at the diner, as well as the vision we shared and that I'd seen a flash the first time I put on my dad's ring.

Jodi's face is impassive. Once I'm done talking, she takes another sip from her mug, then stands and goes to the hutch in the corner of the room and opens a cabinet at the bottom. After rummaging for a few seconds, she pulls out an envelope and a white taper candle. I recognize the candle as the same kind she sells at the shop. She brings the candle and a holder to the table and sets them on the top, in front of me. The envelope she keeps near her. "Witches," she says as she settles back down in her chair, "are able to channel and control energy. They can manipulate elements—earth, air, fire, water. Krissa, I told you once that people can use crystals to direct energy, you remember that?"

I nod.

"Anyone can do it. Some stones naturally harness certain energies. So, if you wear something made with tiger's eye, for instance, it can draw in prosperity and pass it on to you. No experience needed. But if you want to, say, come into some money, just wearing the tiger's eye might not be enough. That's when you might want to cast a spell to really focus and channel the energy. Now, anyone can find a spell and cast it—I mean, there are a billion sites on the Internet. But not everyone possesses the ability to really make it happen. Some people are naturally gifted with those abilities—that magic. And those people are witches."

The cadence of my heart increases. They're real. I don't know why, but I was sure Jodi was going to tell us we were being silly— of course there aren't real witches. But there's no humor or malice in her eyes. She's not lying to us now.

Owen shifts in his chair. He's still holding my hand and his chest brushes against my shoulder. "So that's it, then. We're witches."

Jodi shakes her head. "I don't think so."

"But you just said—"

She holds up her hand. "I said witches use magic to manipulate the energy of nature. Accessing *time* is completely different. Witches can't do that."

"Well, who can?"

Jodi picks up the envelope from the table, fingering it with trembling fingers. "Look, I'm about to tell you something, and I'd really like it if you could try to cut me a little slack and not go straight to pissed teenager, okay?"

"I'll try," I say, not sure what Jodi could say that would upset me. I eye the envelope. "What's that?"

Jodi takes a deep breath and releases it slowly. "I lied to you. When you asked me if I was in contact with your dad. I mean, I'm not really in contact with him, but he's been in contact with me—infrequently, of course—over the years. He'll send me odd notes—and I do mean odd. Often there's no context and I've got to figure them out on my own."

A chill courses through my body and I shiver. Owen squeezes my fingers. "Why would he do that?"

She shakes her head. "He didn't just leave to leave. He wouldn't have left you and your mom if he didn't think it was important—that he had no other choice."

Heat creeps into my cheeks and I turn my face away from Owen. A wave of shame envelops me. I haven't told him about my parents, and I don't like that he's here to find out from Jodi. I want to believe what she's saying, but I can't bring myself to. What could be more important than being there for my mom and me? And what about once Mom died? Why did it fall on Jodi to take care of me? I stuff down the questions swirling in my mind. "What's in the letter?"

Jodi unfolds the envelope's flap and carefully pulls out the contents. She slides it to me and I move it so Owen can see too. The piece of paper I press flat on the tabletop is a scan of what appears to be a very old list of some sort.

"A genealogy," Owen says quietly. "A family tree."

I look at Jodi. "So, what? There's something weird about our family tree?"

She shakes her head. "Not ours. Yours. This is your mom's family."

I slide the paper closer to me and lean in so I can get a better look at it. I scan the bottom of the page, but my name isn't present. Neither is my mother's. "How do you know?"

"Believe me, that took some digging. This is all your dad sent me. No note, nothing else. I had the same first instinct as you and wasted weeks trying to tie this list to the Barnette line. But it's your mom's family line. Your dad wanted me to know something about her." She leans across the table and points to a spot toward the center of the page. The spidery handwriting is difficult to make out.

"Anderson Witacre?"

"That's what gave me the hint I needed. Hang on a sec." She stands and rushes out of the room. I hear her footfalls against the hardwood floors as they recede and then return to the dining room. She holds a large, thick black book emblazoned with gold foil lettering.

I squint at the title. *"Founding Families?"*

She snorts as she puts the book down on the table. It makes a solid thump as the spine connects with the hard wood. She lets the book fall open to the middle before flipping forward and backward in search of something. "Yeah, this is something some of the families in town got together to write a few decades ago."

"Let me guess: members of the founding families?"

"You're quick." She skims a page and points at it triumphantly. I lean in to see what she found.

"Anderson Witacre? Is that the same—"

"The same guy? Yeah. Back in the early 1800s, he and a group of others founded Clearwater."

I attempt to understand the implications of Jodi's revelation, but nothing comes to me. "So, my mom's ancestors are from Clearwater too? Alright, both my parents can tie some family members to this town. No offense, but, what does that matter?"

"I'll admit, even I didn't understand the depth of what this meant until just now. See, your dad's sent me lots of little things over the past five years. Sometimes it's mysterious family trees, sometimes it's pages from journals kept by early settlers. From what I can tell, for generations, people have been drawn here to

Clearwater. There's something about this area that pulls certain kinds of people in."

"Witches?" Owen asks.

She nods. "Yes, but not just witches. Like I said, dealing with time isn't really a witch thing."

I glance at Owen before turning back to her. "Well, who deals with time then?"

"Psychics."

Owen leans back in his chair, removing his hand from mine for the first time. "You're messing with us, aren't you?" The chair legs scrape against the hardwood floors as he pushes it back to stand. "You had me going there for a minute."

Jodi stands too. "I'm being serious."

Owen shakes his head, running a hand through his hair and causing it to stick up on the side.

I turn to him. "You're willing to believe in witches but not psychics?"

He sighs, resting his hands on the back of the chair he was sitting in. "I don't know. It's just... It's all so crazy, isn't it? Witches, psychics, magic, visions... I mean, it can't really be real, can it?"

Jodi's shoulders slump, her face resigned—sad, even. "I'm not lying about any of this."

The candle on the table flickers to life and I jump. Owen places his hand on my shoulder.

Jodi offers a small smile. "I'm a witch."

Chapter Twenty-One

It takes me a moment to register Jodi's words. It takes me a moment longer to remember to breathe.

"How'd you do that?" Owen asks.

Jodi shakes her head. "To be honest, I'm a little surprised it worked. It's been a long time since I've practiced. But I guess it's like riding a bike."

He navigates around his chair, sitting down again. "What do you mean, it's been a long time since you practiced? Are you a witch or not?"

Jodi closes her fist and the candle flame extinguishes. "Like I said, some people are born with magic in them. It seems like abilities build over generations. I'm guessing my grandmother, Hannah, had magic in her—that's how she knew about herbs and crystals. And my dad is the one who taught me. But I never really noticed anything particularly magical about him. I never sensed it—even when I was practicing."

I rest my forearms on the table, leaning toward Jodi. "Wait—if you're a witch, and it runs in families, doesn't that mean... You said I'm not a witch."

She bites her lower lip. "I had a friend back in high school whose mom used to make some extra money by telling fortunes and holding séances. But my friend never had an inkling of psychic ability. What she did have was magic. From what I can piece together, when a psychic and a witch have a kid, one set of abilities or the other wins out. Nature doesn't seem to like having both the skillsets in one body. But sometimes, it happens."

The meaning in Jodi's eyes makes me flush. "No, I'm not... I can't, you know, light candles without matches."

"But what about the things you told me about?" Owen asks, his voice quiet. "Things breaking and exploding around you?"

Jodi sighs. "I had my suspicions when I saw what was in your school file. It's not surprising for these kinds of things to happen if you've got no outlet for your magic. Sometimes it builds up so much it needs to be released. And if you don't know how to direct it, it can go haywire."

"You had your suspicions?" I ask, my voice quivering. "Were you ever going to tell me about what you thought I was?"

Jodi shifts. "I'm not sure."

Her words are a dagger in my back. "So, what? Were you just going to keep it to yourself?"

"I thought it was for the best! You have no idea what you could get yourself into. I told you I haven't practiced in years. It's been nearly two decades since I cast a spell."

"Why?" Owen asks.

A faraway look settles in Jodi's eyes. "When I was in high school, just a little younger than you two, a friend of mine figured out what she was—what we were. She learned about the town's history and the founding families. She brought together a small circle of us—of witches. Oh, we thought we were *so* special. My friend found her family's grimoire—this book full of spells and other magical things. Every time the circle got together, we'd try something new—whether it was getting a plant to grow quickly or lighting a candle or using wind to move objects. It wasn't easy— not at first—but the more we did, the better we got. And the better we got, the more we were convinced we were capable of.

"But we weren't quite as capable as we thought we were. And one night, my friend got in over her head. Magic ended up killing her."

"Crystal Taylor." My voice is quiet when I speak her name. "That's who you're talking about, right? Lexie and Crystal Jamison's aunt?"

She nods. "After Crystal died, the rest of the circle stopped practicing. It didn't seem fun anymore. It didn't seem worth it." She looks at me. "Magic can have consequences."

I look at my hands. I only just found out I have magic inside me and it feels like it's already being taken away. "You don't want me doing magic, do you?"

She runs her fingers along her eyebrows before pressing her fingertips to her temples. "It might be better—safer—if you work at controlling your magic. Not *using* it, but controlling it."

Owen snorts. "That's easy for you to say. You use magic all the time, don't you?"

"I just told you I haven't cast a spell in years—"

"That's not what I mean. All the stuff you sell in your store—the teas, the candles, the jewelry—that's all witchcraft, isn't it?"

Jodi sighs. "Not exactly. Everything has an energy and I know a lot about how to use those things." She reaches a hand across the table toward me. "And I'm willing to teach you everything I know. There's magic you can do without casting spells and practicing the craft." She presses her lips together and her mouth twitches, like she wants to say something more, but she doesn't.

A knock sounds at the door and I jump. Jodi curses under her breath. "I completely forgot—I'm going out to lunch with some old friends—Shelly's friends." She stands and takes a couple steps toward the front hallway. "Be there in a sec!" she calls through the door before turning back to me. "I'm sorry. We can talk about this more later, okay?"

I want to tell her it's not okay, I need to talk about this now, but the words stick in my throat. She just lost her friend; I know too well what losing someone is like to keep her from spending time with people who might be able to ease her pain. I nod and she smiles at me before heading for the front door. It opens and Jodi's voice mingles with an unfamiliar female voice. It's not until the door closes and I hear the receding footsteps of people stepping off the porch that I look at Owen.

"How you doing?"

He reaches forward and takes one of my hands. Pressing it between both of his, he looks into my eyes. "I should be asking you."

Heat rises in my cheeks. "I'm... fine. I always knew there was something strange about me. I'm actually a little relieved that there's an explanation."

A smile tugs at the corners of his lips, but only for a moment. "That's not what I mean. I saw you go all tense when Jodi mentioned your dad. And I... I saw in my head that you didn't want me to hear about him."

I look down at our hands, pressing my lips together. "I'm sorry. I didn't mean for you to see that."

He shakes his head. "And I didn't mean to see it. But that's not the point. The point is you don't have to hide things from me. You haven't said anything about why you're here in Clearwater, and I haven't pushed because I could tell it hit a nerve. I figured when you got comfortable around us—around me—you'd open up."

"I'm sorry." I pull my gaze up to meet his, the hurt in his eyes stabbing my heart. He's right. He deserves my honesty. I swallow and take in a deep breath. "Five years ago, just after my twelfth birthday. That's when these things first started happening. I mean, I guess I was always a little more in tune with what people were feeling, but around the time I hit twelve, things just started going nuts. I'd hear these... voices... in my head. And at first I thought I was going crazy, but I realized the voices weren't coming from me—they were coming from other people. I was overhearing people's thoughts. And at first... at first it was awesome." I smile at the memory. "I suddenly knew whether or not the boys my friends were crushing on liked them back. I knew all the answers the teachers were looking for during group discussions. But then one day at my friend's birthday party, I got mad at her. I don't even remember for what anymore—it was something stupid. We got into it, yelling insults back and forth. And then suddenly it came to me—the perfect thing to hit her with. A secret—a big secret—one she'd never shared with me, never shared with any of her friends." I squeeze my eyes closed as the memory plays out in my mind. "The look on her face when I said it... I wish I'd slapped her instead. Everyone heard it. Looking at her, at what I'd done to her, I felt terrible. I felt worse than terrible—I felt empty."

Owen squeezes my fingers. I know part of him wonders what

the secret was, but he won't make me tell. He allows me the time I need to regroup before going on.

"She attacked me. I couldn't even blame her. I didn't fight back. She knocked me over and just started punching me and I took every punch. We were at one of those pizza arcade places—you know, with all the games and the giant singing rats? And as she hit me, every one of the games started going berserk, lighting up and spitting out tickets and regurgitating tokens. By the time the adults got to us to break the fight up, the place was insane. Kids were running around, screaming, grabbing tickets and tokens. And the littler kids were screaming and crying, pressing their hands over their ears because it was so loud. My dad was a chaperone at the party and I'll never forget the look on his face when he got to me. He took me by the shoulders and pulled me up to sitting. As soon as his hands were on me, all the machines stopped freaking out. And his face—he was terrified. My dad was terrified of me."

I bring my free hand up to cover my eyes and am surprised to find my eyelashes are wet. I wipe my cheeks, smiling apologetically at Owen. He presses my hand between his.

"My dad left soon after that. I knew it was my fault he left, and I thought maybe—maybe—if I learned to control it, he might not be scared of me anymore and he might come back. But he hasn't come back. Not even when my mom—" I cover my mouth with my hand, choking on the word. Died. My mom died. A sob escapes my lips and I stand, releasing Owen's hands and starting toward the kitchen. It's bad enough he had to hear what he already heard; I don't want him to have to deal with this.

I'm a few steps from the kitchen when Owen's hand descends on my shoulder. He spins me and pulls me into his arms before I can react. He wraps his strong arms around my back and I nestle my head against his chest. I'm getting the front of his shirt all wet but I don't care. He won't let me care about that. His hand finds the back of my head, his fingers rubbing gently at my scalp as I cry. His other hand massages my back in slow, gentle circles.

Minutes pass before he speaks. "I'm sorry," he murmurs.

Bringing my hand to my face, I wipe my nose with my shirt sleeve. "I try not to think about it. When I think about it—about her..." I sniff. "Well, you can see what happens."

He reaches his hand out and wipes a tear from my face with his thumb. "I can't imagine what you're going through. But if you ever need someone to talk to, I'm here, okay?" A smile stretches across his face. "You can cry all over my shirt whenever you want."

I laugh, eyeing the sizable wet spot I've left in the center of his chest. "Yeah, I'm sorry about that."

"Don't be. I'm serious. Anytime you need me, I'm here for you."

His blue eyes smolder when he looks at me and my stomach flutters. He trails his fingers down the side of my face and I lean toward the touch. The cadence of my heart increases as he shifts toward me, the same way he did last night at the dance.

His cell phone chimes and the spell is broken. A spasm crosses his face as he pulls the phone from his pocket. "It's my mom," he mutters, glancing at the screen. "I'm sorry—I'm supposed to take my sister to this Halloween thing..."

I nod, shooing him with my hand. "Go. I understand."

His face tightens as he looks at me. He leans in for a hug before heading toward the front door.

His footsteps fade and a pressure constricts my chest.

Owen knows my secrets now. What's more, some of my secrets are his, too. In the span of a couple hours, everything I thought I knew has been destroyed, yet I am at peace. As crazy as everything Jodi just told me sounds, I accept it without question. I finally know who I am.

Chapter Twenty-Two

The day of Mrs. Cole's funeral dawns clear and bright, a light frost reflecting the late October sunlight. It's a Tuesday, but I don't dress for school. Clearwater High is closed today since so many of the teachers and students will be at the funeral.

I put on the black skirt Jodi lent me for the occasion. I don't have a black dress. I wore purple to my mom's funeral. Purple was her favorite color. The skirt is a little big on me, but it doesn't look bad once I pull on my sweater. It looks cold, so I don my black leggings, too.

On my way downstairs, I stop by Jodi's room. She stands in front of her dresser, trying to clasp a necklace at the back of her neck. Her fingers tremble and she can't quite get the ends to connect.

"I'll get it," I murmur, crossing to her.

"Thanks." She offers a tight-lipped smile when she hands the necklace to me.

I turn the pendant over in my hand. A purple stone the size of my pinky nail is set in the center of a circular ring of white gold. "It's pretty."

She turns her back to me and I lower the necklace over her head. "Amethyst. Helps with grief."

I do up the clasp and smooth the fabric on the shoulders of her dress.

When she turns back to me, her hand is on the stone. "The last time I wore this piece was at Crystal Taylor's funeral. It seems fitting to wear it today too." She picks up a brush from the top of her dresser and runs it through her hair. "You really don't have to come, you know. Shelly was my friend. She was your principal and you only knew her a couple weeks."

"I don't mind," I say, although it's not entirely true. I don't really want to go to another funeral—not so soon after my mom's. "You shouldn't have to go alone."

Jodi holds open her arms and I enter into her embrace. I hold her tightly and she squeezes me so strongly I find it hard to breathe. She sniffles a few times and I hold on until her breathing returns to normal. "Thank you, Krissa."

"Sure."

Jodi puts her shoes on and the two of us head out of the house and to her car. During the car ride, she doesn't turn on the radio and neither of us speaks.

The funeral home is just outside of downtown and the parking lot is nearly full when we arrive. Jodi locates an empty spot in the back corner and we make our way to the entrance.

The mood in the building is somber. Jodi is no more than a few steps through the door when someone calls her name. She walks over to a group of some women her age and they all embrace. Some of them have tissues in their hands and they dab at their faces at regular intervals. I stand over by a wall, not wanting to be in the way. I figure I'll just keep an eye on Jodi and follow her when she goes somewhere.

Besides this one, my mother's is the only funeral I've ever been to, and I'm not sure what the etiquette is. I barely remember anything about my mom's funeral, truth be told. I figure the best course of action now is to do my best to mimic Jodi.

"Krissa?"

I look up at the sound of my name and see Lexie standing near a wall, looking like she's trying to stay out of the way. She's wearing a simple black dress and a chunky turquoise necklace and I smile, glad for some color in the area.

"I didn't know you were coming." I keep my voice low. "Jodi and Mrs. Cole have been friends since high school, I guess. I didn't want her to have to come alone."

Lexie nods. "I'm here with my dad. He's a bit older than Mrs. Cole is... Was. But apparently his sister was pretty good friends with her back in the day. You know, Crystal Taylor?" Her eyebrows cinch together. "I wonder if Jodi was friends with my aunt Crystal too?"

"She was," I murmur.

Lexie's eyes brighten with intrigue. "Really? I wonder if she can confirm my theory. Do you think she'd know if my aunt was a witch or not?"

My stomach knots and a flush warms my cheeks. The thought of Lexie knowing the truth about the witches of Clearwater, of knowing what I really am, unsettles me. If she knows I'm a witch, she might lump me in with Crystal Jamison, and I don't want her to think of me that way. I don't want to lose her friendship. "This probably isn't the best place to ask her about it."

Her face falls and she sighs. "You're probably right."

Jodi removes herself from her group of friends and scans the foyer for me. She smiles at Lexie and waves for the two of us to follow her down the hall. At the door to the room is an easel with a sign spelling out Mrs. Cole's name: Shelly Tanner Cole. I try not to look at it as I pass.

Soft piano music plays at the front of the room. All around us are the sounds of low murmurs and tears. Jodi finds a spot near the back and the three of us settle down.

A slide show plays at the front of the room, displaying Mrs. Cole's life in images. There are pictures of her as a baby, held by a smiling mother and a proud father. There are pictures of her ripping open presents on Christmases and with cake smeared on her face on birthdays. As the show progresses to her teen years, the woman I knew becomes more visible: Mrs. Cole smiling beside a trophy, Mrs. Cole with her arms slung around the shoulders of a pair of girls. One of the girls looks familiar and, with a pang, I recognize my aunt's face.

Silent tears stream down Jodi's face and another realization strikes me: I didn't cry. At my mother's funeral, I didn't cry. It was too quick, too surreal. I listened to the words the funeral director said, but I didn't hear them. The words were generic. It could have been anyone's funeral.

All around me I hear murmurs of comfort and sadness, I see the shaking of shoulders as tears fall. Beside me, even Lexie is sniffling. Mrs. Cole has been a part of these people's lives for a long time, and I feel like an outsider, intruding on their grief.

Yet I have grief of my own. Yesterday with Owen was the first time I allowed myself to cry for my mom. I tried so hard not to think about her for too long, for fear that I'd lose it, and guilt swells within me now for not allowing myself to remember her. She deserves better from me. We were alone in the world. If I don't dwell on her memory, if I don't grieve for her, who will?

At the front of the room, a gray-haired man in a tailored suit enters and begins speaking. I don't hear him. The air in the room seems thin and I struggle for breath. I have to get out of here. I can't sit in this room with the oppressive weight of these people's grief pressing in on me.

I stand and scramble over Lexie to get to the aisle. She makes a move to stand and follow me but I shake my head. I need to get away, to be alone. I don't want to explain to her. I don't want to have to explain anything.

I push through the swinging door at the back of the room and rush down the hall toward the entrance. I shove open the heavy glass door and step out into the chilly October air.

Gulping in great breaths, I settle myself on the cold concrete steps. The world blurs and I rub at my eyes, tears spilling onto my fingers. Everything I felt yesterday with Owen returns, amplified now by the sadness of all these people, and my own guilt. A sob claws its way up my throat and out of my mouth, and my whole body shakes with the force of it. I long for the feeling of Owen's arms around me again, but he's not here. No one's here with me.

I hear the sound of shoes on concrete and feel someone settle beside me on the step. The hand that touches my shoulder is small and warm. Lexie. I don't look at her, I can't look at her. And though she doesn't ask, I have to tell her. I have to share something of my mother with her just to alleviate some of the crushing weight of bearing her memory by myself.

"When I was five, I was afraid of thunderstorms. I would

scream and cry until they were over. My parents tried everything they could think of to distract me—cartoons, stories, games—but nothing worked. And then there was this crazy storm and the power went out and I was just freaking out. My dad wasn't home and my mom was beside herself trying to deal with me. So she built this giant fort in the middle of the living room and told me this story about how it was a magical place where thunder couldn't reach. She found an old radio and turned it up really loud and put flashlights in the corners of the fort and started doing this crazy anti-rain dance. And it was just so ridiculous, I couldn't stop laughing at her." I suck in a breath. "My mom died," I say, my voice trembling. "That's why I'm here in Clearwater. Jodi took me in because I don't have anyone else. My mom's dead and my dad's gone and I've got no one else. I'm alone. I'm all alone."

Her hand slides around my shoulder and she hugs me close to her. "I'm sorry. I didn't know."

The voice isn't Lexie's. My eyes snap open and I turn. "Crystal?"

Crystal's eyes, usually so cold, are clear and open as she looks at me. "I saw you come out here. You looked like you needed someone."

I shift away from her, wiping at my face with the backs of my hands. I don't know what to say to her. I bared a piece of my soul, one of my favorite memories of my mom—something I haven't told anyone—not Owen, not Lexie or Bria. My stomach twists.

"I'm sorry about your mom." She sounds genuine. "If I'd known…"

I wait for her to continue, but she doesn't. Irritation flares in my stomach. There's no excuse for how she's treated me. "If you'd known, what? You wouldn't have been a complete bitch to me since my first second of school here?"

Crystal's mouth opens in surprise, like I've slapped her. The shock makes me wish I *had* slapped her. My grief is overtaken by another emotion: rage. I stand and round on her.

"It doesn't matter that I just lost my mom. That shouldn't be the reason you feel bad for treating me the way you have. You should feel bad about that because it's *terrible*. You're a terrible person. You're nothing but a bully—so afraid you're not as good as everyone else that you make everyone else feel like shit so they don't notice how insignificant you are. You're *nothing*. And I'm done being pushed around by you or anyone else. So, if you don't mind, I'd like to sit here alone and grieve for my mother!"

Crystal looks small, seated on the stairs below me. Her lower lip trembles and she tugs at the ends of her hair. "I'm sorry," she repeats. She stands and ascends the steps toward the entrance, but she stops halfway there, turning back to me. "I've been trying, you know? I've been trying to be nice to you, or haven't you noticed? I can't take back the way I treated you when you first got here, but I'm trying to make up for it now."

I snort. "Yeah, right."

She looks down at her shoes. "I deserve that. But... I misjudged you. And I want the opportunity to start over."

I cross my arms over my chest. "That isn't up to you. You don't just get to decide you get a second chance."

"I understand. But I hope you'll consider it. I think you'll find... we're more alike than we are different."

"Why? Because of the whole founding families thing? Lexie told me how you're obsessed with it."

"Well, that's part of it, but..." She shakes her head. "I don't expect you to understand."

How can she be so condescending? I ball my fists. "What don't I understand? That you're a witch? That you and your little witch friends think you're special and other people don't matter?"

Crystal's eyes widen and I can tell she didn't expect me to know what I know. It takes a moment for her to regroup, her expression switching from surprise to excitement. "How long have you known?"

I shake my head. "Doesn't matter. What matters is I'm not interested. I have friends—real friends. People who like me for who I am, not for what I am or what I could do for them. So all this contrition is wasted on me. I don't want to have anything to do with you."

She takes a few steps toward me, intensity building in her eyes. "How can you say that? Have you ever actually done it? Magic? On purpose, I mean—not just the outbursts you can't control—like in history class."

I bite the inside of my cheek. I don't want to admit I haven't, but she seems to have surmised as much on her own.

"You don't like me. I get it. If I'm honest, if I were you, I probably wouldn't like me either. But we can't go back and change what's happened between us. Believe me when I tell you that you owe it to yourself to learn how to control your magic. It's more amazing than you can imagine." She takes another step toward me, so she's barely an arm's length away. "I know what it's like when the magic just kind of erupts out of you. It's scary. But once you actually learn how it works, how to use it, that doesn't happen anymore. You can control it."

My insides ache at the idea of being able to control the magic I possess. I spend so much time afraid that if I'm too upset something crazy will happen. What would it be like not to carry that burden? And if I could do some simple spells—like light a candle the way Jodi did—what would the danger of that be? But it's Crystal. Can I really trust her? Do I want to learn more about my magic if she's the only avenue? Jodi offered to teach me about herbs and stones and other items that possess magical qualities, but she didn't seem too keen on me learning to use my magic. Whatever happened to Crystal Taylor all those years ago scared her away.

Crystal opens the small purse she carries and pulls out what looks like a receipt. She places it between her hands and presses her palms down on it, closing her eyes. Her lips move soundlessly for a moment before she hands the paper to me. I stare at it. The black ink has reordered itself. It doesn't display the name of the store or the items purchased anymore; instead, a phone number and address are spelled out in neat script.

When I look back up at Crystal, she is moving toward the door we both exited through. "If you ever want to talk—if you ever want to *learn*—call me." She looks at me a moment longer before crossing the rest of the distance to the main door. She opens the door and takes a step through before turning back to me. "You don't have to be alone."

Chapter Twenty-Three

Jodi goes out with friends after the funeral. She drops me off first, and I change out of the leggings and black skirt into my favorite jeans. I try to get comfortable in the house, but my conversation with Crystal keeps replaying in my head. *You can control it. You don't have to be alone.*

When Jodi talked to me about my magic, she used the word *control* too, but she meant something different from what Crystal did. Jodi wants me to learn to rein it in, to tamp it down. What Crystal offered me is more appealing. Why would I have this power in me if I'm not supposed to use it?

The air in the house is thick and oppressive. I need to get out. I find one of Jodi's jackets in the hall closet and pull it on over my sweater before heading out the door.

My feet crunch through scattered leaves as I walk down the sidewalk. I breathe in deeply and exhale pale clouds of vapor. Someone nearby is burning leaves and I close my eyes as I take in the scent.

The autumn day is thrumming with energy and I at once feel connected to and separate from it. Jodi said witches can manipulate the energy around them, and for the first time I wonder if it's possible. Perhaps it's the conversation with Crystal buzzing around in my mind, but it occurs to me I might be able to tap into the pulsing world of power around me.

Two blocks down, there is a tiny bridge over a small stream. I leave the sidewalk to follow the water. The sound is soothing and the sunlight glistening off the rippling surface is beautiful. I haven't gone too far when I see a fallen log running parallel to the bank, its bark worked off and the wood smooth; clearly this is a place people frequent.

But no one is here today. The only sounds as I settle on the log are the twittering of birds, the rush of the water, and the skittering of leaves against the ground.

Maybe I don't need Jodi or Crystal to teach me to use my magic. Now that I know what it is, maybe I can learn to control it myself.

Except I've never tried to do magic on purpose. I don't even know how to begin. Anytime something has happened before, it's been because I've been upset or scared, and I don't know how to conjure those emotions from nowhere. I could think about my mom again and try to overwhelm my system with sadness, but I quickly disregard the idea: If grief were a trigger for me, then something would have happened earlier with Crystal or yesterday with Owen.

But if I'm trying to control the magic, I also shouldn't have to rely on being overly emotional. Instead, I close my eyes, focusing on the sound of the stream. Jodi mentioned that witches manipulate elements, like water. Perhaps I can somehow channel the energy from the natural world around me.

I clear my mind, filling my head with the gurgling and flowing of the stream. Water is a powerful force. Given enough time, it can cut through rocks. Given enough force, it can take down buildings. Something that strong should be respected.

A breeze blows by, ruffling through my hair. The scent of burning leaves reaches me even here. I press my palms against the fallen tree below me, against the cool and unresisting wood.

There is magic here. I am magic here.

I meditate on those two sentences, repeating them over and over in my head until they mean everything and nothing at once.

A strong shiver courses through my body, pulling me from my thoughts. My eyes snap open and I'm aware suddenly of how cold I've become. I flex my fingers, but they feel wooden, unyielding. My ears burn.

How long have I been sitting here? I inhale deeply but there is no trace of burning leaves in the air. I stand up and look around. Everything is the same as it was when I sat down. I bite the insides of my cheeks, attempting to quell the wave of disappointment rising in me. I have no idea what I'm doing. I don't know how to control whatever magic I might possess. I can't stop it and I can't make it happen. Frustration builds and my stomach muscles clench. Maybe Jodi and Crystal are wrong—maybe I don't have any kind of special abilities. Maybe I'm just a freak like I've always thought. Or maybe Jodi is right and I should just try to forget about it all—crush it when it appears.

But in my gut, I rail against the idea. No, there's something inside me, something deep and desperate. And I need to know how to use it. How can I go through life without understanding it? There's a piece of me that needs to be acknowledged and accepted, the same way I've been since I've moved here to Clearwater.

I can't ignore it. I need to know more.

And there's one person who can help me.

Chapter Twenty-Four

The piece of paper Crystal gave me at the funeral is still at the house, but I don't need it. The phone number and address are seared into my mind. Even though I don't know the town well, I have no doubt I'll be able to find Crystal's house. It's like I'm being pulled there by my own desire to understand myself.

It takes half an hour for me to find Crystal's street. The houses here are nothing like in my neighborhood: Instead of Victorian behemoths, these houses are all newer one-story homes with identical lawns and decorative trees on every curb.

I hesitate as I step onto the porch. She made her offer sound open, but it's still presumptuous of me to show up here without warning. What if she's not even home? I don't think I want to deal with her parents. What do I tell them if they ask why I'm here?

I lift my hand to knock on the door, but pause before making contact with the wood. This was silly. I shouldn't have come. I turn on my heel and am almost to the stairs when I hear the door open.

"Kristyl?"

I turn to see Crystal Jamison standing in the doorway, a look of confusion on her face. I take in a breath and move a step closer to her. "Krissa."

She nods. "Of course." She pushes the door open. "Would you like to come in?"

I press my lips together. The answer is no. The idea of actually being in Crystal's house doesn't sound appealing at all. But she might be the only one who can answer my questions. "Thanks." I step past her and stand in the hallway. I glance into the living room adjacent to where I stand and see no one.

"My parents are out," Crystal says, correctly interpreting my unspoken question. "We can talk about anything."

She walks into the living room and I follow her, sitting after she's taken a seat. "I need to know how to use it. You said you'd help me learn."

Crystal's face lights up and she covers my hand with hers. "I'm so glad. At the funeral, I was sure you weren't going to be able to get past how I treated you."

"I'm not sure I have. But... Jodi doesn't want me to learn to use magic." My stomach twists; I feel like I'm betraying my aunt by admitting it. "She wants me to control it, that's it. But I don't think that's enough."

She nods. "You're right. It's not enough. Not when there's so much we can do. When you learn how to use it, the crazy, unexpected things stop happening, and the things you can do are... well... limitless."

A thrill courses through me at her words. Limitless. The idea is intoxicating. "Did you ever still have the unexpected things happen? Like me?"

"What, like making an entire school building shake?" She smiles. "No, never like that. But I think I understood it earlier than you. See, I've been doing magic since—"

"Before ninth grade." I remember what Lexie told me about Crystal becoming obsessed with her aunt the summer before high school began.

She doesn't seem surprised that I know this. "That's right. I mean, when I look back, yeah, there were a couple little things that happened before I started learning to control the magic—you know, like a light flickering or something falling off a table. Things that never really registered as weird, but that probably were magic, now that I think about them. But those things always happened when I was frustrated." She bites her lower lip. "That's why Bridget and I were messing with you that day in history. You know, the wind in your hair, the pencil falling off the desk. I figured if we could get you frustrated enough, something might happen." She rubs at the back of her neck. "I didn't expect the whole shaking building thing."

"So you knew then? That's why you started talking to me about earthquakes and all that? Why not just come out and say something?"

"I still wasn't sure. The earthquake thing threw me, for real. I was waiting for you to admit it." She shrugs. "I guess I can't blame you for not confiding in me, though."

I release a breathy laugh. "How did you figure it out for sure?"

She clasps the crystal pendant around her neck. "The day you found this. This pendant—this shard of crystal comes from a much larger crystal, a very old piece. This bit has power in it, but it's nothing compared to the power in the whole crystal. When you touched this, it could sense who you are—what you are. Didn't you feel it?"

"I did feel something when I touched it." An image of the green eyes flashes through my mind again. I wonder if Crystal knows about them. I open my mouth to ask, but she's talking again.

"When I got the necklace back, I could feel what it sensed in you."

"So, that's how you can tell if someone's a witch? Make them touch your necklace?"

Crystal smiles. "That's one way. When I first started learning about all of this, I started checking into descendants of founding family members. I found out that some of them have magic. But some of them don't."

"Like Lexie?"

She shifts uncomfortably. "I've never seen any evidence that Lexie's special."

I snort. It's clear she doesn't know her cousin at all if that's her impression of Lexie.

A spasm crosses her face, but it's gone in an instant. "I *have* found others, though. At first it was just me and Bridget. Now every time we add someone to the circle, we all get stronger."

"Who else is in your circle?"

"Take a guess."

I shrug. "No idea."

She smiles and motions to my ankle. My fingers touch the anklet Jodi gave me and I take in a breath. "Fox?"

"Yeah. Why else would girls fall all over him wherever he goes? Haven't you noticed he's not nearly so alluring since you've been wearing that?"

I think back to the dance, how I felt like myself around him for the first time since we met. "Wait—are you saying—?"

"That it's a spell that makes all the ladies go crazy for him? Absolutely. So, yeah, Fox and his older brother Griffin are both witches, too. Do you know Zane Ross?"

"Barely. Owen thinks he's trouble, just like Tucker Ingram."

The corner of Crystal's mouth quirks upward. "Oh, he is."

A jolt of energy courses through my mind and I can sense some of the meaning behind Crystal's smile. I shake my head to clear it of the image of Crystal and Zane together.

"But that's all I've found—just the five of us. We're a small circle, and we're pretty close. I mean, Zane's a bit of a bad boy and Griffin's kind of a dick, but when push comes to shove, I trust them both."

"Do they know about me?"

"They know I suspect. But I haven't told any of them that I know for sure. Not even Bridget."

I'm struck by the kindness of this simple gesture. There's nothing to stop her from telling these friends of hers—this circle. But she's done me a courtesy by keeping the information to herself. "Thank you."

"I told you, I want to make up for the way I treated you before. I want to prove to you that we can be friends. That I can help you." She closes her eyes and takes in a breath. For a second, I wonder what she's doing. Then, the lamp on the end table beside her begins to hover. It raises several inches in the air before settling itself back in its original spot. She opens her eyes and smiles at me. "I can teach you how to use your magic."

An ache builds in my chest. I want that, more than I can express. I'm ready to embrace who I am—all of it. "Let's do it."

"Okay. Give me a sec." She stands and leaves the room. Her footsteps move down the hall. In less than a minute she returns, holding a white pillar candle. She sets it on the table as she sits on the couch beside me. "We'll start small. We're going to light that candle."

She holds her hands out to me, palms up, and I place my hands in them. "That's small? Lighting a fire?" My mind returns to the other day when Jodi did that same thing. It seemed impossible when she did it. "Shouldn't we start with something... easier?"

Crystal smiles. "It's a really basic spell, don't worry." She closes her eyes and takes in a deep breath. "Just relax."

Taking a breath, I close my eyes, focusing on her hands against mine.

"Okay, now, just breathe in slowly and then breathe out slowly—just a few times to quiet your mind."

I do what she suggests, but my mind is far from quiet. Anticipation courses through my body, causing my heartbeat to speed up. A grandfather clock is ticking, wind is whining against her house. A warmth spreads through my hands and up my arms, taking me by surprise. I open my eyes, but Crystal's face is just as it was last time I looked. I close my eyes again.

"Everything has energy. The herbs your aunt grows—they're all full of potential. Some can be used for good, some for bad. They have energy in them that can be unleashed by someone who knows what they're doing. It's the same for everything else in the world. Everything's got energy, power, that can be used. Feel the energy. It's all around us—in the wind outside, the air in this room, in the ground under this house and the water in the river at the center of town. Breathe in and take in some of that energy."

I take a breath, managing to calm myself. I try to remember the sense of peace that overtook me by the river. It was easier to feel the energy there, in nature, but when I focus, I'm able to connect with the things around me here too.

"Now," Crystal says, her voice quiet. "Think about a flame. Think about the way it bursts to life when you strike a match. Then think about that candle, and match the idea of a flame to the wick of that candle. Got it?"

My eyes still closed, I try to follow Crystal's directions. "I think so."

"Okay. When you're ready, imagine the wick of that candle igniting into flame and say *fire*."

A thrill of dread courses through me. That can't be it—it can't be that easy. I can't be ready to make fire appear, not yet. But Crystal's hands continue to grip mine firmly and I know I need to try. How will I know whether or not I can do it if I don't at least attempt it? I conjure the images in my mind and murmur, "Fire."

Heat builds in my abdomen, making me gasp. My eyes fly open and I look at the candle, but nothing has happened to it. Still, the heat in my core increases and I panic. Standing, I release Crystal's hands. Her blue eyes snap open and she stares at me, open-mouthed. "What's wrong?"

Before I can respond, the pressure inside me erupts and the candle's wick ignites. The flame shoots up at least a foot in the air and I scream, backing away.

"Fire *out*," Crystal says, her voice high but firm, and the flame disappears, leaving the faintest trail of smoke behind.

I release a shaky breath. My fingers tremble as I bring them to my mouth. "Oh, my... That was..."

"Incredible," Crystal whispers. "I've never felt power like that before. Do you know how many times I had to try before that spell worked? And don't get me started on Bridget. Even now, she's hit or miss with that one. But you... Krissa, you have no idea what kind of power you have."

"I don't want to know," I say, shaking my head. "That felt... dangerous. Crystal, if I can shake a whole school building when I don't know what I'm doing, what will I be capable of when I *do* know? It's too much... Maybe Jodi was right. I need to learn to control it, not how to use it."

"Are you crazy?" Crystal stands, crossing the room to me. "How can you say that? If there's *that much* magic inside you, do you really think you can just ignore it? You owe it to yourself to explore your potential. The circle—"

"That's really what this is about, isn't it?" I ask, realization dawning on me. How could I have been so foolish as to believe she wants to help me for my sake? "Your circle. You don't want to help me manage my magic, you want to increase the magic of your circle."

She shake her head. "No. No, I want to help you."

"And you're telling me my magic has no bearing on you or Bridget or Fox or any of them?"

Her eyes flicker off my face. It's all the answer I need. I push past her and head for the front door. "I can't believe I thought I could trust you."

Crystal calls my name but I ignore her. Before I know what's happening, I'm on the street, running. I don't even know where I'm going. I just want to put as much space between me and Crystal as possible. The magic that surged in me was powerful and frightening. She said she'd never felt anything like it, which means no one in her circle has as much magic in them. What would happen if the rest of them could tap into the same power as me? How much stronger could Fox make an attraction spell if he had more magic? What other kinds of spells might he or the others attempt?

No, Jodi had the right idea all along. Magic is dangerous. It needs to be controlled.

Chapter Twenty-Five

At school the next day, Crystal has the sense to give me my space and not approach me about what happened at her house. During lunch, I try to lose myself in conversation at the table, but it's hard to engage in my friends' light-hearted banter when I feel so burdened by the knowledge of my magic. It's like now that I've used it once, it wants me to use it again and again. I feel the incessant tug of it on my consciousness.

Halfway through lunch, Owen moves to the spot next to me, opposite Lexie. "Hey, you okay today?"

I force a smile. "Yeah. I'm fine."

The look on his face tells me he's not convinced. Under the table, he taps my leg with his hand. When I don't respond, he taps it again, more insistently. Biting my lower lip, I slip my arm under the table and slide my hand into his.

Electricity jolts through me as our palms touch. I feel it flow through my arm and into the center of my body. To all the world, we could just look like a couple holding hands. Except we're not a couple. And we're not just holding hands.

The best way to describe it is an echo. In my mind I sense the reverberations of Owen's thoughts, but nothing is distinct enough for me to understand. I focus on the sensation until an idea thrusts itself into my awareness. *Is this because of Mrs. Cole? Is it because of your mom?*

It's not Owen's voice in my head, it's my own. I'm reminded of when Mrs. Ortiz gives sentences in Spanish for us to translate: I can hear what she's saying in Spanish, but I translate the concepts in my head. Only now, my mind is translating Owen's feelings.

I'm not sure how to respond to his question. The answer, of course, is no—I'm not thinking about death today; I'm thinking about magic. I could tell him; he already knows my secret. But how will he react if he knows I went to Crystal? Will he tell Jodi I tried to use my magic instead of following her directions to control it? And if he doesn't tell Jodi, do I want to saddle him with another secret, force him to lie to my aunt?

Guilt swells in me as I release his hand. "Yes," I lie.

Concern creases his eyes and he slides his arm around my waist, pulling me against him. Across the table, West raises an eyebrow at us, but I don't care. I allow Owen to hold me close, wishing my biggest problem was grief.

When the bell rings, Owen walks me to fourth hour, keeping his arm around me as we navigate the halls. When he pulls me in for a hug outside my math class, he holds me longer than usual, like the acceptable time frame for a platonic hug means nothing after he held me for so long while I cried. "If you need to get out of here, say the word. We can cut class and I'll take you home."

I laugh. "Thanks for the offer. I'll be okay."

Bria waggles her eyebrows at me when I walk into the classroom. My cheeks burn as I take my seat beside her. "If you have something to say, say it."

She shakes her head. "I'm not saying anything."

Fox and Zane walk in just before the late bell and Mrs. Hill looks at them disapprovingly. The two are generally the last to arrive to class, and for the first time, I wonder why. Are they practicing magic between classes? Or, more likely, reaping the benefits of the attraction spell Fox uses to make the girls all fawn over him. Every time I think about that, it makes me angrier.

I try to pay attention as Mrs. Hill goes over the problems from last night's homework, but even in the most ideal circumstances, my attention has a tendency to wane during math. Therefore, when the class breaks into motion about halfway through the hour, I'm taken by surprise.

Fox scoots a desk up beside mine. "Be my partner?"

I turn to Bria, who would be my first choice for a partner, but Zane has already turned the desk in front of hers so they face each other. When I hold my hands out to her, she shrugs, motioning with her eyes to Zane. I sigh when I interpret her look: He's cute and she doesn't want to pass up an opportunity to work with him.

Reluctantly, I turn back to Fox. "Cast a spell on her too?"

"No. Crystal felt bad that things went sideways with you yesterday. She thought it might help for me to talk to you."

I bristle. "She told me she didn't tell anyone about me."

"She didn't. At least, she didn't tell me about you until after you left her house. She's worried about you and she figured you wouldn't want to talk to her again."

I cross my arms over my chest. "That doesn't make it okay. She doesn't have the right to go around telling people."

"Oh, come on. Clearly she told you about my little secret. Now I know yours. Tit for tat." His eyes flicker downward and he flashes a grin. "So to speak."

I roll my eyes. "No wonder you need magic to get girls to talk to you."

"Hey now, be nice." All humor leaves his face and his eyes soften. "Seriously, I just want to help you."

"Yeah, right. You want to help yourself. Crystal admitted as much yesterday. She said every time you guys add someone to the circle, all of you get more magic. That's really all you want from me, isn't it?"

"No," he says, his voice firm. "I mean, not that more magic doesn't sound good to me. But it's not what you're thinking—not really. Adding more people to the circle just adds more power to the spells we cast *together*." He leans forward, lowering his voice. "I want to help you because I already *have* magic, and I know how awesome it can be. I want you to experience that too."

I shake my head. "That's where you're wrong. It's not just some cool trick. It can be dangerous."

Fox waves away my concern. "You tried your first spell and you got scared. So what? Do you give up on everything that makes you a little uncomfortable?"

"I'm talking to you, aren't I?"

He grins, leaning closer to me. "I make you uncomfortable?"

My instinct is to shrink backwards, away from him, but I fight it. It's what he wants me to do. Instead, I press my fingers against the lump under his shirt. "It might have something to do with that rose quartz you wear around your neck."

His eyes narrow at me in confusion. "That's not the first time you've mentioned rose quartz. How do you know that?"

The simple answer is that I saw it, but I can't tell him that—can't tell him I once visualized his bare chest. I attempt to arrange my face into a nonchalant expression. "It's an attraction charm, isn't it?" The words bubble to my lips like they've been on my mind all along. I inhale his scent—the spice along with the slightest sweet floral note. I smile. "And a sprig of lavender in your right front pocket. Also used for attracting romantic attention."

He studies my face. "How are you doing that? Is it a spell?"

It's not a spell—at least I don't think it is. I'm pretty sure this knowledge comes from my psychic side—but I'm not going to tell him that.

Fox leans in closer. "Magic comes naturally to you, whether you want to admit it or not. It's part of who you are. Why deny it?"

I consider his words. What happened yesterday was scary, to be sure, but he has a point. "I want to be able to control it."

The corner of his mouth tugs upward. "Well, as with anything, it takes practice. You can't learn to control it without learning how to use it. It's as simple as that."

The bell sounds and the classroom erupts as students start grabbing their backpacks and heading out of the room. I stand but Fox blocks my way. "Look, just give us a try. The circle—we've all been where you are now. You can learn from us. And I bet there are a few things we could learn from you."

I try to edge my way around him, but he anticipates each move. I sigh. "Okay," I say, looking up into his stormy eyes. "Okay. I'll try."

He smiles. "Good. We're meeting tonight at my house. Give me your phone—I'll text you the address."

I hesitate. I don't want to give him my phone, but I do. He taps the touch screen a few times before pulling his own phone from his pocket. He hands mine back to me and allows me by. I don't waste any time heading out of the room. Before I make it to the hall, I hear his voice behind me.

"Seven o'clock."

I turn and nod. "Seven o'clock."

Chapter Twenty-Six

If Jodi is suspicious when I ask for the car keys after dinner, she keeps it to herself. Or at least she tries. She thinks I'm going out with Owen. I don't correct her: I doubt she would react positively to my hanging out with Crystal and Fox and learning how to use magic.

Fox's house is just a few blocks from Crystal's and its year of origin seems to fall somewhere between Jodi's house and Crystal's: Its construction is stout and solid, made of heavy red brick. Leaves from the tall tree by the road litter the front yard and the only hint at landscaping is a rather bedraggled garden gnome leaning against the small front porch.

I park, but my hands remain firmly on the steering wheel. Going into the house would be so simple, but a fear lurks inside me: What if walking in signifies more than I mean it to? Crystal said I wouldn't have to be alone, and Fox said the circle and I could learn from each other. I don't want to step in to something I can't step out of.

A thump sounds on the roof of the car and I jump, a squeal escaping from my lips. Outside my window stands a guy wearing a soft leather jacket over a gray tee-shirt. His form is slender and his face is hollow and angular. His brown hair is just long enough to fall into his eyes.

"You the girl Fox said was coming?" he calls through the glass.

I nod and he steps back from the door. I turn off the engine and climb out of the car, the guy's eyes on me the entire time. After I slam the door behind me, he jerks his head toward the house and starts for it. I follow. It's too late to turn back now.

I feel like I should introduce myself, but he doesn't seem interested in knowing my name. When he gets to the front door, he opens it and walks right in. I hesitate at the threshold but cross it quickly when he glances back.

Fox emerges from a door down the hall and smiles. The guy who led me in heads off through the dining room and into the kitchen without a word. Fox raises his chin after the guy when he passes out of sight. "I see you met Griffin."

I shrug. "I wouldn't exactly say we've met."

He nods. "Yeah, that's Griffin for you. Not very chatty." We're standing in the living room; the curtains are drawn and only the hall light is on, so the room is mostly in shadows. What I can make out is covered in shirts and pants in varying states of cleanliness. There is mail stacked up on the dining room table, along with plastic shopping bags and old takeout containers. Game system controllers litter the area directly in front of the television. He sweeps his hand around. "So, what do you think?"

I bite my lower lip. He doesn't sound like he wants my honest opinion.

He senses my inner struggle and grins. "I know—kind of a bachelor pad. But with just me and Griff here most of the time, that's what happens. It could use a woman's touch. Care to volunteer?"

I cross my arms over my chest. "So, are the others here or what?"

A rough chorus of laughter from the basement answers my question. I head in the direction Griffin went and Fox follows me.

The basement is dim, even though a bank of fluorescent lights flickers ominously near the center of the room. The walls are covered in faux wood paneling and most of the space is consumed by two couches and three recliners in varying states of disrepair. Crystal sits on the couch directly opposite the stairs, talking with Zane Ross. Griffin stands off to the side, looking less than politely disinterested as Bridget chats away. When her eyes land on me, she approaches me and links her arm through mine like we're the best of friends, like we've done this every day for our whole lives. She smiles brightly and steers me toward the unoccupied couch.

Fox settles beside me, a smile stretched across his lips. "Welcome to the club."

I shift closer to Bridget. Not that I care to be any closer to her, I just want to put as much space between me and Fox as possible. I still wear the charm Jodi gave me, and so far I've felt like myself around Fox, but I don't want to test its limits.

When I'm seated, Crystal ends her conversation with Zane and turns so she can address the room. But her eyes fix on me. "Krissa, I'm glad you decided to come."

I nod, not sure how to respond.

Zane leans toward me. "Crystal says you guys tapped into some serious magic the other day." His eyes are wide, full of admiration. "You think you could show us how you do that?"

I press back into the couch cushions. "I don't..." My eyes travel from Zane to Crystal. "I thought you guys were going to help me."

From his spot against the wall, Griffin snorts. "No fair not sharing."

I shake my head. "It's not that I don't want to share, it's just—I don't know how to do anything yet. Crystal said you guys could help me control it. Fox said you would help."

A broad grin crosses Griffin's face. "Fox says a lot of things to pretty girls."

Beside me, Bridget sniffs audibly.

"We *will* help you," Crystal says. "That's the thing about the circle. We all help each other. And I'm sure Krissa will show us how she can tap into such strong magic, but she needs to understand how to use it first." Her hands go to the back of her neck and she unclasps the necklace from which her crystal pendant dangles. "How much has your aunt told you about crystals?"

I shrug. "A little. She says they're for harnessing and channeling energy."

Crystal nods. "Different crystals have different properties. And some are stronger than others. This necklace is made out of a very old, very powerful crystal."

Griffin affects a loud snore. "Boring," he sing-songs. "How many times are you gonna tell this story?"

"*Krissa* hasn't heard it," Bridget sneers, and a flash asserts itself in my consciousness. Bridget is desperate for attention from Griffin. She tries all the techniques that usually make guys interested: touching his arm when they talk to each other, laughing at his jokes, wearing her tight, low-cut tops pulled even tighter and lower than usual. But Griffin shows no interest in her. I squeeze my eyes shut and rub my fingers over them briefly as Crystal continues.

"Clearwater has a long history full of magic, dating back to the founding families. But for some reason, several generations ago, the magic seems to have just disappeared. I've tried to figure out why, but I can't find anything that explains it. Anyway, this crystal has been in my family for generations. It was entrusted to the Taylor line to protect because it's so full of power. My grandpa was responsible for it, and once he died, my aunt Crystal took it upon herself to look after it. And once she took possession of it, the most amazing thing happened: Magic started returning to Clearwater. There was something special about Crystal Taylor, and once she got her hands on the crystal, she started being able to use magic. And so did some other people."

I nod. I had learned as much already from Jodi.

"Now, magic in its natural state can be wild—that's the thing about magic that scares you, I think. But if a circle anchors its magic to a crystal, it serves as a kind of tether that keeps the members connected to nature. Having that kind of connection can keep unintended things from happening." She gives me a meaningful look.

I glance from face to face around the circle. "How do you know this?"

Crystal smiles. "I found my aunt's book of shadows. It's full of all kinds of information about magic—some spells, some thoughts, some history and understanding. She was trying to convince her circle to anchor itself to the crystal before she died. In her book of shadows, she explains how the anchoring spell would make the magic more accessible and it would amplify the circle's natural abilities."

"That'd be nice," Zane says, interlacing his fingers behind his head and leaning back into the arm of the couch.

"Then why don't you do it?" I ask.

"Well, we need to find it first." Crystal holds the pendant again. "This is the only piece I've found from the crystal. I've gone through boxes at my grandma's condo and through all my mom's stuff from when she was growing up. I even asked Lexie's dad about it. But no one's seen the crystal in years."

I press my lips together, trying to understand what she's telling me. "So, if you can't find that crystal, why not just use another?"

Griffin throws up his hands. "Thank you. Finally, someone with a bit of sense."

Crystal casts him a withering look before turning back to me. "It's not that easy. Like I said—some crystals are better than others for certain tasks. And some crystals are more powerful than others. This one's *particularly* powerful. It was used by generations of witches before the magic went dormant. It needs to be a special kind of crystal for the anchoring spell to even work."

"So, you're telling me that in order for my magic to be less... wild, or whatever... we've got to find this crystal so we can all anchor ourselves to it?"

She nods.

"And the crystal is powerful, it amplifies abilities?"

Crystal nods again, smiling slightly. "Yeah, that's right."

I bite my lower lip. "Well, what if we anchor ourselves and it just makes things worse?"

"Worse how?" Fox asks. "Giving us more power? I don't see a downside."

I shake my head. He doesn't understand. None of them do. Have they never had something get out of hand, out of control?

"It takes effort and concentration to connect with the magic," Bridget says, her voice softer than usual. I wonder if this is her natural tenor, if the voice she uses in public is a show. "It's hard for it to go out of control. It's hard to control it to begin with."

Griffin crosses his arms over his chest. "That's why I'm willing to do this anchoring thing to begin with. If this spell will make the magic easier to use, I'm all for it."

Crystal turns to me. "You see, we're not all like you. From what I could tell yesterday, you seem to have a stronger connection to your magic than the rest of us. It takes a lot more effort for the rest of us to do magic at all. The energy is difficult to tap into. Anchoring ourselves to the stone will link us directly to a source of energy." She smiles. "Then we'll be more like you."

I shake my head. How can they not see the danger in this? "If you're used to the energy being hard to access, how do you know what'll happen after you're anchored? If the magic is easier to access, there's a bigger chance something could go wrong."

"What, like you're suddenly an expert?" Griffin asks.

I bite my lip again. Of course I'm not an expert. I consider telling them about some of the incidents that have happened, things I'm only now coming to understand were due to a buildup of magic in my system, the inability to channel it correctly.

What happens when there are six witches without the ability to control their magic? I don't want to know.

"I think it's a bad idea. I may not know as much as you guys do about how to use magic, but I know more than you do about what happens when there's too much of it. You guys remember the earthquake at school a couple weeks ago?" One glance in Crystal's direction tells me she hasn't confirmed it was my doing. "If one witch can do that, what could all of us do if the magic is easier to access?"

Zane stares at me open-mouthed before looking at Crystal. "You said you didn't know whether she did it or not."

I can't help feeling a surge of pride at the awe in his voice. "Yeah. It was me."

Griffin leaves his post by the wall and approaches the couches. "I see what you're trying to do. You're already tapped into some strong magic and you don't want to share with the rest of us. You want us to show you how to use yours, but you don't want us to have any of our own."

I shake my head. "That's not it. I want to be able to control mine so I don't cause any more earthquakes—or worse."

Griffin sneers at me. "Well, help us find the crystal and anchor our magic and we can all learn to control it together."

I look from him to Crystal, incredulous. "What, now you're blackmailing me?"

"Technically, it's extortion." The corners of Griffin's mouth quirk upward in a humorless smile.

I turn to Fox. "To think, I almost bought your act. You were so nice to me today, trying to convince me I need the circle like you guys need me and you'll help me and we can all be a big, happy family. I should've known I couldn't trust you. As soon as I found out about your attraction spell, I should've realized you're not someone *worthy* of trust."

Crystal reaches forward, putting her hand on my knee. "Don't listen to Griffin. I told you, he's a dick. But he is right about one thing: We can learn to control our magic together. Even though it's hard for us to access, the five of us can already cast spells and use magic. There's no reason to believe having access to more magic means we suddenly won't have control over it anymore."

"Do you know that for a fact?" I look from Crystal's face to Bridget's, then to Fox's, Griffin's, and Zane's. None of them meet my eyes. They're just going along with what Crystal tells them. "What happens if we all get access to more magic and we can't control it?"

Crystal's eyes hold the slightest hint of condescension. "That won't happen."

I snort. "You don't know that for sure. You're trying to convince me you've got all the answers, but you don't. You're figuring this out as you go, just like I am. Sure, you've got your aunt's shadow book or whatever, but that doesn't mean you know everything." I stand up, crossing to the stairs. "I can't help you. It's too dangerous."

Crystal shakes her head. "You're going to be sorry. The day's gonna come when you need more magic than you have and you won't be able to do something. And then you'll wish you could come back to this moment and change your mind."

I start up the stairs. "I'll take my chances."

Chapter Twenty-Seven

After school Thursday, Jodi has me stocking dried herbs. The names, scents, and uses are becoming more and more familiar to me, and it's hard to imagine a time when they were completely unknown. As I arrange the bunches, I wonder what it would be like to select herbs to use for magic. Does a person need herbs to cast certain spells? Or do they work like crystals, directing energy whether magic is involved or not? I want to ask Jodi, but I'm not sure if it's an out-of-bounds question.

We haven't discussed magic since the day Jodi first told me and Owen about our abilities. I've wanted to, but I don't think I'll like what she has to say. Though I'm not on board with Crystal's circle's desire to obtain more magic, I'm also reluctant to give mine up before I've really had a chance to use it.

I touch the ring under my shirt. Would things be different if my dad were here? Would he want me to disavow my magical side? In some ways, it seems likely; he worked as an engineer when I was younger, and he liked dealing with facts and figures. He didn't even like movies with elements of fantasy in them and would leave the room if my mom ever put one on.

Jodi touches my shoulder and I jump. "You scared me," I say, releasing a shaky laugh.

"I called your name a couple times. You seemed pretty deep in thought." She reaches for my hand and I look down to see a mangled bunch of rosemary.

"Wow, I'm sorry. I guess my mind was somewhere else." I hand the herbs to her.

"It's okay. I can use these in some tea." She presses her lips together. "Why don't you take a break? Go for a walk, get a coffee?"

I open my mouth to protest but the look on Jodi's face indicates it's not a request. I nod. "That's a good idea."

She smiles. "Yeah. And, no rush, but when you're on your way back, could you bring me a hazelnut mocha?"

I shake my head. "Oh, I see. You really just want me to support your caffeine addiction."

"Am I really that transparent?"

Jodi shoos me out of the store and I head for the coffee shop, not sure where else to go. I sit down in one of the armchairs with my drink and replay last night's interaction with the circle. Did I make the right decision in walking away from them? Part of me is convinced I did; the other part is not so sure. Is the idea of anchoring our collective magic really so bad? What if it's just magic in its natural state that's wild? The term anchor implies stability. Isn't that what I want?

The problem is the not knowing. If I agree to join the circle and anchor my magic with theirs and things get out of hand, there's no going back. Sure, according to Crystal, the circle's magic is limited now. But if the power inside of me gets amplified by whatever is inside that crystal, who's to say what will happen?

I want to ask someone if I've made the right choice, but the only other witch I know is Jodi, and she might be mad at me for talking to the circle to begin with. Owen is the only other person who knows my secret, but he's not a witch, he's a psychic. He might not understand.

For the first time since moving to Clearwater, I feel as alone as I did before my mother died.

I finish my drink and order Jodi's hazelnut mocha. Millie, the store's owner and Jodi's friend, chats with me while I wait. As I walk back to the shop, I remind myself things are different here. I'm not really alone. In all the time since I moved in with her, Jodi hasn't once given me reason to think she'd be furious about me talking to Crystal and the circle about magic. It's only natural to be curious. Who knows? Maybe she'll even be willing to show me some simple spells once she knows how much it means to me.

And if I tell Jodi, I should tell Owen too. I still feel guilty for lying to him the other day. He's my friend and he deserves my honesty. He's been nothing but supportive since I moved in, and I shouldn't reward his kindness with secrecy. He won't be pleased to know Fox is involved, but if he knows Fox is a witch, I can tell him about the attraction spell—and that I'm now immune to it, thanks to Jodi's anklet. I can finally give him an explanation for my odd behavior around Fox.

As I push open the door to the shop, I feel much better than when I left. But all those positive feelings leave me when I enter the store: The whole circle is there, browsing different sections. Griffin is checking out the stones and crystals. Bridget is perusing the books about herbalism. Zane is sniffing around the dried herbs. Fox is weighing different candles. Crystal stands at the counter, chatting with Jodi as she pays.

Jodi glances at me when I walk in, offering a quick smile before turning back to Crystal. I approach the register, setting Jodi's coffee on the counter. "Millie wanted me to remind you to bring her DVD when you guys hang out tomorrow night," I say to Jodi.

Jodi nods but doesn't respond to me.

Crystal doesn't even look at me. Instead, she reaches across the counter and takes Jodi's hand in both of hers. "Thanks for your help, Miss Barnette," she says, smiling.

"You're welcome." Jodi returns her smile, but it doesn't reach her eyes.

Crystal releases Jodi's hand and picks up the bag from the counter. When she walks toward the door, the rest of the circle trails after her.

Jodi's eyes follow them out. When the door closes behind them, she looks at me, shaking her head. "I'm worried about her. I'm worried about all of them."

I'm surprised by her words. "What do you mean?"

The corner of her mouth quirks upward. "You don't have to pretend like you don't know."

"What? That they're all witches?"

Jodi nods. "Crystal's too much like her aunt. And we both know how that turned out for Crystal Taylor."

"You think she's going to get herself killed?"

"I think they're all too young and too foolish to be playing with magic. I mean, come on. Fox and his attraction spell? Does he think he's being clever? Or subtle?" She crosses her arms over her chest. "I'm glad you're smart enough not to get caught up with them."

Part of me bristles. Is she implying that if I were involved with them, I'd be stupid? How can she be so dismissive of their desire to use magic when she dabbled in it when she was our age? "Maybe they wouldn't be like that if they had someone teaching them. A mentor."

Jodi sighs. "Krissa—"

I narrow my eyes. "No. What right do you have to judge them? Look at the things you sell. You have everything here a witch could ever want and you're going to be mad when a couple of them decide to use this stuff for magic?"

Her eyebrows cinch together. "I'm not *mad*, I just—"

"You just don't think people should do magic." I raise my eyebrows, daring her to correct me. "You think it's okay for people to use magical *things* but not actually do magic themselves."

She straightens, squaring her shoulders. "The things I sell here are *natural* remedies. They don't have anything to do with magic."

"They don't have to. But they can. And you think you have the right to dictate how people use these things."

"No, I don't. What are you—" She stops herself, pursing her lip. She presses one hand to her forehead and with the other points toward the break room. "Go get my keys out of my purse."

I'm so surprised by her abrupt request that I do it without asking any questions. When I emerge from the room, she's pointing toward the parking lot.

"Go home. I'll get a ride from Millie."

"Are you kidding me?" I ask. "I disagree with you and you send me home?"

She sighs. "Yes. We can continue this conversation later, but for now, just go home." A breathy laugh escapes her lips. "Look, my parenting bag of tricks is less than limited. If you stay here, I'm just gonna get pissy and start yelling. And you don't deserve that. So, take your moody teenage self home and we can talk about this later, okay?"

"Okay." I grab my things from the back room and head to the parking lot without another word. I guess I was wrong. I can't tell Jodi about the circle or about wanting to learn to use my magic. She won't understand. If I want to learn, I'll have to do it myself.

Chapter Twenty-Eight

On the way to school on Friday, Jodi tells me I don't have to come into work today. We still haven't talked about our fight last night, and we haven't continued the discussion, so I figure it's probably for the best if we're not cooped up in the shop together for hours.

Crystal, Fox, and the other members of the circle continue to give me a wide berth, which doesn't bother me in the least. I'd much rather have them ignore me than try to talk to me about my decision not to join them.

At lunch, Lexie announces that I have plans for the evening.

"Oh, do I now?" I ask, smiling. "And what, may I ask, are these plans of mine?"

Lexie grins, obviously pleased that I'm playing along. "You know the bookstore downtown?"

I shrug. "I know it exists. I haven't been in it."

"Well, once a month, they have a movie night."

"A movie at a bookstore?" I ask, raising an eyebrow. "That sounds a little counterproductive. Don't they want to make people read books?"

Lexie laughs. "All the movies they show are based on books. And it's a good time. You're coming."

"Just you and me?" I ask, casting a furtive glance in Owen's direction.

Bria catches me and rolls her eyes, smiling. "You, me, Lexie, West, Felix... Oh, yeah, and Owen."

"Yeah, so, we'll pick you up at Jodi's shop around six," Owen says.

"Actually, I'm not working tonight."

"Really?" Lexie asks. "That never happens. I was beginning to think you were in indentured servitude or something."

I force a smile, not wanting to let on to the reason for my unexpected time off. "Yeah. We should celebrate."

Bria rubs her hands together. "I never need an excuse to celebrate. What should we do?"

"Let's make an afternoon of it," Owen suggests.

"Make an afternoon of what?" Felix asks as he and West approach the table.

"I've got the day off work and we're gonna celebrate," I say.

West nods appreciatively. "Okay, so, the movie, of course. Maybe we could get pizza beforehand?"

"Yeah, and games at the coffee shop right after school?" Lexie suggests.

Owen grins, bumping my shoulder with his. "Sounds like a plan."

We spend the rest of lunch debating the merits of different games available at the coffee shop. While Jenga is a strong contender, Felix is rather vocal about Apples to Apples while Bria laments the shop's distinct lack of Cards Against Humanity.

The rest of the school day flies by and it seems like no time at all has passed when Owen pulls into a parking space in front of the coffee shop. We're the first ones to arrive and we take care in selecting the perfect table. We've already got our drinks by the time the others show up, and although he can sit anywhere, Owen selects the seat right beside mine. He moves close so our arms press together and my mind fills with the echoey sensation it gets when he sends a thought to me.

I'm glad you've got the night off.

I smile at him. "Me too."

He raises an eyebrow. "Why do you always answer out loud?"

The others join us before I can answer, and I'm relieved. All week, Owen has taken every opportunity to practice sending thoughts to me, but I've only done it myself a few times. Part of me is afraid that if I send something to his mind, I might end up sending too much. It seems obvious to me that to him, we're just friends. We share the psychic thing, which gives us a certain level of intimacy, but that doesn't change the friends designation. If I'm not careful, he might be able to sense how much I wish things could be different—that we could be closer.

Felix wins out and we play Apples to Apples. Owen is particularly good at it and I can't tell if it's because he's such good friends with everyone or because his psychic abilities are stronger than mine. In the end, it doesn't matter because we're all having fun.

On the way to the pizzeria, Bria suggests we stop into Jodi's shop. Once she mentions it, everyone insists it's a great idea and I don't want to correct them.

Jodi is crouched by the wall of candles, selecting boxes from understock. Her smile is genuine when she sees us walk in.

"I'm glad to see you're taking full advantage of your day off," she says, winking at me. Her eyes flick to Owen before they survey the rest of the group, and I feel heat rising in my cheeks.

"We're going to the movie at the bookstore," Lexie announces. "We just thought we'd come say hi first."

"Hi!" everyone choruses.

Jodi laughs. "Well, I hope you all have fun. Don't get into too much trouble."

West shakes his head. "Just a moderate amount," he assures her. "You won't have to post bail or anything."

"We'll have her home by curfew," Lexie says, saluting. She nudges me with her elbow. "What's your curfew?"

I shrug. Jodi's never given me one.

Bria brings her hands up and taps her fingertips together. "Excellent," she says in her best evil mastermind voice.

Jodi refolds the box holding the remaining yellow tapers before standing and turning toward us in one fluid motion. But when she reaches her full height, she sways slightly, her hand going to the shelf behind her for support.

I reach for my aunt. "Are you okay?"

She smiles, pressing her hand to her forehead. "Yeah, just stood up too fast. I'm fine." She shoos us with her hand. "You guys go have fun."

The group waves and turns toward the door, but I bite my lower lip. Is it the lighting in this area of the store, or does Jodi look pale?

Before I can comment, Lexie is tugging me toward the front door of the store.

The pizzeria is buzzing when we arrive and we release a collective groan when we're told there will be a twenty-minute wait. We find a place to sit and Owen uses the time to practice sharing thoughts with me. He smiles every time I share one with him. I do my best to stick to innocuous things, like pointing out someone's hairstyle or which pizza toppings are my favorites.

When we're finally seated, we end up on opposite sides of the table, so we can't continue our exchanges. To be honest, I'm a bit glad for it: It's hard concentrating on what things to send and what to keep back. Besides, with him across from me, I get the chance to watch the way his eyes dance when he laughs and how a dimple forms in his left cheek when he smiles. Felix and Lexie keep up a steady stream of conversation at the table and by the time our food comes, I'm laughing so often my face hurts from smiling.

The pizzas are almost gone when Bria checks the time on her phone. "Crap! The movie starts in ten minutes. We still need to get the check."

"We still need to finish the pizza." West belches, rubbing his stomach lazily.

"Was that your attempt at making room?" Lexie asks, wrinkling her nose.

Owen smacks West on the back. "Only two pieces left. You got this, man."

West shakes his head. "Dude, I already ate twice as much as anyone else."

"I got one," Felix says as Bria manages to wave down the waitress to ask for the check. He takes a bite of the second-to-last slice and holds up his free hand as if to ask who's taking the last piece.

The waitress walks away from the table to go get the check and Bria grabs the last piece. "Fine, if no one else's taking it."

Felix swallows his bite. "Nice. Gotta respect a girl who can eat."

Lexie's mouth twitches but she says nothing. A buzzing shoots through my mind: She's wishing she'd taken the piece in order to have been the recipient of Felix's odd compliment. I pat her hand. Bria said Lexie and Felix seem to have been circling each other for quite some time now. I glance at Owen and sigh, knowing how it feels to have unrequited feelings for someone.

By the time Felix and Bria finish their slices, the waitress has returned with our check. Lexie figures out what each of us owes and we all throw in our money.

"Less than five minutes," Bria announces as we spill onto the street.

"The bookstore's in the middle of the last block," Lexie says to me, nodding in the direction she's indicating.

As we walk, I fall into step between Lexie and Owen. My skin tingles each time my arm brushes against his.

The bookstore is about twice the size of Jodi's shop—a square instead of a rectangle. Shiny covers greet us on the new release rack at the front of the store, but the rest of the shelves seem to contain a strange mash-up of new and used books.

In the back of the store, a few dozen mismatched chairs and couches face a wall onto which a white sheet is tacked. A table is stacked with a popcorn popper and a box full of candy bars and pop cans. There are already a few people sitting in the front, chatting animatedly with each other.

"So, what movie are they showing?" I ask.

Owen shrugs. "*Planet of the Apes*, I think. But I don't know whether it's the new one or the old one. Not that it really matters, anyway. It's more about the company."

He smiles down at me and I feel a warmth spreading in my belly.

"I'm gonna get some popcorn," he says, starting toward the line at the back of the seating area.

I groan. "Seriously? How can you even think of more food right now?"

Lexie links her arm through mine. "Let's go grab seats."

I hesitate for the briefest of moments before heading toward a set of couches. Bria leans across Lexie. "Don't worry. You can save a seat for Owen."

I press my lips together in a tight line and Lexie giggles. Am I really so obvious?

The opening credits are rolling when Owen, West, and Felix join us on the two couches we've claimed. West sits on my left and Owen on my right, while Felix settles between Lexie and Bria.

It's the old version of *Planet of the Apes*, and after I get over the initial cheesiness of it, I actually start to enjoy it. But, as Owen noted, it's not the movie itself but the company that's the most entertaining. While the group is far more restrained than they were when we did movie night at West's house, we're far from quiet. West can only seem to go about ninety seconds between whispered outbursts in my ear which make me laugh so hard that half the time, Owen forces me to repeat what he said. At first I feel self-conscious until I realize that the two dozen or so other people who are seated around us are likewise engaged in quiet conversation.

During an uncharacteristic quiet stretch from West, I take a moment to scan the room for familiar faces. I half expect to see Fox seated somewhere surrounded by a harem of adoring girls, but the only face I recognize in the room is Tucker Ingram's. He sits toward the back with a small knot of people, one of whom is a particularly giggly girl. Tucker tips something from a small silver container into his Coke can, but before I can think much about it, West is tugging at my arm to make another comment about the movie.

About halfway through, I find myself reaching for Owen's bag of popcorn. He catches my eye and mouths *told you*. I shrug, unapologetic. Clearly he expected me to sneak some at some point, since he bought the largest bag available.

The popcorn slowly disappears as the movie plays on. Toward the end, my fingers brush up against Owen's hand as I reach into the bag. A thrill courses through me, accompanied by a flash inside my head. This isn't like the thoughts he deliberately sends to me. Instead of the echo, I see a distinct picture. I know immediately that I'm seeing something he doesn't mean for me to see. Owen is thinking of the night at the dance, when we were dancing together. I pull my hand back quickly on instinct.

I bite my lower lip, embarrassed to have been spying, and sneak a glance at him out the corner of my eye. He offers the briefest of shrugs and an unabashed smile and my cheeks flush with pleasure. He rests his hand in the valley between our legs and my heart flutters. It's an invitation. I slip my arm across my denim-clad leg and rest the back of my hand against the back of his. I call to mind my own recollection of our dance and imagine it flowing out of my head, down my arm, and into his hand. I pick up my memory where his left off: We danced, yes, but then he touched the side of my face and leaned forward. But memory and fantasy are so connected that before I can stop it, I've sent the image I've imagined a hundred times since that night: Owen doesn't stop, no one interrupts us, and his lips press gently against mine.

The overhead lights flicker on and I'm surprised to see the end credits rolling. Owen pulls his arm from mine and a wave of regret washes over me. When I glance at his face, his expression is unreadable. This is exactly what I was afraid would happen: I shared too much. I've made things awkward between us.

"Okay, I'm going to the bathroom," Lexie announces, standing. She looks from me to Bria, a tacit invitation to join her.

"I'll wait outside," I say, and Lexie raises an eyebrow as she and Bria head toward the restrooms. Without waiting for the guys, I head to the front door and out onto the sidewalk. The night air has developed a gentle wind and I rub my upper arms with my hands, attempting to generate some heat. I consider my options. I can wait for Owen; no matter how uncomfortable it would be, I can't see him refusing to give me a ride home. But do I really want to endure the unpleasant silence? I could walk down to Jodi's shop, but she's probably already gone home. Since Owen was my ride into town, she probably assumes he'll be my ride home. Until about five minutes ago, I assumed the same. But now I'm not so sure it would be a good idea. I made a mistake and shared my feelings for him, and now I'm afraid I've ruined everything.

I lean against the exterior wall of the bookstore, focusing on the rough brick where it juts out against my back in an attempt to distract myself from whatever—possibly painful—exchange I'm sure to have with Owen when he emerges.

Several people exit the store. I'm not facing them, but I can tell it's a big group by the number of voices cutting through the night air. I don't recognize them specifically, but I'm sure they go to school with me. They pass by, heading in the direction of the coffee house.

"Hey, Krissa."

When I turn to him, Tucker's eyes are intense, both brighter and darker than usual. He presses the palm of his hand into the brick wall over my shoulder and leans in toward me.

I shrink back as far as I can, my eyes darting toward the group he split off from. No one seems to notice Tucker's absence. They're shouting and laughing as they walk away, and even if I call out, they probably won't hear me.

"Aren't you gonna say hi?" His breath is sweet and there's a tinge of something I don't recognize. A smile stretches across his mouth. "I thought you were a nice girl. Won't you even say hello?"

I dig my nails into the palms of my hands. "Hello," I murmur, not meeting his eyes.

"That's better." He shifts, his body easing closer to mine. "So, I saw you in there. Getting pretty cozy with Owen, huh?"

My back is flat against the wall behind me and the coldness of the bricks cuts through my sweater. "He'll be out here soon. With Lexie and West and Felix."

"We're just talking."

He wheezes out a little laugh and the scent I couldn't name before suddenly clarifies itself: alcohol. I don't know why it didn't occur to me sooner: He was pouring alcohol from a flask into his pop can. Tucker's body is so close to mine I can feel the heat radiating off him, but if I'm quick, I might be able to duck around him, get out from between him and the wall. I take in a breath and dart sideways, but Tucker is fast, grabbing me around the middle and pulling my back snugly against his front.

"Come on, Krissa, don't be like that. You're friendly enough with Owen. I just wanna have a conversation."

I struggle against his arms, but it's no use; his grip is too strong.

My heart kicks into overdrive and I feel heat building in my stomach like it has a million times before, just before something bad happened. For the first time, I don't want to push it down. I understand it. Closing my eyes, I focus my attention on the sensation, on the energy, and like the flame I ignited at Crystal's house or the thoughts I shared with Owen earlier, I imagine exactly what I want this power to do.

The heat within me builds to critical mass. And for once, I'm not afraid.

A hoarse cry escapes my lips as the energy leaves my body. I feel it go, and I sense its direction: behind me. At Tucker.

Tucker's grip on my abdomen loosens and he stumbles backward, a surprised cry emanating from his mouth. I turn and he's on the ground, nearly flat on his back, his eyes wide. A shaft of light appears, stretching across his supine form, and I know Owen has exited the store before I look up to see him standing there. I can feel him.

The fear that filled me only moments ago is nothing compared to the anger radiating off Owen as he approaches us. His eyes are glued on Tucker as he moves so he is standing in front of me, between the two of us.

"What happened?"

"Crazy bitch! We were just talking and she attacked me!" Tucker scrambles to his feet, pointing an accusatory finger in my direction.

"He's drunk, Owen. He had me pinned against the wall and when I tried to get away, he grabbed me."

Tucker snorts. "She wishes. Owen, you better keep that girl in line, or next time I might not be so nice to her. It won't be so easy to get the drop on me a second time."

Owen lunges at Tucker so fast, Tucker doesn't even open his mouth in surprise. He releases a yelp of pain when his head collides with the brick wall of the bookstore, just inches from where I was positioned moments before. "There won't be a next time," Owen says, his voice low and dangerous. "You will not talk to her, you will not look at her, you will not think about her, because if you do, I'll know about it. Is that understood?"

Tucker attempts to peel himself from the wall, but Owen slams him backward again, his forearm against Tucker's throat to hold him in place. Tucker sputters, his fingers digging at the wall behind him.

"Is it understood?"

The door opens again and Lexie, Bria, West, and Felix spill out just as Tucker murmurs, "Yeah, man. Yeah." The four of them freeze, mouths open, as Owen releases Tucker and shoves him roughly down the sidewalk.

No one speaks for several seconds. Finally, Owen breaks the silence. "Krissa, come on. Let me get you home."

A few minutes earlier I was sure I'd have to bum a ride home from Lexie, but so much has changed in the last couple minutes. I walk beside Owen toward his parking spot. He stays in lockstep with me, but he's careful not to let his arm bump mine as we walk. The scene with Tucker replays itself over and over in my mind. The sound of Owen's voice, the force he used when he knocked Tucker into the wall. I know Tucker isn't one of his favorite people, but I never would have pictured Owen capable of such violence toward anyone. I don't know what to think about it.

We don't speak during the drive and I'm thankful Jodi's house is only a few minutes away. In all my experience with him, Owen has been kind and playful. Never in a million years would I have imagined he was capable of the violence I witnessed tonight.

Owen pulls into the driveway and puts his car in park. I place my hand on the door but make no move to open it. I keep my eyes fixed on the glove compartment.

"You're upset," Owen murmurs.

I sneak a glance at him, but he's staring at his white-knuckled hands gripping the steering wheel. "A little."

"But not because of what Tucker did."

Guilt swoops in my stomach. Is that true? In the moment, I was so terrified of what Tucker might do to me, but after the sound of Owen's voice, the look in his eyes, I'm not sure how to feel. "I've never seen you like that."

He shakes his head, running both hands through his hair before turning to face me. "I'm not usually like that. Whatever happened tonight, that's not usually me. But when I walked out and saw what was happening... I could see what was on his mind." He closes his eyes. "I wanted to hurt him. I wanted to kill him."

I shiver. "You can't mean that."

When he opens his eyes, they are filled with a pain I can't identify. His mouth twitches. "The idea of him hurting you. Krissa, I couldn't handle that. I... I care about you too much."

A prickling sensation gathers in the corners of my eyes. "Yeah?"

"Yeah." He reaches forward, caressing my cheek with his fingers. "I'm sorry this night went so crazy. It was going so well until..."

I manage a smile. "It was?"

One corner of his mouth quirks up. "It was so cool to be able to share those thoughts with you. I'm glad... I'm glad you're like me. You can understand me."

I press my lips together. Of course. That's why he cares about me: We're both the same kind of freak. I can understand this strange ability he has. And he can practice on me. I'm his guinea pig. I touch his wrist and pull his hand from my face. "I should get in the house before Jodi starts to worry."

Before he can respond, I open the door and slip out of the car. I was stupid to think Owen might have feelings for me, just me. Tears gather in my eyes and my vision blurs. I'm halfway to the porch when I hear his car door slam. By the time I reach the front door, Owen is at my side. He places his hand over mine when I grab for the doorknob.

"What's wrong?"

I don't look at him. "Nothing. I don't want Jodi to worry."

"Are you mad at me?" He removes his hand from mine. "Are you scared of me now?"

"Of course not." I squeeze my eyes closed and wipe at my cheek when a tear escapes through my lashes. "I'm just..." I turn toward him, opening my eyes. "I'm tired and—"

Owen leans toward me so quickly I can't react. His lips find mine and press there gently, but insistently, like he's been waiting to do this and can't allow another second to pass. His hands cup my cheeks, fingers threading through the hair at my temples.

I don't kiss him back. I stand stock still, too shocked to react.

Owen pulls away, eyes wide and apologetic. "I'm so sorry. I thought... I mean, you're the one who shared..." He hangs his head, running a hand through his hair. "Wow, I feel like an ass. I'm... I'll just go now."

It's not until he's back at the top stair of the porch that my body and mind sync up. I cross the distance between us in two large steps and grab his shoulder, spinning him to face me. He flinches when my hands move toward his face, but I don't slap him. I lock my fingers behind his neck and pull his face down to mine, my lips finally sure of what to do. Owen's hands slide around my waist and he pulls me close to him, so close I can't tell where my body ends and his begins. I part my lips and he deepens the kiss tentatively. I slide my fingers through the soft hair at the base of his neck.

No matter how many times I've imagined this moment, not one of them even dimly compares to the reality.

Chapter Twenty-Nine

I'm not sure how much time elapses before Owen and I separate, but when we do, I feel like a part of me has been torn away. His fingers tuck my hair behind my ears. "I've gotta go," he murmurs.

"I know."

He leans in and feathers another kiss on my lips and I press him away gently.

"Go," I say softly, "or I'm not going to be able to let you leave."

A spasm crosses his face and he takes a step back. "I'll see you tomorrow." He turns and descends the stairs and starts across the yard. Halfway to his car, he spins to face me. "Just... don't change your mind."

I shake my head. "No way."

My hand trembles and my breathing is uneven when I open the door. I attempt to conceal my smile as I step over the threshold, hoping Jodi hasn't been watching through the window, but also not caring if she has. But Jodi isn't in the living room. She's not in the kitchen or the sitting room, either. It's late, but not too late, and I doubt she's in bed yet, which leaves one place she could be: the greenhouse.

I'm halfway down the hallway when I hesitate. My first kiss is something I would feel weird about sharing with my mom—is it something I should be so excited to share with my aunt? I pivot and start back down the hall. Maybe I can call Lexie or Bria. But I go no more than three steps before turning back, the smile on my face too broad to suppress. I have to tell someone, and I want to tell Jodi.

The greenhouse door creaks when I open it. A bank of grow lights against the wall on my right sheds an eerie pallor over the room, the leaves of the plants casting large silhouettes across the floor.

"Jodi?" I peer through the shadows, expecting to find her pruning something or hanging some herbs to dry, but I don't see her. I step further into the room, a thrill of dread coursing through me. I shake it off. Maybe Jodi has gone to bed. She's been having a rough time since Mrs. Cole died, so it wouldn't surprise me if she didn't feel up to staying up late. I sigh. That must be it. I'm about to turn when something catches my eye.

Jodi.

She's lying on the floor, legs bent at right angles, head resting on her arm, hair splayed around her. For a moment, I'm convinced she's asleep. But the sweeping dread sinks lower in my stomach as I approach her. "Jodi?"

She doesn't stir and my heartbeat picks up. I shake her shoulder but she doesn't respond. I shake her harder, frantic. She rolls onto her back and her eyelids flutter.

"Hey, wake up."

It takes almost a full minute before Jodi's eyes open and fix on mine. "Where... What...?"

"You're in the greenhouse."

She tries to sit up, but I push her back toward the ground. "I came out here after I got home from work..."

"What *happened*?"

Her head rocks from side to side. "I was watering the plants and... I think... I got dizzy, so I reached for the table to hold onto." She presses her hand to her forehead. "Maybe I slipped and hit my head?"

The light in the greenhouse isn't good, but I don't detect a cut or bruise. "Have you eaten today?"

Her eyes squeeze shut. "A yogurt and a granola bar... Maybe."

I sigh. "Jodi."

"I know," she murmurs.

I pull my phone from my back pocket. "I should call

someone..."

She shakes her head. "You don't need to do that. Just... help me to my room."

I do as Jodi asks, but it doesn't sit well with me.

"I think you should go to the hospital," I say, watching as Jodi settles back against her pillow and pulls the blanket up over her arms.

"I don't need to go to the hospital. I just need to eat more tomorrow."

I press my lips together. "You should eat now. I'll go get you something."

"No," she says firmly. "My stomach's a little sour. I'll call someone tomorrow if I'm not feeling better. For now I think I just need some sleep."

A knot twists in my stomach. I don't like this. What if there's something really wrong with her? What if I come to wake her up tomorrow morning and she doesn't open her eyes...?

I shake the thought from my head. No, she's fine. She just hasn't been sleeping or eating right—she's been too upset about her friend's death. She'll be fine tomorrow.

I turn off her light and close the bedroom door behind me. Instead of heading to my room, I go down to the greenhouse. I don't know what all the herbs are yet, but I know enough to select some to make a tea for her tomorrow.

It takes me longer than I anticipate to collect the herbs and ready the tea kettle so it's set to boil first thing in the morning.

When I finally go to bed, my sleep is fitful at best. I drift toward unconsciousness, my mind replaying the kiss with Owen, the way his body felt against mine, but then my thoughts turn to Jodi on the floor, the icy cold fear that filled my body at the sight.

When my eyes snap open at a little after six Saturday morning, I feel as if I haven't slept at all. Groggy, I leave my room and make my way to Jodi's, easing the door open just enough to peek in at her. In the dim light, I can't make out her face, just the outline of her body. I hold my breath, waiting for movement. I don't want to wake her, but I also want to make sure she *will* wake up. I step into the room and squint through the darkness. I detect the rise and fall of her chest and find I'm able to breathe again too.

I make my way to the kitchen to double check that the tea is ready to be brewed as soon as Jodi wakes up. The task doesn't take long and I'm too full of nervous energy to sit down, so I start putting together a small buffet of breakfast choices. I'm cutting up an apple when I hear Jodi coughing. I turn on the tea kettle before heading upstairs.

Jodi's coughing fit ends just before I enter her room. Her complexion is ashen. "That doesn't sound good."

She props herself up against her headboard. "I feel so strange. Like, I don't feel sick in my head, but my body feels really worn down."

"You should eat. I made you a little spread to choose from. Do you want me to bring it up here?"

"No." She slides her legs off the edge of the bed. "Help me downstairs."

Between Jodi's dizzy spells and coughing fits, it takes us several minutes to get to the sitting room. I help her settle onto the couch and cover her with an afghan before heading to the kitchen for her breakfast and tea. When I hand her the mug, she sniffs it and smiles. "Good job."

Jodi selects bites of food to eat and makes faces as she chews each one. I watch her carefully, my arms crossed over my chest. "You've got to eat."

"I know. It's just... It all kind of tastes like sawdust."

"I don't care. I don't want you passing out again."

Jodi manages a half smile. "Yes, ma'am."

She works her way around the plate slowly and manages to eat only about a quarter of what's there. She's more successful with the tea and even requests a second mug.

When I set the second cup of tea on the coffee table, she asks, "Could you run to the shop for me?"

My stomach clenches. She wants me to open the store? "I don't think I'm ready. I mean, I'm learning the ropes, but I'm still not really good with the cash register—"

Jodi waves a hand at me. "Don't worry, I'm not asking you to run the shop." She holds up her cell. "Devin can't get there until around noon. Could you just put signs up in both the doors saying that's when the store will open and apologizing for the inconvenience?"

Relief sweeps over me, but I don't stand. "I don't want to leave you."

She smiles. "You won't be gone long. Besides, I've got a couple friends coming over to check up on me."

"Is one of them a doctor?"

"No. No doctors."

She doesn't need to tell me who they are. A thought buzzes in my mind: She's called the members of her old circle. They don't practice anymore, but they possess more knowledge of magic and healing than I do. Instead of relying on me to fumble through figuring out which herb is which, she's calling in reinforcements. "It's good you're calling them," I say, standing.

She shakes her head, letting out a breathy laugh. "That'll take some getting used to. Are you finding it's easier to direct your abilities now that you know what they are?"

I nod. "I've been trying to practice—with Owen." I can't suppress the smile that upturns the corners of my mouth when I say his name.

Jodi opens her mouth, most likely to tease me, but a coughing fit overtakes her. I move to her side, grabbing the mug off the table and pressing it into her hand. When the coughs subside enough, she takes a series of small sips of the tea. I press my lips together and she shakes her head. "Go. I'll be fine."

I don't want to leave her, but I know I should. She's right: I won't be gone long. I would insist on waiting until her friends get here, but the store is supposed to open in ten minutes and it would be rude to leave customers outside with no knowledge of why the doors are still locked. "Call me if you need anything." She nods and I take in a breath. "If your friends can't figure out how to help you, promise you'll call a doctor."

Jodi holds up two fingers. "Scout's honor."

A sense of dread sinks in the pit of my stomach as I leave the house, but there's nothing I can do except get back as quickly as possible.

Chapter Thirty

A black Honda is parked in the driveway when I get home, and a champagne minivan sits in front of the house. Jodi's friends have arrived. I park Jodi's Focus behind the Honda and head into the house with the bag of supplies I grabbed from the shop. I feel a little silly with them—it's likely Jodi has all of these things here—but I wanted to bring them just in case.

I hear voices from the sitting room when I enter the house. I close the door behind me and open my mouth to let Jodi know I've arrived, but something stops me. It's not the words that are being said—their tone is too low and the sounds too indistinct to make out—it's the feeling of the room. A darkness, a dread, wraps itself around me like a blanket.

Curious, I edge toward the back of the house, taking care to avoid the creaky floorboards near the middle of the hallway.

"That's just it—the tea *should* be working."

The note of apprehension in Jodi's voice makes me pause. Is she talking about the tea I made for her?

"Maybe just give it a little more time." The woman's voice is familiar an it takes me a moment to place it: Millie, the owner of the coffee shop downtown.

Jodi wheezes. "You forget who you're talking to. I'd put my knowledge of herbal remedies up against anyone's. Believe me when I say something's not right."

"I'm not saying I don't believe you," says a man whose voice I don't recognize. "I'm just not sure what you expect the two of us to do."

"As much as I hate to say it, I'm afraid whatever's wrong with me isn't going to be cured by homeopathy alone. I'd do it myself, but..." Jodi coughs a few times. "Whatever's affecting me is affecting my connection with magic, too."

My heartbeat picks up. She's talking about magic with these people. Why would she call them instead of telling me about it?

"You know we don't practice anymore," the man says.

"Come on, David. Are you telling me you haven't cast one spell in the last eighteen years?" There's a hint of doubt in Jodi's voice. Silence stretches for a few beats before she says, "That's what I thought."

"Still, what do you really think we can do?" Millie's voice is quiet.

Pages rustle. "There are a few healing spells. I've got most of the supplies in my greenhouse. If you could give them a try..." Jodi trails off.

My muscles tense and heat flushes through my body. She wants them to cast spells for her. I don't know if I'm more mad that she plans to use magic after telling me that I shouldn't use mine, or that she wants *them* to do it and not me.

Couch springs squeak and feet shuffle against the hardwood floor. They're about to walk into the hallway. Not wanting them to know I've been listening in, I creep back to the front door and open and close it firmly. I take in a breath to steady my nerves before calling, "Jodi, I'm home."

Jodi and her friends poke their heads out into the hallway, each of them looking like they've been caught doing something naughty. I do my best to rearrange my face into a mask of innocence, like I really have just walked in.

"Ah, you're back," Jodi says. She nods toward her friends. "You know Millie, of course. And this is David Cole. David, this is my niece, Krissa."

David is shorter than I imagined he would be from his voice. His hair is dark and wavy and there's the shadow of a beard on his face. He meets me halfway down the hall and holds out his hand for me to shake.

I place my hand in his tentatively. "It's nice to meet you." His surname sticks in my mind and I almost ask if he's any relation to Mrs. Cole, but one look at his face makes the words stick in my throat. Up close, his eyes are puffy and his face has the pallor of a person in mourning. He's Mrs. Cole's widower. Releasing his hand, I hold up the bag of supplies to Jodi. "I grabbed some things from the shop. I don't know if they'll help, but..."

She takes the bag from me and peers inside. She smiles and another coughing fit overtakes her. When it passes, she nods at me. "This is good. Thanks."

"You're welcome."

The four of us stand in the hallway and I get the feeling David and Millie are uncomfortable with my being here. Since Jodi has reached out to them to do magic on her behalf, it's possible they don't know about by abilities.

"How about I boil some water?" I suggest when it's clear no one else is going to say anything. As I walk toward the kitchen, Jodi holds the bag out to me. I take it, and something on Jodi's palm catches my attention. "What's that?"

"What?" Jodi asks, but she starts coughing before I can respond, holding her right hand against her mouth.

I wait until the fit passes before reaching for her hand. I turn it so her palm faces upward and my stomach sinks when I see a dark red mark there, like a smear of strawberry jam. "This. Jodi, what's this?"

Jodi's eyes go wide when she inspects her palm. "I don't... I have no idea."

"I've seen it before. At the dance. When Mrs. Cole was taking our tickets, I saw it."

David closes the distance to Jodi and inspects the mark. "Oh, my..." He nods vaguely. "Wednesday before she... Shelly was in the kitchen making dinner and she passed out. We both just assumed she burned herself."

Jodi sways and grips David's shoulder to steady herself. "I was wrong."

The color drains from Millie's face. "What does that mean?"

"I've been thinking whatever's affecting me is organic, natural—

just strong. But if Shelly had this mark too it can only mean one thing. It's a curse."

Jodi's words seem to fill up the space around us, consuming the air. It takes several tries before I'm able to take in a full breath.

Millie's hand goes to her chest. "You mean someone's doing this *to* you? Someone did it to Shelly?"

"It can't be a coincidence," says David. "The mark—it's exactly like the one on Shelly's hand."

"Which means," Jodi says, her voice quiet and calm, "whatever happened to her is happening to me."

Millie shakes her head. "No. We're going to figure this out. Now that we know what we're up against—"

"Now that we know what we're up against, what?" David snaps. His eyes flicker to me momentarily before he continues. "Do you remember what it would take out of us to do something simple like make something levitate? I can't imagine the kind of power someone would have to have to do something like this."

"He's got a point," Millie says. "Who's strong enough to cast a curse like this? Is there anyone in town who's even practicing?"

David snorts. "Of course there is. Shelly told me she had suspicions about Jenny Jamison's daughter and her friends."

"Come on—a bunch of teenagers?" Millie crosses her arms. "David, think about how little we could do at their age. Do you really think they'd be capable of something like this?"

"Don't sell them so short," Jodi says, her voice quiet. "They're stronger than we were—I can sense it in them. But, no, I don't think they're behind it."

"Then who?" Millie asks.

She shakes her head. "It doesn't really matter, does it? We can worry about the *who* after we take care of the *what*. David, you said that Shelly passed out the Wednesday before she died?"

A spasm crosses David's face. "Yes."

"And before that she seemed perfectly healthy?"

He nods. "She was just at the doctor that Monday for her yearly physical, and she was in perfect health."

Jodi jerks her chin toward the greenhouse. "We should get to work. The way I figure, at best I've got two days."

Her words cut through me. "Two days? Wait. You can't mean—"

"That I'm going to die?" A muscle jumps in her jaw. "Unless we can figure out how to break the curse, then yes. I'm afraid that's exactly what's going to happen."

I feel as though the air has been pressed from my lungs.

David pulls his cell from his back pocket. "I'm calling Ryan Alcott."

As he walks toward the living room, Millie begins ticking names off on her fingers. "You, me, David. Shelly, Crystal. Sarah Riddell... I guess Ryan really is the only other one left."

"He's down in Ohio, last I heard," Jodi says.

Millie puts a hand on Jodi's shoulder. "He'll come."

My brain finally kicks into gear. "What can I do? To help?"

Jodi shakes her head. "No. I won't involve you."

I gape at her. "But you guys don't have the power you need." I lean toward her, lowering my voice. "Crystal said I've got more magic than she's ever felt before. I can help you."

Jodi's expression is stony. "I won't risk it. We don't know who's behind this. Shelly, me—my whole circle—we disbanded after Crystal Taylor died. If magic really is the motivator for whoever's casting this curse, it doesn't seem to matter if you're practicing it or not. Revealing the kind of power you have could put a target right on your back."

"So, what? You not letting me help is protecting me?"

A relieved look crosses her face. "Yes."

Tears gather in the corners of my eyes. "Who's going to protect me when you're dead?"

Jodi presses her lips together but says nothing. There's nothing she *can* say. And I can't just sit here. Pivoting on my heel, I head toward the front door.

I hear Jodi calling after me, but I ignore her. She can't stop me from helping her. She's the only family I have left.

Chapter Thirty-One

My vision is completely obscured by tears by the time I reach Jodi's car. I open the door and slide into the driver's seat before wiping them away with the edges of my sleeve. I can't fall apart right now. If Jodi needs more magic to break the curse that's hurting her, then I need to acquire more magic.

Fortunately, I have a lead about where to get it.

I pull my cell from my back pocket and tap through the contact list. Pressing the phone to my ear, I hold my breath as the ringer sounds once. Twice.

Crystal picks up in the middle of the third ring. "Krissa?"

"Gather the others," I say without preamble. "I'll help you find the crystal, but we've got to do it now. Call everyone, set up a meeting or whatever. And as soon as we find it, I get to use the crystal. You can have it once I'm done, but I need it first. Those are my conditions."

"What do you need the crystal—"

"Take it or leave it."

I hold my breath as seconds of silence tick by.

"Oh—okay," Crystal says finally. "I'll have everyone meet up at Fox's house."

I bite my lower lip. "As soon as possible. Please."

The drive to Fox's place doesn't take long. The lone car in the driveway tells me I'm the first to arrive, but that doesn't stop me from approaching the house. I knock on the front door and wait for a response. When none comes, I knock again. I try the doorbell. After a few moments, no one comes to the door, so I lift my hand to pound on the wood. Just as I bring my hand down, the door swings open and Fox only just manages to avoid my falling fist.

His gray eyes are wide. "Whoa, what's up?"

I push past him into the house. The living room is just as disheveled as I remember it, with dirty laundry strewn everywhere. The air smells stale. "Didn't Crystal call you?"

"I think Griffin was on the phone with her."

I walk through the dining room, toward the stairway in the kitchen. "The circle's heading over here. I'm going to help you find the crystal."

Fox follows me down to the basement and sits on the couch adjacent to the one I take a seat on. "I thought you weren't going to help. You know, the perils of having too much magic and all that? I thought you were too worried we wouldn't be able to handle our magic once we anchor ourselves to the crystal."

I shift on the cushions. "Yeah, and I'm still concerned about that."

The corners of his mouth turn downward. "Then why are you helping?"

"Does it matter?" I ask, not making eye contact.

"I wouldn't ask if it didn't." Fox's voice is low, but persuasive. Even with my charm firmly in place, he's still magnetic. The attraction spell he uses amplifies what he already possesses.

I don't want to tell him. Telling him will make it real. But I owe him, I owe the others, the truth about why I need more magic. "It's my aunt."

"Jodi?" His eyebrows cinch together and his eyes darken with concern. "What's wrong?"

I press my lips together. I forget that he's known her longer than I have. "Whatever killed Mrs. Cole... She didn't just get sick. It was magic that killed her. A curse."

He stands and begins to pace, agitated. "This isn't good."

"You're telling me? Fox, she's all I have."

He looks at me and the expression on his face reminds me how little he knows about my past—how little anyone around here—

besides Owen—knows. I turn away, but he moves toward me. "What do you mean?"

I shake my head. "It's nothing."

"Clearly that's not the case." He crouches so he's at eye level with me. "Look, I get it. You know about the attraction spell and now you think you can't trust me. Hard to trust a guy who uses magic to mess with girls' heads. But, look." He pulls at the collar of his shirt. He's not wearing the rose quartz necklace. I inhale, and there's no trace of lavender in his scent. His mouth twitches. "I want to be the kind of person you can trust."

A pang shoots through me. I had no idea my opinion of him carried so much weight. I take in a breath. "My dad left me and my mom five years ago. I haven't seen him since. I have no idea where he is. And it was hard, you know? But my mom and I were making it. But then about a month ago..." A lump forms at the back of my throat. "Jodi's all I have now."

Fox takes my hands, squeezing them with a gentle pressure. His palms are warm. "We won't let anything happen to Jodi, okay? The circle—we're family. We'll take care of you."

A prickling sensation creeps into the corners of my eyes and I pull my hands from his to rub the feeling away. Shuffling on the stairs announces the arrival of others and Fox stands, putting distance between the two of us.

Crystal and Bridget enter the basement first, followed by Griffin and Zane. Griffin collapses into a dilapidated arm chair. "This'd better be good."

Crystal rolls her eyes as she and Bridget sit beside me on the couch. Zane claims the adjacent couch and Fox leans against the wall, his expression clouded.

Once everyone is settled, Crystal sits up a bit straighter, squaring her shoulders before addressing the group. "Krissa's reconsidered things and she's decided to help anchor our magic."

A shiver courses through me. That's not exactly what I promised, but I don't correct her. All I want is the crystal. If it can amplify my natural magic, it might be enough to lift Jodi's curse. What the circle does with it after that doesn't concern me.

"That's great," Griffin says, holding out his hands. "Except, of course, for the fact that we don't actually *have* the crystal. Unless you suddenly know where it is."

Crystal purses her lips. "That's what we're here to find out."

Griffin rolls his eyes and I look at Crystal. "Okay, so, how do we do that?"

Crystal stands and crosses the room to a small dresser tucked in a corner behind the armchairs. She opens the top drawer and begins rifling through it. "It's simple, really. We just need to do a relatively simple spell to figure out where it is."

"We've done a locater spell already," Griffin mutters. "Multiple times."

Crystal ignores him. "Every time, it takes us to the same place: the house my aunt Crystal died in." She returns to the middle of the room with an armful of candles that look like they came from Jodi's shop.

I scan my mental images of buildings in the town, but I haven't seen a burned-out shell of a house. Something like that would stand out in a place like this. "Did they rebuild the house or something?"

Crystal shakes her head. "Not exactly. After the fire, my grandma sold the property and moved so she wouldn't be reminded. It's been almost twenty years since she died. They tore down the original structure. There's a new house where the old house used to be."

I nod. "And you're not thinking this crystal is in the new house."

"There's no way," Bridget says, even though my statement doesn't necessitate a response. "I mean, we've been thinking maybe it's under the house—like under the basement or something. But we can't get a clear enough lock on it. The locater spell isn't that specific."

"And, what? You're thinking I'll help it be more specific?"

Crystal opens her mouth to speak, but Fox cuts her off. "It's not as ridiculous as it sounds. The first time we did the spell, it was just me, Bridge, and Crystal. That time, it got us over on that side of town, but that was it. Each time we've added someone to the spell, it's been a little more accurate."

I bite the inside of my cheek. It makes as much sense as

anything, considering that until recently, I thought the idea of magic was just fantasy. If I have to participate in this spell to save Jodi, I'm willing. "Okay, how do we do this?"

An expression flashes over Crystal's face, but it's too quick to read. She reaches out toward Bridget, who hands over Crystal's purse. After a moment, Crystal pulls out a map. She unfolds it and spreads it on the floor, surrounding it with the candles.

Bridget slides off the couch and kneels on the floor beside a candle. Fox and Zane follow suit and, with a groan, so does Griffin. I'm the last to take a place in the circle, and when I do, it's between Bridget and Fox.

Crystal closes her eyes and the candles flicker to life. She unclasps her necklace and places the quartz shard in her hand. "Now, focus on this piece of the crystal. Direct all your energy toward locating the rest of it." She reaches her hands out to Fox and Griffin, who are on either side of her, and the three clasp hands. Fox reaches for me with his free hand, and I reach for Bridget. When Bridget and Zane connect, a current of energy thrums through me, tingling my palms. A smile touches Crystal's lips and Griffin curses under his breath.

Fox squeezes my fingers. "Damn, girl. Crystal was right about you."

My cheeks flush at the compliment. This spell will work. It has to. We'll find the rest of the crystal and I'll be able to save Jodi.

"Find the crystal," Crystal murmurs. "Find the crystal."

The others join in her chant, then I do too. I stare at the map, unsure exactly what I'm waiting for. The tingling sensation grows where my skin touches Fox's and Bridget's, and heat begins to fill my core. I focus the magic rising inside me on locating the rest of the stone.

The map explodes in flame and I gasp. The others seem unfazed and I struggle not to jump back from the heat. Just when I'm sure my face is going to burn, my hair singe, the fire dies out entirely, leaving just a small scrap of paper behind.

The candles extinguish and Crystal releases Griffin's and Fox's hands before leaning forward to look at the remnant of the map. When she pushes herself back, disappointment is evident on her face. "Exactly the same as before. It's the house, but there's nothing more specific than that."

Griffin snorts, standing. "What did you expect? For writing to appear giving you step-by-step directions or something? I told you before, this is a waste. You're obsessed with this crystal, and I get why, but we're never gonna find it. We'd be better off finding another rock to anchor ourselves to."

Crystal shoots back a comment but I don't hear it. Something about the map grabs my attention. It appears to be shimmering. For a moment I wonder if the edges are still on fire, but that's not exactly what it looks like. I tug on Fox's sleeve. "Do you see that?" I ask, nodding toward the scrap.

Fox looks down before turning back to me. "See what?"

"Does the map look strange to you?"

"What, besides being a charred scrap of paper?"

I press my lips together. Maybe if I could see it more closely. I reach across the floor and pinch the piece between my fingers.

That's when it happens.

My body goes icy and I can't move. A bright flash of light obscures my vision before I'm plunged into darkness. Crystal and Griffin's argument fades, the room disappears, and I'm surrounded by blackness.

By degrees, the world comes back into focus. But I'm no longer in Fox's basement. I've never seen this place. The furniture is heavy and ornate, the style old-fashioned and stuffy. The walls are painted pale yellow. There are features similar to Jodi's house—the crown molding, the shape of the room—but it's not Jodi's house.

Footsteps thunder down the staircase and I crouch down, not wanting to be seen by whoever is moving toward me. I scan the room for a place to hide. But before I can move, the person reaches the bottom of the stairs.

And looks right at me.

My heart thunders in my chest as I look into her dark blue eyes. My mind gropes for an explanation for my presence in her house, but it comes up empty. How do you tell someone you were doing a magic spell and suddenly found yourself in their living room?

The girl's eyebrows cinch together. She's pretty in an elfin sort of way, with a chin that comes to a gentle point. Her dark blond hair is pulled into a ponytail high atop her head. There's something familiar in the lines of her face.

"Mom," she calls.

Adrenaline courses through my body. Is she going to have her mom call the police?

"Mom! Can you hear me?"

A woman emerges through a doorway behind me and I'm boxed in. There's no way I can escape from here now even if I wanted to. I watch her, but her eyes don't land on me at all. Instead, she looks at her daughter. "Yes, I hear you. What is it?"

"I'm going out. Can I borrow the car?"

Relief sweeps through my body, followed by confusion. Why are they acting like I'm not here? Unless I'm *not* really here. Unless this is just a vision, like the one I had of my dad in my room at Jodi's house. I take in a deep breath.

The mother rolls her eyes. "What did I say about taking the car on a school night?"

"Please, Mom. I'm just going to run out for a little bit. I'll be back way before curfew."

"Who are you going out with?"

The girl shifts, digging the toe of her left foot into the hardwood floor. "No one..."

"By 'no one' do you mean Dave?"

A blush rises in the girl's cheek and she doesn't deny it.

The mother shakes her head. "I know if I ban you from seeing him it'll just make you want to see him more, but you know I don't trust him."

"Come on, Mom. It won't be just him. Shelly will be there too. And Jodi."

My heart begins hammering in my chest again. Shelly? Jodi? Dave? Can she mean who I think she means?

The mother sighs and holds her car keys toward her daughter. With a squeal, the daughter scurries over to her mother, placing a kiss on her cheek as she takes the keys from her hand.

"Thanks, Mom!"

"Just... Promise me you'll be careful, Crystal."

Crystal Taylor sighs. "I will, Mom." She offers a smile and as she turns toward the front door, she tucks something into the back pocket of her jeans. As she reaches for the doorknob, the crystal glints before it disappears.

The blackness is complete as it envelops me again, but I'm ready for it this time. I hold my breath until the sounds of Fox's basement start to tune in once more. Crystal and Griffin are still sniping back and forth. My eyesight comes back and I look down at my fingers, still pinching the tiny scrap of map. I release it quickly.

"Did it burn you or something?" Fox asks. "You sure let go fast."

I stare at him. Didn't he notice I've been still for minutes? Didn't anyone notice? Then again, maybe time didn't elapse the same out here as it did for me. But why did it happen at all? Why would I have a psychic flash about Crystal Taylor triggered by the charred piece of map? Unless it was part of the spell. Maybe it never worked for them before because they needed someone who could access time, not just magic.

Fox narrows his eyes at me. "Krissa, what's wrong?"

"I know where it is."

The room falls quiet and the eyes of the circle turn toward me.

Crystal claps and pumps her fist triumphantly. "I knew this would work!"

"You did not," Griffin murmurs.

Crystal ignores him. "Where is it?"

I bite my lower lip, not sure how to explain. Fox nods encouragingly and I take in a breath. "I think it's in Crystal Taylor's old house."

Griffin throws his hands up, exasperated. "We already knew that. That's very helpful, thanks."

"No, you don't understand. I think it's in Crystal Taylor's house back before she died—before the fire." I press my lips together, turning to Crystal. "It's not the *where* your spell was missing. It's the *when*."

The silence in the room is absolute. Bridget is the first one to recover. "Wait, you're saying the crystal we've been looking for was destroyed? How are we gonna get it, then? I'm fresh out of time machines."

"Shut up, Bridge," Crystal says absently as she presses herself to standing. She walks over to the dresser, opens a drawer, and pulls out a worn-looking journal. It's open and she's leafing through it before she takes a seat on the couch. "I think I saw... but I guess I never thought..."

I look at Fox to see if he has any idea what she's mumbling about. He shrugs.

"Here it is."

I take a seat beside her. "What is that?"

"It's my aunt Crystal's book of shadows. Well, not just hers—it's been in the Taylor family for generations. It's also part journal. And at one point... It didn't register with me before, but now..."

"Will you spit it out already?" Griffin asks.

Crystal casts a death glare at him. "It's a spell for traveling in time. For going back to a specific moment. But she was never able to do it. She couldn't get it to work for some reason."

Zane sighs. "If she couldn't get it to work, why do you think we can?"

Crystal's eyes are alight when she turns to me. "Don't you see? Because we finally got this location spell to work. Krissa able to see back into the past when she touched the map. Maybe my aunt wasn't strong enough, or she didn't have enough people in her circle. But if Krissa can see the past, maybe we'll be able to go there."

I shift, rolling my shoulders. It's not just that Crystal has added another person to help with the spell, it's the person she's added. Me. As a psychic, I can access time. That's why the locater spell finally worked. And that's why the spell we have to cast next will work. "So, we're gonna go to the past to get the crystal?"

"No," Griffin says, standing. "No. We can't do that. I mean, let's just set aside the fact that it's not possible. Even if we *could* somehow work a spell to go back in time, you have no idea what the consequences for going back and changing the timeline could be. I mean, come on. Haven't you ever seen any movie about time travel *ever*?"

Crystal waves a hand at him vaguely. "We'll just have to be

really careful. I don't know why I didn't see this sooner. My dad says this shard I wear was found in the remains of the house after the fire. They never found the rest of it. So, that's when we need to go back to: the night of the fire. Clearly it was there. We'll just have to steal it before it gets burned up."

Griffin crosses his arms over his chest. "This is possibly the stupidest thing you've ever said."

"Shut up, Griffin," I snap.

Bridget nods appreciatively while Griffin gapes at me. The plan sounds ridiculous, but with all I've experienced today, it doesn't seem like it's too far outside the realm of possibility. And if it'll save Jodi, I'll do it. I look at Crystal. "Okay, let's get started, then."

She looks slightly taken aback. "We can't do it right now."

"Why not?"

"We don't have everything we need." She runs her finger down the list of items on the page. "I don't even know what some of this *is*, let alone where to get it."

"Let me see it." I reach for the book and, reluctantly, she hands it to me. I skim the list. "Yeah, I recognize these names. Jodi's got all this stuff at her shop. I can go pick it up right now and be back here in half an hour, tops—"

Crystal squints as she reads the spell. "We still can't do it until tomorrow. It looks like you have to let the quartz sit covered with the herbs to charge or something."

An icy wave of dread courses through me. "Tomorrow?" I look at Fox. "Tomorrow might be too late."

"We've been looking for this thing for months," Zane says. "What's another day gonna hurt?"

Fox presses his lips together, but he doesn't answer Zane's question. He sits on Crystal's other side and looks over her shoulder at the spell. After a minute, he looks up at me. "She's right. The herbs and the quartz need to infuse with each other for twenty-four hours. Tomorrow's the earliest we can do it."

I pull my phone from my back pocket and snap a picture of the spell. "I'll go get everything from the shop and I'll come right back so we can get things started. Let's plan to do it at noon tomorrow."

Everyone nods in agreement and I waste no time climbing the

stairs and heading for Jodi's car. I can only hope twenty-four hours from now won't be too late.

Chapter Thirty-Two

David and Millie decide stay the night, along with a man named Ryan Alcott, who drove up from Ohio. These are the remaining members of Jodi's circle.

They must be using magic, because no matter how I try, I can't hear what they're talking about. Anytime I poke my head into the sitting room, the four of them go quiet. They don't want me to know what they're discussing.

Jodi looks worse than ever in the morning. There are bags under her eyes, and I'm sure she was up coughing half the night. She tries to smile when I bring her a mug of tea, but I can feel the guilt radiating off her.

She knows she's going to die.

I don't ask if she's made arrangements for me. If the spell works and I'm able to locate the crystal, neither of us will need to worry about that.

At eleven-thirty, I leave the house. I don't bother telling anyone; they're all avoiding me anyhow. I expect to be the first one to arrive at the park near the river where Lexie and I once spent an afternoon swinging, and I'm surprised when Fox is already there.

I get out of Jodi's car and sit next to him on a bench overlooking the river.

"How's she doing?" he asks.

I shake my head. "It's bad."

"This is gonna work," he says, bumping his shoulder against mine. The gesture is so reminiscent of Owen, my heart aches. He called me yesterday afternoon to see if I wanted to go out, but I didn't feel right leaving Jodi. I told him she was sick, but I didn't tell him how bad it is. It's with a pang I realize the only one outside of Jodi's circle who knows the truth about what's going on is Fox.

The rest of the circle arrives before noon and I'm thankful for their punctuality. Crystal leads us all along the river, away from the playground, to a clearing out of sight of the park.

"Why are we out here?" I ask.

"We don't want to draw attention to ourselves," Crystal explains. "If this works, I don't want to end up in the middle of a street or in someone's basement. Much safer this way. Besides, flowing water is good for drawing energy."

Zane sets a large canvas bag on the grass and Crystal begins pulling out a half dozen silk pouches full of herbs and stones. Under her direction, we remove the quartz crystals from the bags, leaving the mix of herbs inside them. Once we've formed a circle with the small stones, Bridget steps back and squints at it.

"It's not very big," she says, wrinkling her nose.

"It doesn't need to be," Crystal says. "Only one of us will be inside it."

My ears perk up. "Wait—what do you mean? I thought we were all going."

Griffin snorts. "Yeah, because that doesn't sound like a recipe for disaster. It's dangerous enough sending one person back in time."

Zane crosses his arms over his chest. "Man, if you're so worried about it, why're you even here?"

Griffin's mouth twitches, but he says nothing.

"*Because*, if we do this, if we get the crystal and anchor our magic, he wants in on it." Crystal rolls her eyes before turning her attention to me. "This spell is gonna take a ton of magic even to get one person back. There's no way we can get all six of us there and back, and I, for one, don't particularly want to get stuck in the past."

A chill courses through me. "If we can't all go back, who do you propose we send?"

She looks at me like the answer is obvious. "Me, of course."

I bite the inside of my cheek. "Why you?"

Her eyebrows hitch upward. "It's my family's old house. I've heard all the stories about the little hiding places. I know which room was whose. I mean, I guess I could tell all this stuff to someone else, but I was under the impression time was of the essence."

Anger boils in the pit of my stomach. She could have mentioned all of this yesterday, when there was still time to learn all these things, but she didn't. Now, she's right. It's too late. "I'm going too."

She shakes her head. "No. No way."

"I'm going." I can't stand the thought of sending Crystal to take care of this. What if she doesn't find the crystal? I know she wants it so we can anchor the magic, but if that doesn't happen, it won't be the end of the world for her. If we don't find that crystal, I'll be an orphan by morning.

"Don't you trust me?" Crystal asks, her eyes wide and innocent.

The heat builds within me and out of my peripheral vision I see a fallen log begin to rock back and forth gently.

Fox claps a hand on my shoulder. The heat dissipates and the log stops trembling. "I don't think this is about a lack of trust. Krissa's stronger than you—stronger than any of us. You might need magic like hers to get you back."

Crystal's mouth twitches for a moment before she nods. "Okay, fine. But just the two of us."

I turn to Fox and smile. "Thanks."

"Why is it that when you say *thanks* it sounds like an accusation?" He chuckles but quickly sobers, reaching out and squeezing my upper arm. "I want you to be able to save Jodi."

A prickling sensation gathers in the corners of my eyes and I'm glad when Crystal clears her throat, moving to the center of the circle.

"I think we should get started," she says. "Krissa, come stand next to me. The rest of you, spread out around us. Lift your arms out toward each other."

Fox, Zane, Bridget, and Griffin follow Crystal's directions. She turns to face me, closing her hand around the pendant that hangs from her neck. She holds her other hand out to me and I take it, squeezing firmly.

Crystal closes her eyes. "We need to focus on a specific moment in time," she says, her voice low. "The day of the fire. It was a Saturday night. My grandma was out of town for the weekend."

I'm not sure exactly how to do what Crystal is asking us to do, so I just clear my mind, trying my best to connect with the energy flowing between our interlocked fingers. She probably knows the details of this day better than anyone. Lexie says she's been obsessed with her aunt since before freshman year. In that time, I'm sure she's found out as much as she can about the day Crystal Taylor died. I direct the swell of magic rising within me to Crystal, hoping she knows what to do with it.

My palm begins to tingle and Crystal grips my hand more tightly.

"Iter per tempus. Deducas nobis."

Although I don't understand what she's saying, I take up the chant, repeating the words as best I can along with her. Slowly, the others join in, until we're all speaking the words in firm, clear voices.

A winds stirs around us, tugging at my jacket, slipping through my hair. Around me, the air seems to thrum with energy. White light fills my vision and I welcome it, knowing it will lead me into the past.

I expect the blackness when it overtakes me; what I don't expect is the sensation of pressure over my entire body, like I'm being pressed in on all sides. I gasp for air and my lungs begin to burn. Something's gone wrong. There's no air here. Wherever we are, it's not the past. I try to reach out with my hand to grab for Crystal, but nothing is around me. Nothing is under me. I'm suspended in nothingness. My lungs strain and scream for oxygen and a fire starts raging in my head.

When I think I can't take it for another second, I am assaulted by sensory information: light, the chirping of birds, the sound of children squealing off in the distance, the feeling of grass under my feet—and air. I gulp huge breaths. Crystal stands in front of me, her face alight.

"Wow," she says, her voice low and reverent.

I survey our surroundings. The stone circle Crystal built is gone, as are Fox, Griffin, Zane, and Bridget. The trees around us look smaller. I feel a surge of excitement course through me. "It worked."

Crystal grins. "Yeah, it did."

I start to move but she holds her hand up. After glancing around the clearing, she scurries off and picks up a two-foot-long stick about as thick as my thumb from the tree line. When she returns to my side, she jams it into the ground so it stands up. "So we can find our way back to get home," she says. "Now, let's do this." She starts walking along the river, toward the playground and Main Street beyond.

I follow close on her heels. "What's the plan?"

"Okay, from what I've put together based on what my dad's told me, what I've heard from my grandma, and town rumors, it happened at night. She had the house to herself because my grandma was out of town and my dad and Lexie's mom didn't live at home anymore. Now, the story goes she lit candles and fell asleep while they were still burning, and somehow one got knocked over and started the fire. But I don't think that's what happened. I think she had her circle over and they were trying a spell and things got out of hand. Maybe the spell's what made the crystal splinter. Even if it's not, we know the crystal had to be in the house during the fire—otherwise I wouldn't have this." She clutches the pendant around her neck.

"So, what? We just go to your grandma's house and wait for a fire?"

She shrugs. "It seems the most direct approach. Not that I believe Griffin about messing up the space-time continuum or anything, but I promised to keep my interactions with the environment to a minimum."

"Okay." I take in a breath.

We pass by the playground and I'm surprised it's different. While the structures from our time are made of plastic and rubber, this one is all wood and metal. We make our way to the street and head over the bridge toward downtown. In so many ways, Main

Street is exactly the same: The people milling around are nearly indistinguishable from the ones from our time, except perhaps their clothing, and the fact that no one is holding a cell phone.

My breath catches as we draw near Hannah's Herbs. The shop looks exactly the same, and I almost expect to see Jodi spill out of it, heading down the street to pick up a drink at the coffee shop. Instead, the girl who exits has honey-brown hair and high cheekbones. My stomach clenches and I sigh.

I don't realize I've come to a stop until Crystal tugs at my arm. "Hey, you alright?"

I nod. "Yeah... It's just..."

"Weird, right?" She bites her lower lip. "You wanna go in?"

I shift forward on the balls of my feet for a moment before catching myself. "No, I can't."

"Oh, come on. Just go in, for a second. You don't have to talk to anyone."

The idea is appealing. My grandmother died before I was born and my grandfather died when I was just a few years old, and the idea of seeing them makes my heart flutter. Maybe Jodi's in there. It would be funny to see a young version of my aunt. Or maybe... maybe my dad is in there.

I turn away from the shop, shaking my head. "No, I shouldn't. It's a bad idea."

Crystal rolls her eyes. "You sound like Griffin. What's it gonna hurt to just take a peek? It's not like one look will destroy the world. Aren't you curious?"

"What about your promise to Griffin?" I don't think he's right, but I also don't think poking around in the past too much is a good idea.

When it's clear I'm not going in the store, Crystal gives up and we start back down the street. The sun beats down on us and I wish I weren't wearing long sleeves. It must be a different time of year now than in our own time. I'm sweating by the time we finally make it to the old Taylor house. It's closer to downtown than Jodi's house, but it was clearly build during the same era. There are no cars in the driveway and I take it as a sign there's no one home.

"How are we gonna get in?" I ask.

"Around back," Crystal says, leading the way up the driveway.

I glance around the neighborhood nervously. There are four girls doing cartwheels in a yard down the street, but no one else is in sight.

Crystal ascends the back porch stairs confidently and goes straight for the door. She reaches for the handle and twists, but nothing happens. "It's locked."

I nudge my way beside her, reaching tor the doorknob. "What do you mean, it's locked? I didn't think people locked their doors around here. I'm half-surprised Jodi locks up the shop."

Crystal shakes her head. "I don't know. I mean, maybe my grandma doesn't feel safe since my grandpa died, or maybe Crystal doesn't feel safe since her mom's not home."

"So, what do we do about it? Is there a key hidden somewhere?"

"How would I know that?"

Irritation flares up inside me. "I thought you knew everything about the house. Wasn't that what you were saying before?"

She ignores me, moving from the back door to a nearby window. She presses at the sill, trying to push it open.

"They lock the door but they're going to leave the window open?"

"Have you got a better idea?"

I don't. I glance around the backyard. It's the middle of the day. If a neighbor comes outside to let out a dog or take out the garbage, they'll see us and our chance will be blown. I move to the opposite side of the door from Crystal and try another window. It's stuck tight and I stifle an irritated groan. I was right not to trust that Crystal would be able to get this done. She can't even get us into the house. Is there another way to get the crystal? Perhaps we could find her aunt somewhere in town and stealthily pickpocket her. I shake my head. That's no good: first, I don't know how to pickpocket someone, and second, there's no promising she has the crystal with her. It might be in the house. Frustrated, I bang on the wooden windowsill, wishing it would budge. A small click sounds and I press on the window again. To my surprise, it slides up easily.

"Psst. Crystal."

The window is low enough and wide enough that I can climb through with minimal effort. Crystal follows closely behind. I feel a strong wave of déjà vu when I look around. I was just here—only now I am *really* here. If Crystal Taylor walks into the room now, she'll see me.

"Where do we hide?"

"This way." Crystal leads the way to the stairs. We ascend and I tense at the loud creaks they make as our feet touch them. I really hope no one is home. There was no car, but what if Crystal Taylor is just sitting in her room?

Crystal doesn't seem to share my concern. She walks purposefully toward a room at the top of the stairs and eases open the door, which is already ajar. The hinges creak as it swings open. Crystal grins over her shoulder. "This is her room." She walks in, her eyes roaming the space.

My heart begins thundering in my chest. I don't like being out in the open like this. "So, what? We're just gonna pop out and yell *surprise* when she gets here?"

It's a long minute before Crystal turns her attention back to me. "Of course not." She walks past me, back out into the hall, and to the room next door. "This is my aunt Bonnie's room. According to my dad, the closets back up against each other and there's a little trap door. Crystal used to sneak through it when she had nightmares and climb into bed with Bonnie."

I follow her to the closet and cringe as she begins shoving clothes and shoes out of the way. Once she reveals a square of wood that doesn't match the rest of the wall, she smiles, settling down in front of it. She pats the spot beside her and after a beat, I sit too.

"How do we know they're gonna come up here?" I ask, attempting to find a comfortable position.

"Where else would they go for a sleepover?"

"In a giant house when no one else is home?" The folly of our plan lays itself out before me and I can't believe we're here without a better idea of how to accomplish our goal. Crystal, on the other hand, seems completely at ease.

"Better settle in. We're gonna be here for a while."

Chapter Thirty-Three

Heavy footfalls on creaky stairs jar me from my doze. When I open my eyes, it takes a moment for me to remember where I am. *When* I am. Crystal sits beside me, her eyes bright and alert. I wonder if she's been like that the whole time. I shift my weight and wince as a pins-and-needles sensation overtakes my left leg.

"Show time," Crystal whispers to me. She moves closer to the crack in the trap door and I press my lips together, irritated. I wonder what time it is and how long it'll be before the fire starts. And, more importantly, I wish I had any idea about how time was progressing back in our own reality. Have we been gone for hours? Or when we come back will it be like we never left? My stomach churns as I think about Jodi. How much time does she have left?

Five girls and two guys filter into Crystal Taylor's bedroom. Crystal shifts so she can get a better look through the crack between the board and the wall, and I jockey for the same position. I'm just as curious as she is, although I figure we've got two different ways of thinking about this. For her, this is a chance to learn about the aunt she never knew, the one she idolizes. For me, it's about saving the aunt I have.

In Crystal Taylor's room, the group chats idly. A girl with bushy dark blond hair settles atop Crystal's bed and the blond guy joins her. Crystal and a girl with dark brown hair pull beanbag chairs out of a corner and begin placing them strategically on the floor. A girl with light brown hair moves toward the closet.

Instinctively, Crystal and I both move backward. My heart

thunders in my chest. We've been found. Everything is ruined.

Seconds tick by and the wood blocking the opening remains firmly in place. The girl doesn't call out; no one comes running into the room we're hiding in. Crystal and I lean forward, peering through the crack again.

The girl is back in the main part of the room, setting candles in a circle in the empty space inside of the ring of beanbag chairs. When the last one is in place, she holds her closed fist out by her side. As her hand opens, the wick of each candle ignites.

She turns back toward the closet and I gasp as I catch a glimpse of her face. Jodi. She's young, probably younger than I am, but there's no mistaking her.

Crystal looks at me. "Did you know she was here?" she mouths.

I shake my head. I knew Jodi and Crystal were part of the same circle, but I had no idea Jodi was here the night Crystal died.

"Okay, everyone, let's sit down," Crystal Taylor says, settling onto one of the beanbag chairs. Jodi sits on the one to her left and, I realize with a pang, Shelly Cole—or Tanner, as she would be called now—sits to her right. I scan the other faces and recognize David Cole and Millie from the coffee shop. The blond guy who was sitting on the bed earlier is Ryan Alcott, who drove up from Ohio to help Jodi. The only one I don't know is the girl with the bushy blond hair. I recall Millie mentioning another name at the house earlier: Sarah Riddell. This must be her.

"I bet you're all wondering why I invited you over today," Crystal says after everyone has taken a seat.

Ryan snorts. "Yeah, since the last time we tried to do a spell it was such a rousing failure."

Crystal presses her lips together.

Shelly crosses her arms over her chest. "So, maybe that spell was a little advanced for us. It doesn't mean we should give up on magic all together." Her eyes flick briefly to Jodi.

"I never said that," Jodi murmurs. "I just think we should stick with simple spells. You have no idea what the consequences of messing with more complicated magic could be."

Crystal Taylor's eyes brighten. "I think we can solve that. When we did the spell before, things got out of hand because we don't have enough power to control the magic. But I found this spell that'll help us amplify our abilities."

An excited murmur rises among the group. Beside me, Crystal Jamison sits at attention.

In the room, only Jodi seems unimpressed by Crystal Taylor's revelation. "How?"

Crystal turns to her. "Now, before you say no—"

Jodi throws up her hands. "I can't believe it. The *crystal*?"

I hold my breath. Are they talking about the same crystal we've come for? I scan the room, but it's nowhere to be seen.

Crystal Taylor shakes her head. "I don't know what your issue is with it. You sell all different kinds of stones at your parents' store. How is this rock any different?"

"If it's not any different than any other rock, then why are you so obsessed with it?" Jodi counters.

"We already know the crystal isn't just any old hunk of quartz," Millie says. "We've all felt its power. We all know doing magic is easier when you're holding it." There's a hint of bitterness in her voice; maybe Crystal Taylor has trouble sharing.

"That's the problem," David says. "There's only one crystal and there are seven of us. It doesn't have enough power to go around."

Crystal leans forward in her beanbag chair. "But what if it does? *That's* the spell I want us to try. If we can get it to work, it'll release the magic from the crystal."

"Wait—what do you mean, 'release' it?" asks Ryan.

"Where's it gonna go?" asks David.

A chorus of questions rises up and it's difficult to pick out what the others are saying.

After a few seconds, Crystal is able to restore order. "There's energy trapped in here, and if we release it, we can channel that energy into us."

David rubs his hands together. "Okay, when do we get started?"

Jodi presses backward into her chair. "I don't think this is such a good idea."

"Oh, come on, Jo. Don't be chicken."

Jodi shakes her head at Crystal. "I don't know how you can be so flip about this. I've told you before, you don't know what you're messing with here. You find this crystal and your family's old grimoire and you suddenly think you're this all-powerful witch or something."

"Better than not being a witch at all," Crystal murmurs.

Jodi looks around the room at each member of the circle. "Look, I know the idea of getting more magic sounds good, but I also know more about this stuff than you do. Whatever power's locked away in that crystal, what if it's there for a reason?"

Crystal snorts. "Yeah, for us to use!"

Jodi rolls her eyes. "Come on. You can't be that self-centered to think your family's been passing this thing down from generation to generation just so you could use all the magic inside it."

"We," Shelly says. "So *we* can use it."

"You guys are all being stupid," Jodi says, standing. "If you want to mess with magic beyond what you're capable of, go for it. I'm out."

The flame of the candle nearest Jodi shoots up high—almost to waist height. Jodi jumps away from it. "Knock it off, Crystal."

Crystal stands, but the flame doesn't change. "If you know so much, why don't you stop it?"

I take in a breath. Is this how it starts? Is this what causes the fire? I still haven't seen the crystal. This can't happen yet.

One by one, the other candle flames jump higher until there's a wall of fire encircling the two of them.

"We've got to move," I hiss at Crystal.

"Not yet."

The candle flames extinguish all at once. Jodi's face is impassive as she looks at Crystal. "Just because I don't show off doesn't mean I can't do all the little parlor tricks you can. But that's all they are, Crystal. You think these tiny spells you can do mean you're the master of all magic or something. Believe me, if you're not careful, it's gonna master you." She turns on her heel and moves toward the door.

"If you leave, you're missing out. You'll be sorry when we've got the magic and you're still poor little Jodi who can make a tea for any occasion but who can't do any real spells."

"I'd rather be exactly who I am—exactly *what* I am—than get caught up in whatever you think you're about to do. I promise you, Crystal, nothing good's going to come of it."

The door creaks and Jodi's steps echo through the house. I bite my lower lip. Why is Jodi so against this spell?

Back in the room, Crystal Taylor makes a show of slamming the door after Jodi. "We don't need her anyway. Good riddance."

"Crystal... Maybe she's got a point," Sarah says, her voice quiet.

"Do you want to leave with her, Sarah?" Crystal casts a cold glare at the people who remain in the room with her. "If any of you want to leave with Jodi, feel free to go now."

There's a tension in the room as each person shifts, considering doing just that. But the seconds tick by, and no one makes a move for the door.

A look of satisfaction crosses Crystal Taylor's face as she surveys her friends. She smiles slowly before going to a drawer in her dresser and pulling out an old leather-bound tome and opening it up to a page toward the middle. "Let's get started."

The earlier sense of excitement has faded completely and tension has thickened the air.

Crystal calls out directions. Shelly puts a large metal bowl in the center of the circle of candles. David and Ryan sprinkle some herbs inside of it, and Millie adds a few chunks of quartz. Crystal Taylor puts the large book down beside the bowl before going to her bed. She picks up her pillow and pulls something from it. My pulse quickens as it dawns on me: This is where she's hidden the crystal. She unwraps the dark cloth surrounding it and picks it up, caressing its jagged edges with her fingers.

Shelly crosses the room to Crystal. "Are you sure about this? Maybe Jodi's got a point."

Crystal's glare is icy. "Are you serious?"

"Well, maybe. It's just... She's right, you know? About not being able to do much magic—not yet. Remember last week when we were practicing the automatic-writing spell and half our papers burst into flames? I'm not saying we shouldn't try the spell. I'm just saying maybe we need to wait a little. Practice more. Then, when we're stronger—"

"You don't understand—this spell, this is what's going to

make us stronger. You can't imagine the magical power that's contained in this crystal. If we do the ritual correctly, we'll be able to tap into that magic—"

"You think," says Millie.

"Excuse me?"

"You think that's what'll happen. Let's be honest here, Crystal. That old grimoire of yours isn't exactly legible and the spell you want us to do isn't actually in there."

Crystal looks as if she's been slapped. "How do you—"

"I looked, okay? I looked. I know, that's against rule number one or whatever, but I was curious. Sue me. You went to the bathroom and I got curious about how you were just now finding this spell. I mean, come on. We all know you've read through that whole book a dozen times. So I looked at the page you had it open to and what you want us to do is not what that spell is designed for. The spell in your book is an anchoring spell, not a releasing spell. You have no idea if you're even doing it right—"

"It's the same thing," Crystal insists, "except instead of leaving the energy in the crystal, we're releasing it to live in us. But if you're not, maybe you should leave, like Jodi did."

Millie relents. "I'm not saying I want to leave..."

The flame of the candle nearest to Crystal flickers to life. "I can't trust you," she murmurs. Another candle ignites.

Millie's eyes go from one candle to the other. My breath catches and I ready myself for action. If things get out of hand—maybe this is what begins the fire. "Crystal, don't be like that. Your problem lately is you don't trust any of us. You're changing, and you don't even see it."

"It's not me who's changed. You never used to go through people's personal belongings and—"

Millie shakes her head. "Maybe Jodi is right. You know what? I'm leaving too. Good luck, Crystal. If getting more magic makes me more like you... maybe I don't want more magic."

Footfalls recede through the hallway and down the stairs. Crystal looks at the four remaining people in her room. "If you all want to leave, that's fine. Go. I'll do it all by myself."

I hold my breath, waiting for someone to move.

A brief eternity passes before Shelly sighs. "Are we doing this or not?"

Crystal directs the remaining members of the circle to stand equidistant from each other. When they lift their hands toward one another, their fingers close but not touching, I'm reminded forcibly of the way Fox and the others looked while they were doing the spell to send me and Crystal Jamison back here.

Crystal Taylor bends down, setting the crystal in the metal bowl. She consults the spell in her book before resuming her spot in the circle. "Repeat these words with me: *Libera nos vir potens hominis. Effugium tuus vincula.*"

Slowly, the others take up the chant. I glance beside me at Crystal Jamison, but her attention is focused fully on her aunt.

Through the crack, I see the flames of the candles rise and fall rhythmically. The air feels heavy, electrified.

A loud snapping noise sounds in the room. A wind rushes past me and I spin around, afraid someone else has come in. The window by the bed is open, but there is no one who could have opened it. The curtains billow, rising as they fill with air. I turn back to look at the circle; the girls' hair is whipping around their faces. Slowly, the crystal rises from the metal bowl, taking on a luminescent quality as it hovers several feet above the ground. The furniture begins to rattle against the floor.

Something is happening. I don't know what it is, but I can feel it's not good. Whatever Crystal Taylor thinks she is doing, this is not it. An overwhleming force presses against me, like a tangible thing.

I'm not the only one who senses it. Millie screams and falls to the ground. "Crystal, stop it! Something's wrong!" She flails on the floor before finally pushing herself back to her feet, only to scramble out of the room. Over the rush of wind, I hear her feet thundering down the stairs.

If Crystal Taylor notices, she doesn't show it. The candle flames leap at regular intervals around the group as they continue to chant.

A picture frame slips off the wall and flies across the room, smashing against the floor inside the circle. Shelly jumps back but then returns to her original location.

Sarah releases a hoarse cry. "It's not worth it! I need to get out of here! I need to get home!" Ryan pulls her close to him, leading her out of the room.

A pulse of energy radiates from the crystal outward, knocking Shelly to the floor. "Crystal!" she screams. From here, I can feel the weight of whatever pushes against her. "We have to stop! Crystal!"

Crystal opens her eyes, but there's something different about them. They seem brighter somehow. And when she speaks, it's no longer her voice. The voice is rougher, more masculine. "You cannot stop the power. The magic is returning, and it will seek atonement for sins. The children of the children will not be spared."

David leaves his position in the circle and crouches beside Shelly. Putting his arms around her middle, he pulls her from the floor and the two of them stumble toward the door. My heartbeat is thundering in my ears. It is going to happen any second—I feel it. How are we going to get to the crystal and get out without burning along with Crystal Taylor?

I begin to pry at the board between the closets. Crystal grabs my hands. "What are you doing?"

"We have to be ready," I say, wrenching my hands from her. "It's going to happen any time now."

Hesitation flickers across Crystal's face for a moment before she grabs hold of the board and helps me pull it off. It's so loud in the house with the wind rushing and the furniture shaking and items flying around the room that the creak and groan of the wood being torn loose is barely audible, even to me. Crystal Taylor's eyes are closed again and she doesn't cease in her chanting. I crawl through the opening into her closet, Crystal close behind me. I can see the luminous quartz hovering just feet from where I crouch. With her eyes closed, Crystal Taylor might not notice if I grab it and run. But I can't do that; I have to wait until the very last second.

The crystal begins to glow an ominous green color and spin in midair. Before I have time to wonder what could be causing it, something explodes out of the stone like a wave. It knocks me backward into Crystal Jamison and for a moment I'm afraid we're too late and the quartz has been destroyed. My fears are quickly allayed when I see it still pulsing with the green color. Another shockwave emanates from it, but even though it's stronger than the last one, I'm ready for it this time and barely shift backwards. Crystal Taylor isn't so lucky. She stumbles back and knocks over a candle, the tall flame of which ignites the quilt on her bed.

This is it. The fire. It's now or never.

I lunge forward, snatching the crystal out of the air. It is warm in the palm of my hand, as if it's been sitting in the sun all day. A pulse of energy courses through me, much stronger and more intense than the one I experienced when I touched the shard from Crystal Jamison's necklace. There is magic in it, all right. It's a deep, thrumming power I've never experienced before. But I can't let myself dwell on it. As soon as it's in my hand, I start for the door and down the stairs. The front door is unlocked and I run through it, stopping only when I reach the street in front of the house. I bend over, sucking in breath for a moment before straightening and grinning. "Got it." But Crystal Jamison is nowhere in sight. I look back to the house but don't see her. Smoke is already pouring out the open windows upstairs. Where could she be? She was right beside me.

I didn't check after the second wave of energy to see if Crystal was alright. I was so focused on my task, I didn't even think about her. A shiver courses through my body. What if she's knocked out, just like her aunt? I look down at the stone in my hands and back at the house. If I get the crystal but let my friend die, what good is that? I have to go back.

The flames have already traveled to the front door. I marvel at the speed at which they're moving. I attempt to see beyond the wall of flames, but there's no way I can get in through here.

I have to do something, fast. This fire isn't going to go unnoticed for long, and I can't be found here. The back window—maybe I can still get in that way. I take off at a sprint around the side of the house, colliding with something as I turn the corner and falling to the ground.

Crystal Jamison coughs as she holds her hand out to help me

up. "We've gotta get out of here."

I allow her to pull me to my feet and follow her to the sidewalk in front of the house. She walks quickly, but not so quickly as to draw attention to us. I keep pace with her.

"What happened?"

"You ran out so fast," Crystal says, her voice low. "I tripped when I tried to get out and by the time I got to the front door, there were flames everywhere. So I went out the back."

My eyes scan the neighborhood for signs of fire engines or witnesses, but I see nothing out of the ordinary. The sun has long since set and there's a chill in the air that wasn't there on our walk to this house. "Now what?"

"We have to get back to the clearing where we arrived. The spell is still active. All we have to do is get back to where we started and the circle we cast in the future should pull us back there."

"Should?" I ask as we turn the corner.

Crystal doesn't respond. Our pace is so quick that by the time we get to Main Street, I'm panting. It's Saturday night so people are out on the town; I try my best to avoid eye contact. All I want is to get back to the present and use the crystal to heal Jodi. We've spent so much time here already; I have no idea how much time has passed back in our real life.

Beside me, Crystal gasps. I glance at her and see she's rubbing her chest where her necklace usually rests. "It's gone."

For a split second, I wonder if it fell off her somewhere. "It never existed." I hold the crystal out toward her. "Since this never broke up in the fire, you never turn the shard into a necklace."

She reaches for my hand. "Let me hold the crystal."

"What? Why?"

"I just..." She presses her lips together. "I want to see if it feels the same."

I hesitate. "You remember my terms for helping you, right? I get to use the crystal first."

Her fingers twitch. "I remember. I'll give it back. Just let me see it."

I hand it to her as we cross the bridge over the river. We're not far from the park now. We pass by the play structure, which is abandoned at this hour, and follow the river toward the clearing.

Beside me, Crystal slows. I turn, irritated. "Come on. We've gotta get back." But something's wrong. Her eyes have glazed over and her mouth hangs open. What could be happening to her? Is there some kind of complication from smoke inhalation I don't know about? Her mouth begins moving soundlessly and I cross to her, taking her by the shoulders and shaking her. Her gaze doesn't snap back to reality; instead, she starts chanting the same words her aunt was chanting before the fire started. I grab for the crystal and pry it from her fingers, but it won't come loose. Whatever Crystal Taylor was trying to do, it's still happening.

I don't know how I know it, but I'm positive I can get us back without finding the spot where we arrived. I felt the magic in that crystal. Maybe using it for something other than whatever spell it's in the middle of will snap Crystal out of this trance. Or maybe it'll make us both burst into flames. I have no idea, but I have to try. Giving up on pulling the crystal from her hands, I settle for closing my hand over hers. I close my eyes and focus on the power emanating from the crystal. I remember the words Jodi said to me on my first day in Clearwater—that all time exists at once. I imagine the steady stream of time as a river, rushing indomitably forward into the future. In my mind's eye, I see that stream freeze, making it possible to move from one point to another. I allow the magic within to crystal to rush into me, mixing with the magic building in my core. I need to get back to the present, back to Jodi.

A bright flash overtakes my vision for an instant before darkness rushes in. As the crushing sensation presses over my body, another wave of energy blasts from the crystal. My body is hurled backward, my fingers slip from Crystal's hand, and I fall into the void of timelessness.

Chapter Thirty-Four

I land with a thud on the grass and take in deep, greedy breaths of air. I try to open my eyes, to move, but I can't. Panic rises in my chest. What's wrong? What did I do? Are we stuck in some kind of limbo between times?

Hands seize me by the arms, pulling me upward. At first I think Crystal is helping me to my feet, but the hands are larger than hers, the person stronger. With a mighty effort, I manage to open my eyes. The person in front of me is blurry. I can hear his heavy breathing.

"Are you alright? I came upon the clearing and there you lay—"

There's something odd about the man's words. Did we go back in time instead of forward? "Where's... Crystal?" I try to escape the stranger's grip, but my arms are like lead. "Crystal?"

There's a moan from the ground beside me and I manage to throw off the stranger's hands. I crouch and grope at the grass. The moon is full, providing a decent amount of light, but my vision is still blurry. "Crystal?" My fingers brush her body and I scramble to her side. I rub my eyes and blink a few times before she comes into focus. Her eyes are half closed and her head is moving back and forth. I don't know what's wrong with her, but she might need help. I curse myself for leaving my cell in the car. I turn to ask the guy who helped me up to call for help, but he's disappeared. Besides Crystal, there's no one in sight. What if I did the spell wrong?

"Help!" I yell. "Fox! Bridget! Help!"

Crystal's eyelids flutter and open briefly before closing again. I should be heartened by the fact that she's attempting to regain consciousness, but I'm terrified. What was that chanting she was doing before we passed through time? Did we even end up when we were supposed to? "Bridget! Zane! Fox!" They said they'd wait for us. What if they didn't? It's as dark here as it was in the past; it must be hours since we left. "Griffin!"

I hear shouts in the distance. Seconds later, Fox and Bridget appear around a cluster of trees. When they catch sight of us, they take off at a run.

"What happened? Why aren't you back where we started?" Bridget kneels beside Crystal, placing her hands on Crystal's cheeks. "What's wrong with her?"

"I don't know," I say.

Fox puts his hands on my shoulders, orienting me so I'm facing him. "Are you okay?" his gray eyes seem full of genuine concern.

Crystal gives a low moan and sits up so suddenly Bridget jumps back and lets out a yelp. Crystal's eyes open and she takes in her surroundings.

"Wow—what happened? How'd we get here? The last thing I remember is holding the crystal and..."

"The crystal," I say, scanning for it in her hands. They're empty. "Where is it?"

Crystal shakes her head. "I don't know."

I drop to my hands and knees, my hands running over the grass. It has to be here. It has to. We used it to cross back to this time, so it had to come with us. I need that crystal. I need it to save Jodi.

Something presses against my heart when I think of my aunt. What if I'm too late?

My fingers brush against something cool and sharp. I pick it up and take off at a run in the direction Fox and Bridget appeared from. That must be the way back to civilization. Shouts follow me, but I ignore them. I pump my legs as fast as I can and run toward the parking lot.

Every second that ticks by as I drive back to Jodi's house feels like an eternity. I push the door open and hurry into the house, not bothering to close it behind me. "Jodi! Jodi?" The living room is empty so I go upstairs to her bedroom. I start to panic. Where are Millie, David, and Ryan? They said they would stay here to watch over her. Jodi's bed is empty and my heart sinks. I'm too late. She must already be gone. Her friends called the cops or the coroner or whoever gets called when someone dies. I've failed her.

"Hello?"

I jump at the voice that comes from downstairs. It sounded like Jodi, but that can't be...

But it is Jodi, standing at the foot of the steps, dirt smeared on her right cheek, pruning shears in her hand as if she plans to use them as a weapon. I rush down the steps and throw my arms around her. "You're okay!"

Jodi returns my embrace tentatively. "Yes, I am. Was I not supposed to be?"

I hold her at arm's length, studying her face. "You... were..." She doesn't look at all like she did when I saw her earlier today. The color is back in her cheeks and she looks healthy, like she usually does. Is it possible she doesn't remember being sick? Did going back to get the crystal keep the curse from happening?

I grab her hand and inspect her palm. There's no sign of the mark.

Jodi presses her hand to my cheek. "You okay? Taking an interested in palmistry?" She smiles, but I can tell there's concern behind it. She's worried about me. The irony!

"I'm good. I'm great, actually." I laugh, giving her another quick hug. "Have you had dinner yet? I'll make dinner."

Not waiting for a response, I hurry to the kitchen. My stomach is growling. I open the refrigerator and inspect the contents.

Jodi stands at the mouth of the kitchen, watching me. "Are you sure you're okay? Everything's fine with you?" Her eyebrows cinch together. "You're not hopped up on some kind of energy spell, are you? I remember Millie did one before midterms one year... Not pretty."

I close the refrigerator door. Why is she talking about me casting spells like it's no big deal? Jodi doesn't want me using magic.

A sinking feeling settles over me. Crystal's pendant, Jodi not being sick, Jodi condoning my use of magic? What else is different now? "No," I say, forcing a smile. "I just feel like cooking. You take such good care of me, I just want to show you how much I appreciate you."

Jodi's eyes cloud for a moment, but then she smiles. "And they say teenagers are moody and taciturn. I already ate, though. It's pretty late. I'm gonna head back out to the greenhouse. Let me know if you need anything."

"I will."

A knock sounds at the front door and Jodi heads for it. I hear the familiar creak of the hinges and smile. Maybe things aren't so different after all.

"It's for you," Jodi calls. I take in a breath and head for the hallway. When Jodi passes me, making her way toward the greenhouse, she murmurs, "It's your boyfriend."

My heart swells at the words. It's funny what can change in just a few days. Last time Jodi referred to Owen that way, I was embarrassed—mortified, even. Now the words are a comforting balm. After what I've experienced today, I want to fold myself up in his arms and breathe in the scent of his body.

I turn into the living room and stop in my tracks. The figure sitting on the couch in the semidarkness doesn't belong to Owen. It belongs to Fox.

"What are you doing here?"

The corners of his mouth twitch as he stands. "You ran off so fast. I just wanted to make sure you were okay. Crystal didn't really know what happened. Her recollection of things is a little fuzzy."

I don't move further into the room. "I'm fine. I just had to come check on Jodi, but she's okay. So I'm good." Fox takes a step closer to me and I back up. "Thanks for checking in on me. Jodi and I were just about to have some dinner, so..." I nod toward the door.

He doesn't take the hint. Instead, he moves closer to me. "Something's up. Tell me."

I shake my head. "Really, I'm fine. Just... tired, you know? I guess that spell just took a bit too much out of me." I try to laugh but it comes out more like a dry cough.

Fox studies me, his mouth twitching. "Look, I'll go if you want me to. But I want to talk tomorrow, okay? Get a good night's rest."

He brushes his fingertips under my chin and I look up. Before I can react, he leans down and presses a tender kiss against my lips. My body tenses, freezes. I'm too shocked to even push him away. But maybe the most disturbing thing is that this doesn't feel like a first kiss. The way Fox's mouth fits against mine, the duration of the contact, the motion of his lips, it all feels familiar. When he pulls away, he smiles and I see a look on his face I've never seen before. He looks more open, more innocent. He tucks a strand of hair behind my ear and walks to the door.

"I'll call you tomorrow." He puts his hand on the doorknob and pauses like he wants to say something else. He shakes his head almost imperceptibly before smiling again and pulling open the door. "Oh, hey! Here, let me hold this open for you."

I move toward the door. Who he could be talking to? Is it Crystal? Or maybe Lexie has stopped by to visit?

"Thank you, Fox," says a female voice.

My heart skips a beat and my throat goes dry. I know that voice. But it can't be. It can't be.

My mother walks through the door carrying several plastic grocery bags. Her eyes light up when she sees me. "Good, you're home. Could you help me unload the car?"

For the third time tonight, darkness presses in on me. I feel dizzy and my vision goes dark before I hit the floor.

Chapter Thirty-Five

I wake up in my bedroom on the third floor of Jodi's house. What an insane dream. Going back in time, kissing Fox, my mom being alive. Maybe whatever Jodi has is catching and making me hallucinate.

Jodi.

I sit up too quickly and the blood rushes to my head, making my vision blacken around the edges.

"Whoa, be careful. Don't want to pass out again."

I lean back on my arms, waiting for the vertigo to pass. When my vision returns, I see Crystal Jamison sitting in a chair beside my bed. "What's going on? What..."

She scoots her chair closer to me, leaning in. "You might want to lie down again before I tell you anything."

Instead of heeding her advice, I sit up, swinging my legs off the mattress and facing her. "I remember... my mom..." I shake my head. "But it can't be—"

Crystal's mouth twitches. "It looks like we may have changed a few things."

I gape at her. "My mom's alive?" The idea of having my mom back fills my heart until I think it might burst. But it can't be true, can it? We went back to a single day in Clearwater almost twenty years ago; my mom died just over a month ago, miles away from here. How can one thing have affected the other? "I'm still dreaming. I have to be."

She reaches forward, covering my hand with hers. "It's not a dream. She's alive and she's here. She actually let me in this morning."

I shake my head. "This doesn't make any sense. If she's still alive, what are we doing *here*?"

The expression on Crystal's face tells me she's been waiting for me to ask. "It didn't take long after we got back for me to realize things weren't exactly the way we left them, and I spent a good portion of last night doing some research. Don't worry—mostly the world's just the way we left it. It seems like the changes are kind of localized—just us, our families."

"Wait—you're telling me that we *changed history*?"

"Just a little."

I lean forward, placing my head in my hands. "What do we do? How do we fix this?"

"Fix it? I thought you'd be happy. Krissa, did you hear me? Your mom's alive! The two of you live here with Jodi. Apparently you've been living here for years. I was looking through my old yearbooks..."

"But I haven't."

"But you *have*. I know it doesn't make sense. I mean, we didn't *do* anything, right? But somehow, just by going back, I guess we affected the future." She shakes her head. "Don't you see? We can't do anything to fix it now. What's done is done. Can't you just... take the win? We found the crystal. And you never lost your mom."

"And I'm dating Fox?"

She bites her lower lip. "I know, right? Weird."

"Crystal, how can you be so calm about this? We've messed with reality."

She shakes her head. "What's wrong with you? Your mom's still alive. Krissa... This isn't a bad thing."

I understand the point she's trying to make. Jodi isn't cursed. That's the reason I agreed to help find the crystal in the first place. If that's the meter by which I gauge our success, then I accomplished what I set out to do. But I didn't expect other things to change. My mom is alive. I can't even wrap my mind around how it's even possible, and it's even more amazing than saving Jodi's life. Still, I can't shake the feeling that it's wrong—that I've cheated somehow. And if something as big as my mom and me living here with Jodi is so contrary to the way it really happened, what other things have changed?

"What else is different?" I ask.

She shrugs. "It hasn't even been a whole day. I think those are the main things."

"What about Owen?" A pain shoots through my heart when I say his name.

"What about him?" She studies my face and her lips part in surprise. "Did you two have a thing? I mean, I knew you were hanging out with Lexie and him, but I didn't realize..."

Heat rises in my cheeks. I never got the chance to gush about my kiss with Owen, and now it's entirely possible it never even happened. A hollowness forms in the pit of my stomach. Less than a day ago, the two of us were standing on the threshold of a relationship. Now, nothing.

Crystal shifts in her chair, pushing it backward just slightly. "There's one more thing."

I take in a deep breath to prepare for the news. "What is it?"

She chews on her lower lip. "I don't know how, exactly, or why, but... your mom's not the only one who..."

I urge her to go on with my eyes. "What? What are you talking about?"

A smile creeps across her mouth, but it blinks out of existence almost immediately. "It's my aunt. Crystal Taylor is alive."

"What? How could that happen?"

Her eyes flicker to the floor. "I don't know. Clearly something we did made it so she could get out. Maybe it was just because we took the crystal. I don't think we'll ever know. But... isn't it great?"

I shake my head. Far from being great, I think this is a bigger problem than my mom being back from the dead. "That's almost twenty years of history she wasn't supposed to be around for. Who knows what she's changed because she's been here?" I stand, starting for the stairs.

Crystal is up in a flash, positioning herself between me and the exit. "Where are you going?"

"I'm going to go tell Jodi what we did. Maybe she'll be able to fix it."

"No!" Crystal pushes me squarely in the chest and I stumble backwards. "We can't tell her. We can't tell *anyone*."

Regaining my balance, I shove her back. "Get out of my way."

She grabs my wrist when I try to push past her. "Krissa, stop. We can't fix this. Think about it, and you'll see I'm right. Even if we could go back, we'd run into *ourselves*. And who's to say that wouldn't make a bigger mess?"

I struggle against her grasp, but her words cut through me. She has a point. Still, there has to be a way to reverse what we've done. Jodi told me magic comes with consequences; I'm learning that firsthand in a major way.

When I stop fighting against her, Crystal releases my wrist, but her posture remains coiled, like she's prepared to spring should I make a sudden movement.

The stairs leading up to my room creak under someone's weight. "Kristyl?" calls my mom's voice tentatively. She ascends to the top of the stairs and smiles when she sees me. "Oh, good, you're up. Fox has already called twice." Her eyes go heavenward and she shakes her head. "That boy. If you're feeling up for it, I made pancakes." She glances at Crystal. "There's enough for you, too, if you like."

Crystal smiles warmly. "Thanks. I'd like that." She casts a loaded look in my direction, like she expects me to blurt out something about traveling to the past and altering the course of events and is warning me not to.

I tamp down the annoyance flaring in me. "We'll be right down, Mom."

My mother squints at us before turning and heading back down the stairs.

Crystal moves to follow her. "We don't want to keep her waiting."

After a beat, I move toward the stairs. At least for the moment, I have to pretend like there's nothing wrong. But how can I do that when my reality has been suddenly rearranged? In a way, it's like I'm in a dream. But dreams aren't real, and neither is this. No matter how amazing it is to have Jodi's curse lifted—to have my mother alive again—it's not reality. By going back in time, we've messed with the natural order of things. We've cheated. The idea twists my stomach.

I don't like it, but we can't tell anyone about what we did, at least for now. I like it even less that we're going to have to find a way to reverse it.

ALSO BY MADELINE FREEMAN

The Naturals Trilogy

Awaking: Morgan Abbey's life changes dramatically when a mysterious stranger shares two secrets with her: she possesses psychic abilities and her mother—who has been missing for a decade—is still alive.

Seeking: When Morgan discovers that her mother might be in danger, she is prepared to dismiss all warnings to bring her safely home. With the help of her friends, Morgan will risk everything in an attempt to save her mom. But forces darker than she can imagine are out there, and before her search is over, Morgan will find that not everything is as it seems—and those she thought she could trust may just be her greatest enemies.

Becoming: Life in the safe house is routine, but routines are meant to be broken—and the reappearance of a familiar face turns life in the safe house on its head. Through relational upheaval and secrets revealed, Morgan has to keep everything together to fulfill her destiny. But when it's time, will she have the resolve to do what needs to be done? Will she be able to kill Orrick?

Shifted: **Season One**

Leigh Evans's perception of reality is about to be shifted.

On the night of her high school graduation, Leigh stumbles onto a secret hiding in her sleepy rural town. What appears to be a case of serial abduction and murder is something darker, more sinister.

Enter Peter and Mollie Monroe, twins trained to hunt down and destroy the things that give people a reason to be afraid of the dark.

When the lives of these three intersect, nothing will ever be the same.

Leigh is thrust into a world she never knew existed, faced with dark creatures and secrets about her own past.

ABOUT THE AUTHOR

Madeline Freeman lives in the metro-Detroit area with her husband, her daughter, and her cats. In the time she should spend doing housework, she rewatches *Fringe*. She also loves anything to do with astronomy, outer space, plate tectonics, and dinosaurs, and secretly hopes her daughter will become an astronomer or a paleontologist.

Be the first to know when new books are released! Sign up for Madeline's mailing list: http://eepurl.com/DARP5

Connect with Madeline online:
http://www.madelinefreeman.net
http://twitter.com/writer_maddie
http://facebook.com/madelinefreemanbooks

26428752R00152

Made in the USA
Middletown, DE
28 November 2015